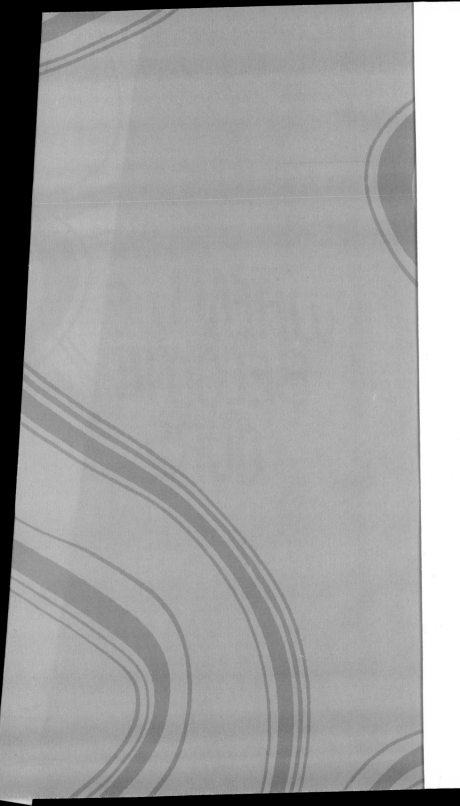

WHEN WE BECOME OURS

WHEN WE BECOME OURS

OURS

A YA ADOPTEE ANTHOLOGY

EDITED BY

SHANNON GIBNEY & NICOLE CHUNG

HARPER**TEEN**

An Imprint of HarperCollins*Publishers*

TO ALL THE YOUNG ADOPTEES OUT THERE: WE GOT YOU.

—S.G. AND N.C.

CONTENTS

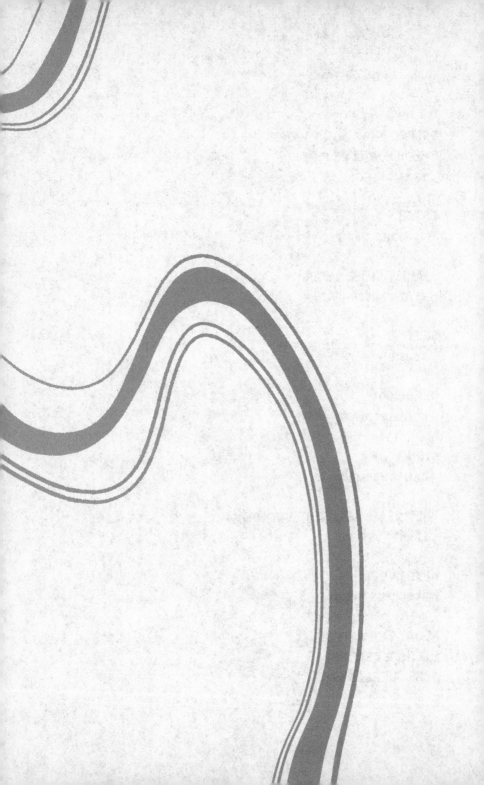

FOREWORD

I use the term "mind-blowing" every time I try to describe what it felt like to give birth to my son seventeen years ago—family I made *of* my body, a brown boy who later, when he was about four years old, would see his own reflection in a photo of me as a child. As a Black girl adopted by a white family, raised in an all-white New England town, I could not have possibly imagined how to prepare for having this child who would look so much like me; a child who would one day grow up and strike out on his own. Even when I saw a Black person in real life for the first time at six years old, or *felt* something indescribable that I didn't have the language to make sense of, or wondered whether Easy Reader on the PBS children's program *Electric Company* might be my birth father—these were seemingly abstract instances that transported me to a kind of paradoxical netherland, where Black people were simultaneously both familiar and foreign.

Nothing in my adoptee experience prepared me for what it would feel like to grow a person inside my body, who would be born with my DNA, and also look like me.

Next year, my son will be off to college. I'd like to think that had there been more representation of transracial adoptees in books, movies, TV, and songs—anywhere, really—I might have been better prepared for the prospect of my child becoming a whole individual independent of me, and of course, his father; that the prospect of him possibly attending college far from home would feel less like a specter of my central adoption trauma, and perhaps more like a thrilling sense of gratitude for my son's independence (I may still get there yet!).

That is what the stories in *When We Become Ours* do for transracial adoptees, and oh, that they would have been available to me growing up. I wish I had known as a girl, then as a young woman, that the shared grief of transracial adoptees is complex, but not insurmountable. And, as the stories here demonstrate so beautifully, that we are more than, and can move beyond, our adoption experiences—our imaginations, especially our young ones, are brimming with ideas, bursting with creative energy, and transforming trauma into new and nuanced narratives. Representation makes us feel less alone. Representation plus imagination anoints us to fly. Read these stories, and then soar.

—**Rebecca Carroll**

EDITORS' NOTE

Dear Reader,

We've always been here. And yet when you're an adoptee, often the last thing you expect to encounter is your own story—any version of it, in any universe.

If you're a transracial adoptee, you may feel like an alien when going out to dinner with your white family, patrons staring right and left, some of them bold enough to ask you outright, *Is that your brother/sister/mother/father?* or *Where did they get you?* Reading the stories and novels assigned at school, you may feel invisible if no characters identify as adoptees, or you may feel misrepresented if they *were* adopted and that fact is played for laughs or used to justify prejudice or cruelty. Or, if you're like us, maybe you've encountered stories of adoptees that just felt *off* in some way, not really vibing with your own lived experience.

Adoption shows up a lot in literature and pop culture. But most of the time, our stories are written by non-adoptees:

white adoptive parents, white writers with no personal connection to adoption, and, increasingly, non-adopted BIPOC folks. The lack of authentic representation—of literature about adoptees, by adoptees—can lead to one-dimensional, even harmful portrayals of adoption and adoptee characters. It contributes to the view that adoptees are *not* the authority on our own lives. It can also lead many adoptees to feel as if they are alone, "the only one," or even "a freak," who no one else sees or understands.

This is the representational void that we and our fellow adoptee contributors are writing into. Stefany Valentine gives us a powerful view of how human difference and prejudice can manifest across planets and loving families in "Almost Close Enough." In Jenny Heijun Wills's "Sexy," an adoptee teen grapples with feelings of isolation that make her more vulnerable to an untrustworthy person. Lisa Wool-Rim Sjöblom illustrates both the limits of "color-blindness" and the close bonds of love and understanding that can be forged between fellow adoptees in her comic "Love Is Not Enough." The ghosts of lost loved ones are everywhere in MeMe Collier's "Haunt Me, Then," while in Eric Smith's "Truffles (or Don't Worry, the Dog Will Be Fine)," loss is both acknowledged and changed through caring for another being that doesn't quite fit in. A young Native girl who doesn't know her tribal background begins to find community through a local Native women's circle in Susan Harness's "Shawl Dance," and two Black adoptee teenagers stumble toward their own voices in Mariama J. Lockington's "Cora and Benji's Great Escape."

Storytelling *matters*. Storytelling can heal, and it can bruise. It can make us feel seen and connected, and it can make us feel alone and strange. We know that adoptees need more stories—by us and for us. We need the freedom to explore our very particular imaginations and identities on the page. As editors, contributors, and transracial adoptees ourselves, we were thrilled to throw ourselves into assembling an A-team of stories from many genres by leading adoptee writers today. The literary, sci-fi, fantasy, horror, speculative, and graphic fiction in this volume points to the complexity, breadth, and depth of adoptee experiences, though we know there are many more stories out there yet to be shared. It will draw you in, make you laugh and cringe, grieve and hope, ask questions and perhaps seek new answers. Most of all, we hope it will spark some flash of recognition in our adoptee readers: the knowledge that our stories have always been with us, waiting to be told and shared, processed and held. The only thing we needed was a forum. And each other. This is when we become ours.

—Shannon Gibney and Nicole Chung

CORA AND BENJI'S GREAT ESCAPE

BY MARIAMA J. LOCKINGTON

"I am too old for this mess," I say under my breath as Mom lines my siblings and me up in front of our minivan in matching, crisp black hoodies that read *Black Is Beautiful* in block lettering with a Black Power fist on the front.

"Cora, please smile. This will only take a second. Then we can get on the road!" Mom yells from the end of the driveway as she places her iPhone tripod in the perfect position in front of us.

"Come on, Coco," my twelve-year-old twin sisters, Amelia and Freya, whisper at me in unison. "We want to leave. Let's get this over with."

"Plus," Freya continues on her own now, "Sam and

Drew-Drew are not going to be able to keep still much longer."

Sighing, I look down the line at Sam, my six-year-old brother, and Andrew, who just turned four. Sam is starting to kick up imaginary dirt with his sneakers like it's his job, and Drew-Drew is swinging his arms side to side and looking wistfully at his abandoned plastic pickup truck a few feet away in the walkway.

I plaster on a smile. "Okay, I'm ready," I say through gritted teeth. It doesn't matter that I'm almost sixteen, Mom still thinks I'm her forever baby. She still has me sharing a room with Amelia and Freya, even though I told her I don't mind moving into her "office" in the basement. But Mom says she needs her "Boss Babe Cave" to be a kid-free zone so she can do all her momfluencer work in peace. I don't understand why she needs a whole basement just to edit reels of our family and ship out feminist cross-stitch pieces from her small Etsy store, but whatever.

"Oh, you guys just look so cute!" Mom squeals before setting the timer and running over to join us in the shot. She is wearing an identical shirt, except hers says *My Kids Are Black & Beautiful*, sans fist. If Dad were home, she'd have him in one too, standing next to her, and then we'd be complete: "The O'Henry Family—A Salt & Pepper Story."

If you haven't guessed already, we—me and my siblings—are the pepper. Each one of us is adopted and Black, and our parents—Lily and James O'Henry from

Madison, Wisconsin—they are the salt.

"Oh, that's just perfect!" Mom squeals, checking her phone as we all scatter and claim our seats in the minivan. The tension in my shoulders eases up a little as I climb into the passenger seat up front. Dad's out of town this weekend for work, so that means I get shotgun, Sam and Drew-Drew will be in the middle seats in their boosters, and the twins get the back row. Mom throws her tripod and ring light in the trunk on top of all our bags, and then she hops into the driver's seat and buckles in.

"Give me just one sec, and then we're off to Camp Unity!"

"Yay!" Everyone in the car cheers, except me.

"Finally," I mutter as I watch Mom open Instagram to post our latest family portrait.

"Cora—help me think of some good hashtags."

"How about, #letsgetontheroad #now."

Mom purses her thin lips but doesn't take her eyes off her phone. "Very funny, Cora. I don't get why you're so moody these days. You used to love this weekend away."

I watch Mom type out her caption: "When your family is Black & Beautiful and headed to Camp Unity." #roadtrip #transracialfamily #momof4 #blackgirlmagic #blackboy-magic #mixedfamily #asaltandpepperstory.

"And posted!" she squeals. "All right, fam bam. Let's blow this Popsicle stand."

And with that, Mom revs the engine and we are finally on the road.

Camp Unity—"A Black Identity Experience" is a family retreat my family has been participating in ever since I was five years old. From Friday through Monday of MLK weekend, a bunch of families just like ours make our way to a big lakeside conference center just outside Milwaukee to be in community, learn about our Black heritage, and take workshops on antiracism or whatever. Well, it's really just our white parents that take the intense workshops—us kids, well, we kinda just get to chill until the final night, when there's a big family celebration, with African drumming, dancing, a raffle, and soul food. It used to be a lot more fun when I was younger—they play a lot of movies for us and have an arts and crafts room, but once you get past the age of like twelve, there's not much for us to do. In fact, if it wasn't for Benji, I would have begged Mom to stay home this weekend. Benji (Benjamina to her parents) is my best friend at camp and has been since forever. Benji was adopted as a toddler, like me, and she lives in Chicago with her two moms and a pug named Lolly and is just six months older than me. I only get to see Benji in person once or twice a year, otherwise we stay in touch via text and email, so at least this weekend we get to be bored together.

When we pull into the conference center a couple hours later, it's midafternoon and the parking lot is full of cars, vans, and SUVs as families spill out of them and head inside to check in. Freya and Amelia immediately spot their friend Lauren a few cars over and run to envelop her in a hug. I leave Mom in the front seat checking her IG account and get Sam and Drew-Drew out of their seats.

"Grab your bags, boys," I say, moving to unpack our luggage. "And don't forget your truck, Drew-Drew."

"It's my butt truck!" Drew-Drew says, grabbing his toy.

"That's not a butt, Drew-Drew." Sam laughs. "It's a dump truck."

"Bump truck!" Drew-Drew tries again, throwing Sam into a fit of giggles.

"Okay, you two. Very funny," I say, but I also have a big smile on my face.

Freya and Amelia finally extract themselves from their huddle with Lauren and come running back over, asking Mom if they can go down to the gazebo and explore.

"You need to get your bags first!" I say before Mom can chime in. "I'm not carrying all your stuff for you like I did when we left the house. What did you even pack that's so heavy? It better not be your nail polish collection. That stuff stinks, and you know people have sensitivities."

Freya and Amelia roll their eyes at me.

"Don't roll your—" I start.

"Girls," Mom chides as she steps out of the driver's seat. "Grab your own bags, please. Let's all get checked in and find our room assignments. You can see your friends at the opening session."

Amelia and Freya scowl.

My pocket buzzes, and I pull out my phone.

Benji: You here yet? My moms are irritating me already. Also—are there more families wearing kente cloth patterns this year or is that just me?

I snort, and quickly snap a picture of my hoodie. Then I type: Just got here. And I can't speak to the African prints, but this is what my mom had us wear this weekend.

Benji: Cora . . . what on this green earth.

Me: It was for her Instagram. I'm taking this off as soon as we get to our rooms.

Benji: You better. I can't be seen with you in that.

Me: Shut up. See you soon. I'll text after we check in.

Benji: 👍

It takes forever to check in, not because it's a super complicated process, but because Mom won't stop talking with other parents, and then Drew-Drew has to use the potty and Sam needs a snack, and by the time this all gets sorted out and we make our way to our dorm-style rooms (one for Mom and the boys, one for me and the twins next door), it's time for the welcome session.

Meet in the auditorium? Save me a seat, I type to Benji as I throw my duffle on the bed closest to the window.

Benji: Yep, got you one. Back row.

I grin and shimmy out of my *Black Is Beautiful* sweatshirt. I replace it with a chunky marigold cardigan; then, in front of the full-length closet mirror, I inspect my fit.

I'm wearing high-waisted, gray-washed boyfriend jeans, my black Doc Martens, and under my cardigan a tight, black-and-white-striped tank top. My hair falls around my shoulders in a series of tight box braids, with teal and purple braided into them. It's the first style my mom let me choose on my own, and she didn't insist on trying to do it herself. I love it. I've been keeping my edges meticulous and even using a toothbrush on them like other Black girls on YouTube do. When I see myself with this hair, instead of the messy twist-out Mom used to try to help me style, I feel like a literal queen, a goddess. I hope Benji likes it too. Benji, who has an open adoption, sees her first mom and cousins every few weeks or so. One of the things they make sure to hook her up with are the most immaculate hairstyles. Every time I see Benji, she's rocking a new do—like Goddess braids with gold beads in them, perfectly sectioned out Bantu knots, or a braided headband crown—and for once I'm gonna be just as cool as she is.

"Okay, Cora, we get it. Your hair is amazing. You look like fricken Beyoncé," Amelia chimes in now as she and Freya come out from the bathroom, where they've no doubt been trying to find a spot to stash their smelly nail polish supply.

"It is amazing," Freya chimes in with no sarcasm. "I wish Mom would let us get braids like that." She looks longingly at me and then pats her two Afro puffs.

"She might let you if you keep asking," I say. "You just

have to be persistent. Wear her down."

"No way," Amelia says. "Mom's feelings would be too hurt. You know how much she loves to do our hair in new natural styles. It's like half of her content on IG."

"Yeah, but it's *your* hair. Not hers," I nudge gently. Ever since they were born, Mom has had their faces all over her social media, doing all kinds of photo shoots and tutorials with them in matching clothes. Then, when the twins were four and I was seven, she took one class with KidStyles in Chicago—an organization that helps white parents learn how to do their Black kids' hair—and immediately decided she was an expert. The twins have always had it worse than me, but this year I finally got sick of it. I told Mom that I didn't want to be in any more of her hair-styling videos. I wanted to go to a salon to get mine done. I think it hurt her feelings, but I still don't get why. She doesn't let us play with her hair, she gets to have hers dyed and layered professionally every few months, so why can't I? In the end, she and Dad gave in.

"That's what I said," Freya mumbles. "It's my hair. Plus, we're too old for some of the hairstyles she puts us in anyway."

Amelia gives her a sharp look and then grabs her by the hand. "Come on, let's go. We're going to be late for the opening."

"Conversation to be continued, I guess." I sigh, grabbing my lanyard, my phone, a tube of cherry ChapStick, and the key to our room. Then I follow the twins down the hallway and out into the cold January air.

In the auditorium, I find Benji right where she said she'd be. I take the auditorium steps two at a time, toward Benji, who is rocking an amazing, curly mohawk with the sides braided up. She's got small gold hoops in each ear and is wearing a lavender jumpsuit, rainbow Doc Martens, and her signature clear cat-eye glasses.

"Cora!" she says, jumping up to hug me. "Excuse me, your hair is fire. When did this happen?"

I hug her back, hard. Benji is my safe place. Her arms remind me to loosen my shoulders all the way, to breathe, to relax. Remind me that I can be myself.

"You like?" I say, flipping my braids over my shoulder dramatically.

"I like a lot. Might have to copy you," Benji says, nodding.

I grin so wide it hurts and then plop down next to her.

The lights dim as if on cue, and Ms. Jade and Ms. Alice— the codirectors of Camp Unity—make their way onstage. Ms. Jade is a tall, stylish Black woman from Zimbabwe, with a massive, sparkling Afro. She is a sociology professor at Northwestern and is in charge of all the camp's workshops and educational programs. Ms. Alice is an average-size white woman with short brown hair. She has a collection of homemade sweaters for every season and holiday, and today she's wearing a black-and-white sweater with the image of Martin Luther King woven on the front. Ms. Alice—well, honestly, I don't know what Ms. Alice does. I think she organizes the raffle and entertainment for the final celebration, and her sons Leo and Thadius were the inspiration for starting the camp.

"I wanted my sons to feel PROUD of their Black skin," Ms. Alice is saying now, a little too loudly, into the mic. "To feel a connection to their roots and their people, and to know they are beautiful! And I wanted to create a space for us, as the parents of Black children, to learn and grow and be better allies. So, welcome new families and old, this is our thirteenth year, and we're going to have a GREAT weekend. To start us off with a song, I'll pass the mic to my co-organizer, Ms. Jade."

"Here we go," Benji whispers as we both stand in the darkness out of habit.

Ms. Jade introduces her Black and brown college students, who are here to volunteer for the weekend, and then she asks everyone to rise for the Black national anthem, "Lift Every Voice and Sing."

"Please join along!" Ms. Jade commands the audience in between two verses. "For those of you who are new, there are sheets with lyrics in your welcome folders."

A bunch of new families start to fumble through their folders or lean over the shoulder of someone who has the sheet. To be honest, I've been coming here for ten years, and even though I know all the lyrics now, I still don't understand what the history of the song is, or why it's even considered the Black national anthem. Ms. Jade and Ms. Alice never explain this. We just all awkwardly sing it because it's something we're supposed to know, as Black people, I guess.

"We sound horrible," Benji says, leaning over, as if reading my mind.

"I know, right. This is a bad way to start a weekend about unity. We can't even sing in key."

Benji stifles a laugh. "They should just play the Beyoncé version and call it a day."

I nod. When I watched *Homecoming* and heard Beyoncé sing "Lift Every Voice," I got goose bumps. It felt like she was singing to me. This just feels awkward as hell, and they make us sing *every* verse, which takes forever.

"Wanna get out of here?" I mouth to Benji, who has stopped singing to look at her phone.

"Immediately, yes," she mouths back.

Nobody notices when we sneak through a side door and into the empty hallways of the center. When we're out, we grab hands and run as fast as we can into the harsh late-afternoon air and toward our favorite place on the grounds: the cafeteria.

The cafeteria is not open yet, but the pop machines work. Benji and I grab cups and fill them to the brim with root beer (our favorite). Then we pick a table in the far-left corner that overlooks the lake, and we settle in. Dinner will start right after the welcome session is over, so really, we've just claimed our spot early before it gets busy. Until then, we have a whole forty minutes to ourselves to do what we love best: exchange poems. Nobody—not a soul in this whole wide world knows I write. Not my parents, not the twins, not my one friend back home, Rebecca, no one. No one, except Benji.

I didn't even know I was writing poetry until Benji helped me understand what it was. I just know that sometimes, the only way I can express all the sadness, anger, anxiety, and loneliness I feel is to open my phone and a new Notes app and type it all out. At first I didn't know what a stanza was or a line break or even what alliteration was. It was Benji and YouTube that helped me figure all that out. Benji—who not only knows she is a poet but competes in poetry cyphers all the time at her performing arts high school in Chicago. Benji—who has never been shy a day in her life and has the gift of commanding a room with her voice no matter if she's reading her poems or just talking. Benji—who never seems afraid that she'll be rejected or that her stories don't matter.

"Okay, so you got something new? I want to hear it."

"You first," I say, thumbing through my Notes app for what I want to share.

Normally, we email or text each other once a week with our pieces, but because we knew camp was this weekend, we saved up. I am trying to decide whether to read what I wrote a few days ago, about feeling like an alien at school, or what I penned in the car ride up here while Mom and my siblings were having a sing-along to *Moana*. I hadn't had a chance to edit today's piece, but also, this is Benji. I can share my most unfiltered thoughts with her.

"No way," Benji says, shaking her head. "You're first. I always send you videos of me reading my poems aloud, but I hardly ever get to hear you read yours. I want a performance, darling!"

I feel my face and neck flush.

With the twins around, it's hard to ever get time to myself in my room. If I want to practice my poems out loud, I have to lock myself in the upstairs bathroom and turn the shower on, and that gets too steamy, not to mention wasteful. But I really, really don't want anyone in my family to know about my poems. They are mine, nobody else's, so normally I just email them to Benji. I glance around the room. There are only a few staff members by the buffet, starting to set things up for dinner. Coast is clear.

"Fine," I say. I take a big gulp of my pop and then lean over the table, closer to Benji. "This isn't finished yet. I just wrote it on the way here, so—"

"NO DISCLAIMERS!" Benji practically yells.

"Okay, okay. Geez. Calm yourself. Here I go," I say, then recite:

> *i see myself in the blurred landscapes*
> *snaking by the windows as we speed*

13

down the highway the snow catching light
catching all the colors of brown and black
and bright
my face in the windowpane distorted and contorted
an illusion of a girl
who is more fiction than fact
more movement than stillness
more wanting than having
more undone than understood
the car travels mile by mile
and all my faces unravel
until I am everywhere
as far as the eye can see
Black and stretching out forever
my body lifted up and out and flying away

until

I am free

"That's as far as I got," I say, after a beat to catch my
breath.

"Wow." Benji whistles under her breath. "That was
amazing. And no, I don't think that's the ending. You need
to keep writing, see what else comes. I was feeling a lot of
the imagery. Especially the part about being 'more undone
than understood'—a whole mood."

"Thanks," I say. I knew Benji would get it. That she wouldn't tell me I was being too dramatic or be confused about why I sometimes feel "distorted and contorted." When kids at school find out I'm adopted, they say things like *Wow, you're lucky* or *Wow, you must be so glad your mom decided to give you up so you could have a better life.* Or my least favorite, *Wow, I wish I was adopted. That must be so cool.*

It is cool, sometimes. But more and more these days, it's also confusing to be me. I have all this sadness, and more and more I find that my poems are full of the ways I don't fit in here or there, blurry landscapes, and trying to see myself more clearly in a foggy mirror. More and more I look at myself and think, *Whose lips do I have? Whose eyes? Who might I have been if I'd been kept instead? Would I still feel so undone?*

And I don't have to say any of this to Benji. When she reads me her poem next, it's different but also full of the same questioning and wondering as mine. It's about going into a store with her moms and getting followed around by the clerk until they realized who she was with. And when she ends with the line, "So step off my neck, Karen, and let me live!" I clap for her, loud and proud across the table, and my claps echo through the empty cafeteria.

"Thank you, thank you," Benji says, standing up and giving a small curtsy. "I'm still working on memorizing it, but I think it's getting there."

"Oh, it's there," I say. "In fact, I bet you could perform it if you tried. You barely looked at your phone the whole time."

Benji gets a gleaming, mischievous look in her eye. "Okay, listen. I have an idea," she says, sitting back down and waving me in closer.

I lean over the table so that our noses are almost touching.

"So, you know how my first cousin, Treasure, goes to University of Wisconsin–Milwaukee?"

"Yeah, she's a sophomore, right?"

"Yep. So, listen. Sunday night, she says the BSU is putting on an MLK celebration with an open mic, and we should come."

"But Sunday night is the final camp celebration. I don't think we can miss it. Plus, how would we even get there?"

"Treasure said she and her girlfriend can come get us. But yeah, we'd have to sneak out. My moms don't know Treasure like that, and I'm only really supposed to be in a car with my first mom."

"I don't know, Benji . . . I mean, won't they know we're not college students?"

"Please. We'll fit right in. Promise. Plus, Treasure will be there, and she's an adult."

"Barely."

"Come on. You know that the final celebration is always the same. Once our parents start dancing along to the drumming and the food comes out, that room is so crowded nobody can tell where anybody is. I bet they will barely miss us. Plus, if they text, we can say we went back to our rooms early to hang out."

I raise my eyebrow. Ditching the final camp celebration *is* appealing. "I'll think about it."

"Okay. Well, think quick because if Treasure is going to come rescue us, I need to text her soon."

"A real open mic? A college open mic?"

"Yes! It will be low-key amazing. I mean, Treasure says it's a whole scene, that all the Black students on campus get together for it, and there's a DJ and pizza and shit. She said it's a whole vibe."

I gulp. It sounds like a dream, but also, I have this feeling that me and my awkward self might mess up whatever "vibe" the event has going for it.

"Okay—well let me know," Benji says. "Looks like dinner is opening up. I better go find my parents in line so I can get my meal coupon."

"Same," I say, standing up with her.

"Meet you back here when we we have our plates?"

The first night of camp (Friday night), they always play a movie for us kids while the parents have antiracist book clubs. Benji and I have made it a tradition to steal cookies from the cafeteria so we can eat them in the back of the movie room and gossip. Tonight they're screening *Black Panther*, which I've literally seen five million times because Sam thinks he *is* Black Panther. So I doubt I will pay attention.

"You bet. See you soon!"

And then we scatter, our words left dancing in the air like ghosts.

The next morning, I lie in my bed listening to the twins giggle under their covers, and I think about Benji's proposal. I know she's right about one thing: nobody will notice if we are gone. In fact, except for last night at dinner, when I grabbed my meal coupon, I've barely seen Mom or the boys, and the twins have been on their own agenda since we arrived. That's the thing about Camp Unity—everyone here is someone's family, and we have the whole conference space to ourselves. So, even though at home Mom keeps a close eye on me and my siblings, here she lets us roam and pick what we want to do while she gets to hang out with all the parents and attend workshops. To be honest, it's really nice not being in her spotlight so much. Mom's love is big and warm, and when she finally puts her phone down, she makes sure each one of us has what we need to face the day. But her love can also feel obsessive sometimes—like if we don't give her back as much energy as she gives us, then somehow, we're letting her down.

"Knock-knock, girls." Mom's voice comes through our door now. "Breakfast is opening in fifteen minutes, so please don't miss it."

Amelia opens the door, yawning. "Good morning, Mama."

"Good morning, Pumpkin." Then she peers around and says, "Good morning, Sweets and Coco."

"Mmmmhmmm," Freya mumbles from under the covers. She is the night owl; Amelia is the early bird.

"Hi, Mom," I say, standing up and stretching.

"What's on the agenda for you all today? I saw they have a bunch of activities for you this weekend," Mom says.

"Freya and I are going to do the origami workshop this morning," Amelia pipes up, pulling out her schedule for the day. "Then, after lunch, we have affinity groups, so I guess we'll be in the Black girls' group with Cora."

"Wait, what?" I say, pulling out my own schedule, which I've barely looked at. "What's the point of separating us out like that?"

"I don't know, but they have a special guest speaker for the boys and one for the girls. So we all have to be there," Amelia continues matter-of-factly.

I groan. I wonder if Benji knows about this.

"So, Coco. What are you going to do this morning?" Mom continues.

I glance hastily over my agenda. "Uh, hmm. Benji and I are gonna do the, uh, the yoga and meditation workshop."

"That sounds nice," Mom says. "Wish I could join you."

I smile at her. I absolutely do not want to do yoga with my mom. In fact, I don't really want to do yoga at all, but it's the only thing on the agenda that sounds remotely low-key.

"Yeah, well, perks of still being a kid at these things," I finally say. "What's on your agenda?"

"Oh, we have a long day ahead of us. We're going to be learning how to decolonize our bookshelves and how to make a road map for success in our white allyship. You know, how we can better understand what it might be like in this world for you kids, and things like that."

"Shouldn't that be, like, a family discussion?" I ask, pulling my sweatshirt over my head. "I mean, like, so we can all talk together?"

Mom shakes her head. "No, I don't think so. It's just for parents. It will be too boring for all of you. You'll have more fun elsewhere."

I nod, but I don't understand how our parents are going to learn to be allies if they never talk to us kids directly. I guess that's why I write my poems. At least the page is there to listen, and anyway, Mom is right. I don't really want to be in a room full of white parents talking about all that. Sounds exhausting.

"Ma-ma, Drew-Drew changed the channel!" Sam screams from the room next door.

"Oh, boy. Okay, Sammy. I'm coming," she yells. "Okay, girls. Have fun this morning. See you at lunch."

We all wave and then scramble to get dressed. When I've pulled on a pair of leggings and laced my boots, I text Benji.

Me: Yoga & Meditation?

Benji: I guess. It's the best of the worst.

Me: Did you see they have us in a girls' group later?

Benji: I did. Sounds interesting . . .

Me: My thoughts exactly.

Benji: Did you think any more about my plan?

Me: . . .

Benji: Ok, we'll talk more later. See you at breakfast.

Me: 👍

We don't talk about Benji's plan at breakfast, or during the yoga and meditation workshop, which turns out to be way cooler than we thought. Ms. Ruby, a Black adult adoptee from New York—yes, her white parents named her after Ruby Bridges—leads us through a guided meditation and then asks us to tune in to the parts of our bodies that hold the most tension. Then she starts talking about how our bodies hold trauma, and even though we might not remember all the things that happened to us as babies or kids, our bodies do. When she talks about how she holds a ton of tension in her shoulders and how, when she met her first mom finally in her early twenties, that tension went away, I feel like crying. It's hard for me there too, my neck and shoulders are always tight and full of knots. I never thought about what I might be holding in them—that maybe it's not just physical, but emotional too.

Then Ms. Ruby leads us through some gentle yoga poses and breath work to help with anxiety, and it low-key feels amazing. I feel peaceful afterward. I think Benji does too, because we hardly speak a word to one another during the workshop.

At lunch, we are so hungry from all the moving and breathing, we shovel food into our mouths and then chat with other kids at our table. I briefly see Mom and the boys at another table and wave. Then it's time for affinity groups, and all of us Black girls shuffle into a room where there are two of Ms. Jade's college volunteers—a Black woman named Tamika and a brown woman named Jessenia. I can tell they are nervous, because they kinda fumble through some icebreakers at the beginning, and we all go around and say our names and one thing we like to do on the weekends. When it's my turn, I say "sleep," but really, I like to write poems on the weekends and watch my favorite spoken word poets on YouTube and text Benji. But people don't need to know my business. The icebreaker ends, and then things get awkward. Ms. Tamika and Ms. Jessenia tell us how hard it can be in this world for Black and brown women, how people are going to assume that we're more grown-up than we are and oversexualize us. Then they ask if anyone has experience with this happening. The room is quiet, and a new girl named Mazie raises her hand.

"So, I . . . uh. Well, sometimes when my dad takes me out to restaurants, people give us funny looks," she begins. "And one time, when we got the check, the waiter told my dad that his 'girlfriend' was beautiful and winked at him. He was talking about me. I'm only fourteen, and my dad is really old, so I don't know why they thought we were together. My dad laughed it off and said I was his daughter, but then he let it go. I felt really gross the whole way home. Like, did everyone in the restaurant think I was dating my dad?"

Ms. Tamika and Ms. Jessenia looked visibly shocked, like they weren't expecting this response at all. To be honest, the whole room is quiet, but then Ms. Jessenia recovers and thanks Mazie for sharing. "I'm really sorry that happened to you," she says. "Has this happened to anyone else—or something similar?"

I bite my lip and catch Benji's eye. She gives me a knowing nod. I have a whole poem about how all of a sudden, now that I have boobs and a butt, the white boys at my school call me a "Big Booty Ho," and how, in the grocery store with my dad one time when I was thirteen, this old white woman glared at me in line and whispered, "Disgraceful slut." Dad didn't notice, because he was paying and chatting with the attendant, but everyone in line behind us heard it. The only person who knew about this was Benji, and even though something like this never happened to her with her moms, she understood why it was so embarrassing. But I don't share this out loud or offer my story up to validate Mazie's. I just feel nauseated, like I might throw up. *What's the point of all this?*

I spend the rest of the session in a haze of anxiety as Ms. Tamika and Ms. Jessenia prompt us through more discussion about our Black girl bodies and how we can try to keep safe if stopped by police, etc.—all things Mom and Dad never really talk to us about directly. Sure, we went downtown to the local rally for Breonna Taylor and George Floyd, and we all marched and carried signs, and Mom got good photos of us all together in the crowds, but we never actually talk about how we—me, Freya, Amelia, Sam, and Drew-Drew—could be next . . . how any day, especially as we get older, we could be targeted. How scared I am sometimes, and angry too that the police keep killing us. But I don't know how to bring this up with my parents on my own. I think it would overwhelm them, so I just write it all down, and that works for me. I don't want to talk about this in front of strangers or with these volunteers who don't even understand what it's like to be adopted. I feel my body start to heat from within and my breath getting raggedy and short, and before I can excuse myself, Benji is raising her hand and asking if the two of us can use the bathroom. She leads me out into the hallway, and we walk and walk for what feels like forever, and then there is cold air hitting my face, reminding me to come back to myself.

"You can breathe," Benji is saying.

"I . . . I can . . . br-reathe," I repeat.

"Good. Say it again," Benji prompts.

"I can . . . breathe," I say, more confident in myself.

"Now breathe," Benji says quietly.

We stand in the cold, watching our breath snake into the

air, until my lungs feel back to normal and my heart rate slows.

"Are you okay?" Benji asks after a beat. "It got real in there."

I shake my head no. Because nothing is okay, and she's the only person I feel I can say that to.

"Can I do anything?" she asks, giving me a hug.

"Yes. You can text your cousin. Let's get out of here," I mumble into her shoulder.

Benji leaps into the air and shrieks. "For real?"

"For real. I don't think I can face the final celebration tomorrow."

"Hell, yes!" she says. "Okay, let me text Treasure."

I need an escape from my life, even if just for a night.

Sneaking out on Sunday evening is simpler than I'd imagined. After another full day of workshops and crafts for us kids, it's time for the Camp Unity final celebration before we all head home in the morning. When it starts, at 5:30 that afternoon, Benji and I make our rounds and say a quick "hi" to our parents and siblings, so we're seen at least once. Then we wait until the hallways outside are empty and everyone is in the room, and we watch the lid come off the first tray of soul food. Then Ms. Alice gets onstage and introduces the same African drumming troupe they hire *every* year, and the room fills with the urgent rhythms of djembes as five Black men and women dance and drum their way to the front of the room. As predicted, all the parents and younger kids go crazy, dancing and clapping along with the music, and soon there is a big crowd up front, where everyone's attention is turned.

Benji squeezes my arm and glances at her phone. "Go time," she mouths.

I nod, taking one more look around to make sure my siblings and Mom are not watching. Then Benji and I slip out into the hallway and run outside, where Treasure and her girlfriend Stephanie have just pulled up in a black Ford Focus.

"What in the Zamunda is going on there?" Treasure shouts from the passenger side as Benji and I hop into the back seat, the drumming still audible from the curb.

Benji chortles, understanding a reference that's totally lost on me. "Thanks for scooping us, Cuz. It's a whole mess in there," she responds. "This is my friend Cora. She's the one who makes me a better poet."

I give Treasure and Stephanie a quick wave, but shyness takes over and I can't find my voice. Plus, I'm still stuck on the fact that Benji thinks *I'm* the one who makes her a better poet. She makes *me* a better poet.

"Bet," Stephanie says, pulling away and out onto the road. "Nice to meet you, Cora. You think you're going to spit tonight?"

"What?" I laugh. "Um, no way. I'm just excited to listen."

"That's not what Benji told us. She told us you both had

new pieces to share," Treasure says, looking back at us. "We should get there in time for you both to get on the list. It usually fills up fast, but we're getting there close to the start, so you should be good."

Benji is avoiding my eyes.

"But I thought the open mic was for students—like who go to the university," I say, already feeling like the biggest nerd.

"I mean it is," Treasure says, "but we won't tell if you don't. Plus, you both look old enough to be freshmen. Nobody will care anyway. It's all love, you'll see."

I gulp and go silent.

"Let's just see how we feel when we get there," Benji finally chimes in. "You think we'll be able to be back by eight thirty?"

"Is that when y'all turn into pumpkins?" Stephanie jokes.

"Babe, stop playin'," Treasure says, slapping her lightly on the shoulder.

Benji laughs. "Well, yeah. That's about when things wind down for the night after the celebration. If we're much later than that, it will be hard to sneak back in without our parents missing us."

"Well, the open mic portion of the event is from six thirty to eight," Treasure says. "So you should be good. We'll get you back on time. Plus, we're only ten minutes away."

I look at the car clock. It's 6:10 on a Sunday night, and I

am speeding fast down a dark street with my best friend and two women who already feel more like kin than my one friend Rebecca back home. Maybe it's also because Benji is here, and these are her people—Treasure is Benji's first cousin, connected by DNA and blood, the kind of family I only ever get to dream about. I can feel how Benji, too, is different. Her speech and body language are softer, easier, and she and Treasure launch into a teasing conversation, the kind of conversation two people who have known one another their whole lives can have. And God, it feels good to be away from camp. I can't wait until I have my real license, not just a permit, and a car of my own. A car is freedom, a way to fly without having wings. One day, I'm going to be able to go anywhere.

Soon enough, we're parking and walking into a big ballroom in the Student Center. It's full of mostly Black folks sitting at round tables, talking and laughing. On one side of the stage a DJ is rocking out as a Chloe x Halle song blares over the speakers, and behind the DJ on a projector screen are images of all kinds of Black leaders, from Martin Luther King to Kamala Harris, Stacey Abrams, and many others I recognize and some I don't. At the sides of the ballroom are tables filled with pizza, sodas, and water, and it is indeed a whole vibe.

"This is amazing," Benji says, articulating my thoughts. "But I can't lie. I'm really nervous."

"Well, if you want to sign up for the open mic, you go up

there to the DJ. He'll get your name on the list," Treasure tells us.

We drop our things at a table toward the middle in back of the room, so when we have to leave, it won't be too obvious, and then Stephanie and Treasure head off to get some food and say hi to a few friends. Benji and I sit at the table, still taking it all in. Benji is tapping her foot fast against the floor, so I know she's trying to make a decision.

"What are you going to do?" I ask her. "Are you going to sign up?"

"Thinking about it. But I can already tell this is going to be a bigger crowd than I'm used to. Will you do it with me?"

"Like come onstage with you?"

"No. I mean like signing up to read your poem too."

"No way," I say. "Never in my life. I'd freeze up there—or, even worse, throw up."

"Come on. Nobody here even knows you. It will be good practice."

"Fuck no," I say, letting the curse word roll off my tongue like I'm grown.

Benji sighs. "Okay, fine. I'm gonna do it. At least come with me to sign up."

I follow Benji to the DJ stand and watch her scrawl her name on the list. She's the tenth person on a list of fifteen, so I guess it is good we showed up a little early.

"Last chance," Benji says, holding the pen out to me with a raised eyebrow.

I shake my head no. "I'm serious. I'm not doing it."

"Okay, okay fine. You better cheer loud for me, though, even if I bomb."

"Deal. And you won't bomb. You're amazing. I bet you're better than most of the college kids anyway."

"You have to say that because you're my friend." Benji laughs. "But I love you for it."

We fill our plates with food and head back to the table to hang with Treasure and Stephanie. Soon the DJ is fading out the music and introducing the event.

"How's everybody feelin' tonight?" he yells into the mic.

"Good!" the audience responds.

"Oh, we can do better than that. Look how many beautiful Black faces we have up in here tonight. To be honest, I didn't even know there were this many of us on campus, and damn y'all are looking good. I said, how you feelin' tonight?"

The DJ is kind of corny, but the audience responds louder this time, and Benji and I even join in with a few shouts of our own. The energy in the room is contagious as the DJ hypes us up more and then plays a track where the voice of MLK is superimposed over a head-bobbing, hopeful bass beat. I even find myself nodding my head up and down along with the track, then catch myself and stop.

I look around, embarrassed to see if anyone has noticed how ridiculous I look, to see if anyone is recording me with their phone to post on TikTok, but just as Treasure assured us, the room really is all love. Nobody seems to care what I'm doing, or that this is by far the most Black people I've ever been around, or that I'm only fifteen going on sixteen and I have no idea who I am or who I want to be. The room is all music, all sway and bodies and breath, all letting go and flowing and not having to be anybody but ourselves.

By the time the open mic begins, I am on my fourth slice of pizza and feeling like my pop must have booze in it, because I'm snapping along to each poet who graces the stage and I'm holding on to each word as if it is gold. When I get a text from Mom around seven, asking Where are you? I don't even panic. I just show the text to Benji, and mouth "I got this," and then, following our plan, I text back:

Got tired of the noise, hanging with Benji in her room.

Mom: It's not noise, it's art from your homeland! You're missing out.

Me: Africa is not my homeland. I was born in Michigan, remember?

Mom: 😐 Ok, fine. You know what I mean. It's your roots.

Me: I'll be in my room by 9. See you later, Mom.

I put my phone in my pocket. Mom has no idea where my roots are, and neither do I. All I know is that I feel more grounded in this ballroom than I have in a while.

"All right, my people," the DJ transitions. "Coming up next on the mic we have the lovely Benji Angelo. Benji is

31

originally from Chicago, and this is her first time on the UW mic. Let's give Benji a big round of applause."

"Wooooooh, go Benji!" I yell. But Benji doesn't move in her seat next to me. In fact, she's shaking, and before I can ask what's wrong, she whispers, "I'm going to be sick, Cora. I can't do this." And then she runs out of the room.

"Benji Angelo!" The DJ tries again. "Don't be shy, we don't bite. It's all love in here. We know you're going to bless the mic."

The crowd agrees, clapping hard with encouragement.

Benji is going to lose her spot. Before my brain can catch up with my body, I am walking toward the front of the room, my phone clutched in my hand. I am walking toward the stage, and then onto the stage, and whispering into the DJ's ear.

"Well, folks. My mistake. It looks like Benji has passed the mic to her BFF to perform tonight instead. So please give a warm welcome to Cora O'Henry."

The crowd murmurs but still claps it up, and then I am alone with a live mic staring back at me. I clear my throat and try to steady my knees, which I am sure are knocking together.

My heart is so loud, the mic must be picking it up, and I can tell I've sweat through my deodorant, because my armpits itch with moisture.

"Hi, everyone," I say, like a nerd. "Um, yeah. I'm going to

read a poem for you, so, uh. Thanks for listening."

What are you doing?! My head screams as I open my Notes app and scroll back to the poem I shared with Benji earlier in the weekend. I've been working on it some more, but I'm still not sure if it's done, done. This could be the biggest mistake I've ever made.

I clear my throat again.

"You got this, Cora!" the DJ nudges. "Let's give her some extra love, folks. This isn't easy, it takes a lot to get up here and share your voice."

The crowd snaps and claps and cheers, and then, through all the noise, I hear one voice, clear as day, yell, "CORA ANABELLE O'HENRY, YOU BETTER SLAY UP THERE, WHOOOOO THAT'S MY BEST FRIEND! WHOOOOOO!"

"Oh, okay, she's throwing out your government name, Cora." The DJ laughs. "I see you got a fan club here tonight."

"I really do," I say with a laugh.

Then I take a deep breath and let all my words flutter out and up into the air, until my voice is everywhere and full of light.

On the car ride back to camp, Benji, Treasure, and I celebrate our open mic triumphs by singing along as loud as we can to Beyoncé's "Formation," the car shaking with the tenor of our voices, fogging up with the heat of our breath. After I'd performed and been met by a standing ovation,

Benji, having calmed her nerves, got another chance to spit her poem. I screamed just as loudly for her as she did for me, and the crowd went wild when she finished. We were the stars of the evening. It felt like nobody could touch our joy.

Too soon, we are back at the conference center, tumbling out into the cold air, waving bye to Treasure and Stephanie as they speed away.

"Did that just happen?" Benji says, jumping up and down next to me. "Did you just get on a stage and fucking kill it? Like, did you see all those people clapping for you? You DID that."

"I did that shit!" I yell, jumping up and down right beside her, giddy with a joy I've never felt. "And so did you!"

And then, because I'm feeling full, because I do know one thing for sure, I stop jumping and pull Benji into a hug.

"Thank you," I say.

"For what, girl?"

"For understanding."

"Understanding what?"

"Everything," I say, motioning to all the silent spaces between and around us.

"Always," Benji says, nodding.

And then, as if on cue, soft snowflakes begin to fall around us. We laugh and open our mouths, letting all the sparkling wetness dissolve on our tongues.

"Cora!" Amelia's voice sounds through our laughter. She and Freya are peeking out of the conference center main doors with annoyed faces. "There you are. Mom says to get back inside, they're presenting Ms. Jade and Ms. Alice with a gift soon. Where have you been?"

"Everywhere," I say quietly as I wave okay to the twins.

Then Benji grabs my hand, and we run inside toward the sound of hollow drums.

THE STAR OF RUIN

BY MEREDITH IRELAND

In the country of Husei, the hills are lush and green. The rivers are wide and the climate is mild. The land provides ample harvests and the waters are rich with fish—no one hungers. The devoted people are loyal to the generous gods.

In the country of Husei, when the Heavenly Queen dies, a new queen is selected by the priests from the common girls. That's right, darling, even you can become royalty one day. The girl, the Star of Heaven, will be adored as the new spiritual leader, bathed in riches beyond her wildest dreams, and spend the rest of her life in the luxury of the Silver Palace.

In the country of Husei, there is the Letting. On the night the Star of Heaven becomes Heavenly Queen, the rivers run red with the blood of the Star's family.

No, don't cry. It is all as it should be.

In the country of Husei, because of the Letting, the gods continue to bless the lands and waters and the Heavenly Queen always remembers the sacrifices made for her crown. We celebrate the lives of those who were lost so that Husei may prosper.

The Prophecy? Oh, I don't think it's real.

Very well.

The Prophecy states that one of the Heavenly Queen's sisters will be the Star of Ruin. She will survive the Letting and bring an end to Husei as we know it.

But it is impossible. No one survives the Letting. There must be a full night of ritual death. There must be pain with joy, or the gods will turn their backs on us and there will be nothing left.

I am going to kill my sister tonight.

My birth sister. Gwan-si. The Exalted Heavenly Queen of Husei.

My sister Tria and I stand in the shadow of the alabaster tower.

"We made it," Tria whispers. She glances at me, and I know with the raise of her eyebrows that she's asking if I really want to go through with this. A final question, a last chance to turn back from a very bad plan.

I nod, and she looks the slightest bit defeated before smiling. It's a small smile that doesn't show the gap in her teeth. Still, she hoists me up on her shoulders. I grip the bottommost windowsill; my small feet slip before barely finding purchase between the slick stones.

"Die well, Song," she whispers.

"Gods save Husei," I say, though I don't mean it. I don't give a crushed fig about the country, or the drought, or the people who rule Husei. What I mean is the gods save Tria and our parents. My family. The one who found a broken, half-dead girl on a riverbank and took her in after the Letting. Who raised her as their own and gave her their surname. The ones who saved my life after my former sister tried to kill me.

My death tonight is nearly assured, but I'm not really supposed to be alive anyhow. And one girl's life is a small price to pay to put an end to all this. Gwan-si owes me a debt. And tonight I'm here to collect.

We were children of the Yew River—one of the rivers that's since run dry in the six years since Gwan-si ascended to the throne. To be honest, I don't remember all of it—my life before. Before Gwan-si chose to participate in the Selection. Before the priests chose Gwan-si. Before the Letting. Before she tried to murder me.

What I remember are small moments. Our father reading to us by the crackling fire. Our mother's laugh and a bit of song over the smell of wildflowers. Eating baked fish with sticky globs of rice. Gwan-si teaching me embroidery. The quiet hum of bees and making honeycomb candy with our little brother and sister. Running along the loose boards of docks on the Yew with Gwan-si. Her tending to my scraped knee, like the good sister she was, after I got into a fight with a boy who called me an ugly name. My ambitious sister wanted to be a healer one day. But most of all, I remember struggling to be more like my perfect older sister.

Like all the families in the village, we were poor but didn't know it. No one went hungry in Husei. But there's a difference between surviving and living. Yet we were happy. We were taken care of and loved.

She was beautiful, my former sister. The priests always look for that—sparkling ebony hair, large brown eyes, and a nearly heart-shaped face. Also mild. They want a placid queen. They call it purity. But in reality, they look for a girl who will stand silently by as they do horrible things.

I remember the day we heard the news of the former Heavenly Queen's death. How it rippled through the village, silencing everyone. Death isn't mourned, especially for a queen who simply returns to heaven. No, the stunned silence was because a new queen would have to be chosen. I gripped Gwan-si's hand, and she squeezed back.

"It'll be okay," she whispered.

It had been fifty years since the Star of Heaven was selected by the priests. Only my grandmother remembered what the Selection was like. And her spotted hands developed a tremor from the moment we heard that the queen was dead.

They came to town dressed in vivid blue silk robes. The high priests were older than my father. All unwed girls were to be presented to them in the center of each village. Before presentment, Mom had brushed our hair and put us all into our only dresses—the rough-spun ones we usually saved for special holy days when we went to temple. All families were forced to attend the presentment, even the boys and others who could not be chosen. No one was allowed to work that day. Sickness was no excuse. Everyone was corralled, like fish in a net.

The last Heavenly Queen had been chosen at age eighteen. Gwan-si, at only twelve, was the oldest of the three of us girls. My parents kept saying the priests wouldn't choose any of us to be queen. Mom's last words to me were, "Stop squirming, Song, you'll dirty your dress and I'll have to clean it before next holy day."

They were wrong. There wouldn't be a next time.

While everyone in the land must attend presentment in each village, participation in the Selection is "voluntary." That is what the high priests say, but if no one steps forward, there are consequences. We'd stood in a line, everyone too frightened to move, and the priests brought forward Oh Ma, the old village storyteller.

"As punishment for this town's lack of piety, the gods demand a sacrifice," the priest said.

Then they slit her throat. The crowd gasped, some screamed, children cried. Some, like me, were too shocked to react at all.

As the old storyteller who used to delight us with her tales lay dying, Gwan-si let go of my hand and stepped forward. Old High Priest Wen set his milky eyes on her perfect face and licked his lips, pointing a bony finger above her head. And that one motion shattered our lives.

"Run, Song! Run!" Gwan-si shouted at me as the priests laid the diamond crown of the Star of Heaven on her head.

But it was already too late.

Soldiers closed in around us, and my entire family was taken to the Silver Palace, a place far from our safe little village. There was no hope of escape. We were thrown into separate empty rooms and kept prisoner until it was the next full moon—the night of the coronation and the Letting.

That night I was loaded into a carriage and brought a short distance to the confluence of the five rivers of Husei. My sister stood still in a white, shimmering dress, illuminated by the moon as the chanting priests killed my grandmother first. Slowly. Gwan-si didn't scream or try to stop them, and then I knew: she wanted this. The power, the luxury, the life of a queen. My mother died bravely, my father screamed for mercy for his children. But there was no such thing as mercy—not to the high priests. The bodies were tossed into the rivers, and then I was next. The priests gripped me and brought me to the edge. The ground was already slick with steaming blood. Gwan-si calmly stepped forward, the red crown of the Heavenly Queen on her head.

"I will do it," she said.

I still relive that moment in my nightmares. The murmur through the circle of high priests. The stares at each other because this had never been done before. Then the dagger handed to Gwan-si.

"Kneel," the priests told me.

I stared at my sister, who'd taken care of me all my life. Her cold eyes stared back at me.

They brought me to my knees, but it was her blade that crossed my throat and her foot that kicked me into the river. And I don't remember anything after that, until I woke up to a gap-toothed girl looking down at me right before I threw up mud.

It's a long, grueling climb up the white tower. If I hadn't trained for this for years, I'd already have fallen. And though I'm comfortable with dying, I'm not in the mood to do so before I accomplish my mission. So I take it one motion at a time—one handhold, or I make one with my dagger, one foot, and then another foot. There's no moon tonight, and the guard who was supposed to patrol this area has already been taken out by Tria.

Tria is not my sister by blood, but seeing as my birth sister murdered our whole family, I don't put much stock in that. Tria and her parents are my family.

Tria is the one who found me on the riverbank, who brought me on her crop sleigh to her home. She shared her bread and her room with me. Her mother stitched and bandaged my neck. It healed quickly, and I tried to be as much a part of my new family as I could. Life was very different in the south than it had been in my northern village, where women took care of the children while the men fished. In the south, everyone worked on the farmland. It took me a while to get used to it, but the farmers minded their own business. No one asked where my parents had suddenly acquired a child who looked nothing like them. I worked harder than they ever asked me to, burning my pale skin in the fields until it finally tanned. They loved me, raised me, but there wasn't a day when I didn't think about the Letting.

"There's so much anger in you," my father said after I bloodied a boy who'd pinched Tria. I was only twelve, and he was fourteen, but I'd dropped him to the ground and left him crying. I was average size for a girl, but the rage from the Letting fueled me far beyond my strength.

"If you release that anger, you can be anyone you choose," my mother said. "You don't have to carry it with you. You can set it down here, Song."

My mother and father both tried to teach me mindfulness, and neither asked me what had happened, how I came to be washed up on the southern riverbank, and I was forever grateful for that. Grateful to have had a second chance—one for revenge.

Tria's at risk with my plan, and I hate that. She's dressed as a beggar girl, but if they search her, they'll find weapons and execute her. It won't matter that she's seventeen—peasant life is cheap, and it's not like they have issues with killing children. I would've kept her out of it entirely, but I can't do this without her help. She's better at poison darts than anyone I know. I need her to cover me while I climb. Just until I reach the top, where Gwan-si will be sleeping. After that, Tria will run back to our family and be safe.

I've waited years, but tonight has come about quickly. The Heavenly Queen arrived at the White Palace, the southernmost stronghold of Husei, last night. Once I saw the royal procession, I knew it was my chance. The Heavenly Queen moves around on the whim of High Priest Wen, based on what that old man reads or claims to read from the Heavens.

I laugh softly to myself as I climb. I could be put to death just for that blasphemous thought. Never mind the attempted regicide.

I'm almost at the top, and I hazard a glance down to make sure Tria has run back like we planned. She hasn't. I can just make out her brown curls in the bushes. I groan to myself. Stubborn girl.

"That's what makes us sisters, you know," Tria said

whenever I told her she was being unreasonable. Like when she lost our marble game but refused to yield. I respected that. The same way I respected how, when I was first healing, she'd sit by me but not ask questions. She liked that I didn't question why there was a second bed in her room or why she was an only child—unusual in Husei.

Silence bound us as much as stubbornness.

When I told her I planned to kill the queen, she didn't ask the reason. Maybe she guessed. Or maybe it's that my former sister isn't terribly popular with the people.

In the years since Gwan-si took the throne, the gods haven't been kind. Famine, plague, and, most important, drought have rocked the country. From what I understand, the southern prefects have had it better than most—the Tsai River still runs. Maybe that's why the White Palace is barely guarded; they think she's safe here.

I finally reach the highest room in the tallest tower, and my limbs are burning. Of course they couldn't have put her on the ground floor. I expect to have to break a window, but I try it, and it's unlatched. Gwan-si did always like a night breeze.

It's midnight when I squeeze through the window, drop silently into a crouch, and scan around the room. My pulse thuds in my throat. The room is empty, and so is the bed, aside from rumpled sheets.

My breath quickens. Did they know? Is this an ambush? A trap? Is Tria okay?

A light suddenly blooms across the room. A small one, on a dressing table.

"What took you so long?" the Heavenly Queen asks.

Gwan-si sits by her silver dressing table, calmly brushing her hair. Her ebony locks are just as shiny, but they're longer than I remember. Then again, she's eighteen. She's changed a lot since we last saw each other—we both have.

"Sorry?" I ask.

I hadn't expected to speak to her. I'd expected to thrust a dagger into her heart at the start of this reunion.

"I've been prisoner for, what? Six years?" she asks. "I thought you would've come to kill me at least a year or two ago . . . if you'd survived."

She puts her hairbrush down and stares at my reflection in her mirror. "You seem healthy. Strong. I'm grateful to the gods for it."

I swallow hard, my head trying to wrap itself around what she's saying. "You're a . . . prisoner?"

"Oh, Song," she says.

Frankly, she sounds disappointed, and that's strange, considering I've come to assassinate her. I have two daggers in my hands, but she hasn't called out for the guards, and she doesn't appear alarmed. If anything, she looks a little bored.

She turns in her seat to face me and gives me a small smile. "I'm glad you're here."

We both wear all white. We once looked alike, but now we don't. She's still pale and delicate like an orchid, and I'm tanned and muscled from working under the sun. Her hair is a long sheath, and I have bangs and the shorter hair favored by the south. The place I washed up in, thanks to her.

"You're glad? You cut my throat."

"I had to—otherwise they would've actually killed you."

"Actually?"

She purses her full lips. "I cut as shallow as possible so they'd think you died, and then I pushed you in the water so the current would take you away. I wasn't sure you'd survive, but it was the only chance. They were angry that you disappeared before they could verify that you were dead . . ." She shudders. Her eyes look vacant as she stares into space.

She's lying. She's lying, so I don't kill her. She's trying to lure me into a trap. She's not a prisoner who is glad to see me. Who'd spared me. She's the all-powerful queen.

But . . . she's telling the truth.

I know what Gwan-si looks like when she lies. I know she's not good at it. She tried to tell Mother she broke a vase once, when I was the one who'd dropped it, but she could never lie the way I could.

It's the truth.

I shake my head. No. This is impossible. For six years I've

47

believed she tried to murder me and then happily ruled from on high, with my entire family dead. But why did I believe that? My gentle sister, who'd wanted to heal and had flayed fish in one stroke, I believed she had tried to slit my throat and missed. When her quick thinking had saved me. And it worked. I was standing here talking to her.

I put one dagger away in the sheath on my chest.

Suddenly the thought enters my head of our little siblings also being found downstream, taken in by loving families.

"Hi-Jen and Jeung?" My voice rises hopefully.

With the quiver of her lips, I know it is a false hope.

Gwan-si swallows hard. She lowers her head but then forces herself to meet my eye. "I couldn't save them. Only you. You survived like I hoped you would. You're strong. You are the Star of Ruin." She refocuses on me. "You can end this."

I shake my head. "What? How?"

"You remember the Prophecy, don't you? Do what you came here to do. Kill me, and the people will believe that the Star of Ruin has come, and Husei will fall. High Priest Wen, the entire priesthood, will lose control of the land. They nearly have, with nothing working to stop the long drought. And then, with him gone, no other girls will be selected again."

I take a step back.

I'd come here to do this. To kill Gwan-si and avenge my birth family, but now . . . I can't. Not when she's the last remnant of my former life. Not when she did all she could to save me, to spare me.

"What?" Gwan-si tilts her head, scanning my expressions like she used to. "No. No, Song. You have to." She grips her chair, her pale skin getting even whiter at the knuckles.

"I can't." I rest the other dagger on her dressing table.

She stares at the blade, her shoulders slumping. "I have stayed alive hoping you'd come one day. Wen would've been just as happy if I died. They would've blamed me for the drought and selected a new queen, murdered another family. But if you won't kill me, this doesn't ever end."

A chill shakes me—the thought of another family going through what we went through. More girls having to watch everyone they love die slowly, helpless to save them.

"We'll kill Wen," I say. I'll burn in the ten hells for just saying this, supposedly, but I really don't care.

"You don't think I've tried?" She smiles, but it's not a happy smile. "He's nearly impossible to get to."

Gwan-si was always smarter than I was. I had more fight; she had more brains. But I try to get my head to work. There has to be a solution.

"The Prophecy doesn't need a dead queen," I say.

"Yes, it—"

I shake my head, remembering our mother's tale. It was a very strange bedtime story, but maybe some part of her knew this was our fate.

"No. It says the Star of Ruin will survive and bring about the end of Husei," I say. "It never says how. And if you're a prisoner, the priests are what need to be ended . . ."

My mind finally catches up. Killing Wen had seemed like the answer at first, but there are a dozen priests who could take his place. Cut the head off a rigi and two grow back. No—something else needs to be done to get rid of the whole rotten priesthood, or nothing will ever change.

"Run away with me," I say. "We'll find allies. We'll figure out how to take them down together."

Gwan-si frowns. "Song . . ."

"Think about it. They can't crown a new queen if the old one is alive. Come with me. Quickly. It's only a matter of time before someone realizes I'm here." I gesture toward the window.

She hesitates, and honestly, I don't have time for it.

"What's the worst that happens?" I say. "We die, and then the Prophecy is complete?"

She gives me another small smile. "I mean, when you put it that way . . ."

"Can you climb?" I ask.

She looks to the side, and that's not convincing. I'm strong, but not strong enough to make it with her on my back.

"Wait," she says. "I have an idea."

She opens a trunk, and inside there are yards of material for dresses and capes. We get to work slitting the softest fabric I've felt in my life and making a long rope, wordlessly working together like when we made fishing nets on the banks of the Yew. It's beyond strange—as if no time has passed at all.

A few minutes later, there's a knock on her door. We freeze with fear.

"Heavenly Queen," a voice says.

She gestures for me to get under her bed while she shoves everything back into the trunk. From under the bed, I see her sit on the box. Her dainty feet don't touch the floor.

"Enter," she says, as calmly as I've ever heard her.

"I saw a light under your door," an old male voice says. Wen. It must be. Why is he welcome in her bedchamber? No, it's not welcome. It's ownership. He's in charge, and she really is a prisoner.

Soundlessly, I shift a poison dart into my hand. My family farms, but they really make a living selling illegal poisons. Poisons to ease suffering, to mercifully sedate, and sometimes to kill.

"I could not sleep," Gwan-si says.

Wen's slippered feet stop in front of her. His silk robes graze the ground.

"But you must, child," he says. "You need your rest. The council of priests has agreed that tomorrow we will begin gathering the sacrifices."

"Sacrifices?" She says it slowly, and I can hear her horror in every syllable.

"Yes. The gods are angry, my queen, and must be appeased. We will gather two girls, sisters, from every protectorate and sacrifice them to the river gods in a ceremony at the next full moon. Their love for each other will bring back the rains."

Gwan-si gasps, and I run the numbers in my head. There are fifty protectorates in Husei. One hundred girls murdered by the priests under the next full moon. I clutch my dart. No, this ends now.

"It is what we must do to ensure the prosperity of Husei, of your rule," Wen says. "Now, let me help you get to sleep, child."

"Please, High Priest," she pleads.

I slide out from under the bed and slither toward them.

"I'd . . . I'd like a warm glass of milk with cardamom," she offers. "That will make me more . . . relaxed. Please."

He sighs. "Very well. I shall ask a servant."

Once he turns his back, I strike, thrusting the dart into his neck vein the way Tria has shown me. It will kill him within seconds.

Gwan-si covers his mouth with her hand to muffle his scream, and then he collapses. I help her catch him and remove the dart. He's a dead man now, even with the dart gone, and I don't want anything traceable to Tria or my parents.

I stare at him. It's a shame it'll be a relatively quick death.

"Hurry," Gwan-si whispers. "He has guards outside the door."

We toss Wen onto her bed and I tie the end of the rope to the drapery hook. The rope is not long enough, but we don't have a choice. We climb out the window, me first and Gwan-si after.

"Burn in ten hells," she says. Then she drives the dagger I'd left on her vanity into Wen's chest.

He utters a gasp. Good. He was still alive to feel it.

We climb down as fast as we can, my hands aching from skidding along the cloth. But the end of the rope is a good ten feet above the ground and we're too far away from the wall to scale down. I hang, then drop into a crouch, and even though I was prepared, pain shoots up my legs. Tria comes out of the bushes.

"Change of plans?" she asks, looking up.

"You changed them first. I'll explain later," I say.

"Okay," Tria says, staring at Gwan-si, who dangles at the end of the rope.

"Jump," I say as loud as I dare.

Another patrolman should've come by. Tria likely took him out with a dart. Unlike my deadly ones, hers are sedation darts and will wear off in an hour. My original plan had been to kill everyone. My sister is more merciful.

I'm waiting for Gwan-si to jump, and I'm thinking about how to kill all the priests when bells ring out into the night. Alarm bells. They must've found Wen's body.

"Jump. We'll catch you," Tria says.

I look over at her, grateful that she stayed. Grateful for her stubbornness.

Gwan-si hesitates but then lets go and falls backward. I catch around her torso and Tria catches her legs. It's enough force to make us stumble, but then we're off and running.

Or two of us are. Gwan-si makes it a few steps before her long gown trips her. She falls onto the grass. I run back, bend, and slit her dress from her thighs to her feet, breaking the hem.

With her legs free, Gwan-si easily keeps pace with us. She looks over at Tria a couple of times as my lungs burn in the sprint.

"Who is this?" Gwan-si asks.

"My sister," I say.

"Sister?" she asks. "Oh, adopted sister."

"Just sister," I say.

Despite running downhill for her life, Gwan-si looks apologetic. "Right. Right. Of course. I'm glad Song has you," she says to Tria.

"I'm glad most days," Tria says, giving her a real smile. It lights her face before it fades.

The last river in Husei, the Tsai, lies before us. I frankly don't like water since almost drowning in it, but it is what it is.

"Can you swim?" Tria asks, looking at my sister.

"I can," Gwan-si says. "But aren't . . . aren't there monsters in the water?"

I mean, yes, but it wouldn't help to say so.

"No," I say.

"Yes," Tria says at the same time.

I turn and make a face at Tria, but there's no time. We have to get into the water and risk the rigi and other river monsters. I'm not sure that any monster is worse than a high priest willing to kill a hundred girls to keep control over the country, though I'm not excited to test out the theory.

"Well, hopefully we won't have to find out," Tria says, pulling a small raft out from under a bush. It's the one we used to get to the shore of the White Palace. The one she was supposed to have destroyed.

"Did you listen to a thing I said earlier?" I ask.

"You're welcome," she says.

I stare at her and then get on board.

"Your Majesty." She gestures for Gwan-si to get in.

We scramble onto the reed raft, and with a push of Tria's pole, we're off, away from the palace, leaving behind the dead high priest and taking a queen.

I keep watch, with Tria's darts at the ready, but we haven't been spotted yet.

So, tonight didn't go as planned.

But I'm alive, and my family made it, and I'm thankful to the gods for that. I don't know what to do now—except whatever it takes to escape. To live and fight another day.

I'm not sure if I am the Star of Ruin—if that's even real. I look to the sky, but there aren't any stars out to guide us.

And just as we start downriver, it begins to rain. The three of us tip our heads back, joy on all our faces. Tria and her oval-shaped face, Gwan-si and her heart-shaped perfect face, and me. For the first time in six years, something stirs in my chest. It's hope. A fragile wish that with my sisters beside me, tomorrow will be better. That together we can change everything.

HOW SLOW THE SNOW IS FALLING

BY MARK OSHIRO

My phone is vibrating as I pull out of the parking lot of my apartment complex.

I don't know what winter is like in other parts of the world, but today in Crenshaw, the sun is out. It's a dry warmth. Mom says that where she grew up—outside of Atlanta—they don't have this kind of heat. It's all wet and sticky. But I'm already sweating, and my skin feels like I rolled around in a vat of honey, so I'm not really sure what the difference is.

I drive toward winter. *Actual* winter. At least that's what Ray told me about Big Bear. "It's covered in snow in January," he said. "So, as soon as you're seventeen and your mom lets you go on solo trips, we *have* to go there."

His backpack is in the passenger seat. I even buckled it in. My stuff is inside it: a change of clothes, some deodorant, a toothbrush and toothpaste. It was all I could grab before I stormed out of the house. But the bag? It's still his.

But he's not here. He's dead.

Tears well in my eyes, and then I laugh because I really don't want to be a cliché so early into this trip. I have at least two hours to go before I head up into the mountains, and then it's another hour until I hit the lake. Our lake. The one we planned on going to—to watch the snow fall. Is it still *our* lake if one of us is no longer here?

Yes.

Yes, of course. Just like the bag. It's his.

Ours.

Something like that.

My phone vibrates again.

I don't answer it.

Everyone drives in California. I guess I do, too, now. Mom taught me all by herself, and she has a tendency to correct every little habit I develop, so that I drive more like her. "You have to be safe, Adrian," she told me once, then pointed at the steering wheel. "Ten and two is safe and true!"

She is full of little sayings like that, ones she made up that literally no other human has ever said before. I hear her in my head now, and I keep one of my hands at six instead as I steer onto the 10. I'm sure she'd yell at me for doing this.

She probably has other things she is angry about right now.

I hit the metaphorical wall: the sea of cars, the parking lot that is the 10. I watch as the estimated time of arrival jumps up twenty minutes on my phone's GPS.

Living here, it's hard not to be well-versed in LA traffic. I generally avoid driving, especially since they built that Expo Line by our apartment. But I couldn't pull off this trip using public transportation unless I was willing to take two subway trains, then the Metrolink all the way out to San Bernardino, and *then* a two-hour bus that snaked its way up Highway 330 until it looped around Big Bear Lake. It was something like six hours in one direction, and the idea of being trapped in a bunch of metal containers with strangers—strangers who might not be vaccinated, who might infect me, who might panic seeing a tiny brown person wearing makeup—yeah, no. I couldn't risk that. Certainly not alone.

Plus, this was always supposed to be a road trip. Road trips are quintessentially Californian. Our state is so damn big that you kinda have to do a few if you ever plan to do anything outside the city where you live. But since it's just me and Mom, we pretty much never had the time or money to go on any.

Until Ray. After he and I became completely inseparable, I got invited on a road trip with him and his family. Ray's parents drove us from Los Angeles out to Joshua Tree, a desert landscape that looked completely fake. Like . . . how can the actual Earth look photoshopped? The Joshua trees themselves were weird enough. They rose from the dry earth, arms branching out and holding what looked like spiky pom-poms cheering on the desert sky. Then there were the rock formations and the cholla cactus and the sunsets. I barely felt like I was on Earth anymore.

That's where Ray got the idea. We were lying on two enormous rocks while Ray's parents chatted with some other hikers. The sun was so hot and piercing that I was certain we were going to melt, and I told Ray that my gender was sweaty and tired. He said his was Dreaming of Snow, complete with the capitalization and everything. I told him that sounded pretty metal, and he sat up and shielded his eyes with his right hand.

"Let's go to the snow next year," he said.

But it doesn't snow in the desert, I told him.

"Sometimes it does."

But what if we come out here and it doesn't snow?

"We could go to Big Bear. Or somewhere else in the mountains."

Isn't snow cold?

"A stunning observation," he said. "Your gender is actually . . . a thembo."

Thembo.

"You know, a himbo, but nonbinary."

Thembo.

I like that, I told him.

"I knew you would," he said, and he lay back down under the sun.

That's how the idea started, and then it grew, and then Ray died.

My phone vibrates as the 10 becomes the 60.

I ignore it again.

California is unnecessarily long, yes, but it's also wide. It's been an hour, and I've just come down over the last set of hills and into Pomona. I've only been here once, back before everyone started getting sick. There's a venue not far from where I'm at called the Glass House, and Ray and I took the Metrolink from Union Station here so we could see this pop-punk band, Meet Me @ The Altar. We had to leave early so we could make sure to catch the last bus back to LA, and we missed the headlining band. I remember being frustrated that the train didn't return to Union Station in the evening because it was apparently only for commuters. Do we not count? I asked Ray.

"Maybe you should ask your mom about driving," he said. "Then you'd at least have another option."

I resist the temptation to get off the 60 and go stand outside the Glass House. I have these urges sometimes to do things that I think will conjure up Ray's spirit. I don't believe he's "out there" or anything. If he really was going to contact me, he'd have done so already, wouldn't he? It doesn't make sense that he'd make me wait for over a year. Plus, we were only at the Glass House for a couple hours, so why would he choose that place to hang around as a ghost?

The traffic finally picks up, but I'm mostly zoning out, because all I can think about is where Ray *would* haunt. Maybe that one thrift store on Melrose where the clerk told us that he didn't know why we wore makeup. At the same time . . . I don't think Ray would be entertained by haunting a musty, overpriced thrift store. It would get old, knocking over racks of clothing or breathing down the necks of unknowing hipsters all the time.

There's no way he'd haunt school. God, what a scam that would be. What if you died and had to go to school for the rest of your life?

I slam on the brakes as a whole blur of red lights flash ahead of me. I glance at my phone, and it's nearly noon. Snowfall is supposed to hit at 2:30 p.m., and my arrival . . . still at two, despite how much progress I've made.

Maybe this is how Ray is haunting me. He's causing traffic because . . . because he couldn't be here. And he doesn't want me to do this. It's punishment.

I roll down the window and stick my head out into the warm, dry air. No. No, I can't believe that Ray wouldn't want me to do this. He wouldn't want me to give up on life just because he isn't around.

Man, this is the fucking worst. I just want to talk to him again.

I grab my phone. Crank up some Raised Fist, something loud and heavy and angry. There are multiple missed calls, all from her, but I can't talk. I just can't.

I see one message, though.

Please be safe.

Is it bad that I want to be unsafe just to spite her?

I impulsively reach down and unbuckle my seat belt, but that lasts a whole five seconds before I wrench it back over my body. Yeah, that's not gonna fix anything, and I don't want to end up dead like Ray.

Dead like Ray. Huh. That would make a good band name.

As I drive on, I am not sure I have a single thought for the next hour, other than replaying seeing Ray for the last time. He was in a hospital bed, and we couldn't visit him, so it was over Zoom. He told me he was certain he was going to get better the next day. I told him he couldn't leave me before we actually formed a band and went on tour. Our band name was The Gay Agenda, and it was too good a name to end up never playing shows.

But he left us in the middle of the night.

Why? Why couldn't he just hold on a little bit longer?

Mom says I have to stop saying that Ray left *me*. That makes it sound personal, like he chose to abandon me when he died. I guess that makes sense, but my brain latches onto this irrational idea as I brake, speed up, maneuver around a stalled pickup truck, and slowly inch toward the mountains.

But she's right. I know it. Ray would never have chosen this.

It better snow. There have been too many disappointments lately.

She calls. I let it vibrate.

I can tell I'm no longer in Los Angeles; everything seems so spread out around here, like the buildings are allergic to one another. My GPS had me head up the 15 to the 210, and now I've got a bunch of industrial-looking warehouses to the south of me and the San Gabriel Mountains looming to the north. There is no snow on them, and I'm starting to wonder if this trip is going to be as pointless as it seems to be. We'd been planning it for so long, and then after Mom pissed me off, I packed my backpack and left. I should have thought this through more. What if the weather app is lying? What if I get up to Big Bear and it's just as warm as it is down here?

What if *that* is the haunting? What if Ray is tricking me into going on this trip, only to have the last laugh when I get there?

I can't even be mad at this wildly irrational hypothetical scenario, because I'd kill someone to hear him laugh again. Not like . . . literally kill someone. Now I get that whole thing of not wishing something on their worst enemy. I couldn't do *this* to someone else.

A black Mazda veers sharply to the right and cuts right in front of me, nearly clipping my front bumper. I honk, but it doesn't matter, because the driver has already changed lanes again and is zooming ahead of everyone, forcing other cars to slam on their brakes.

Never mind. Maybe that person deserves it.

She calls me again.

I almost answer this time.

I don't know how anyone traveled anywhere before phones existed. It seems impossible to me. How did people know which highways or roads to take? I vaguely remember Mom saying that she has a map in the glove box, but I'm not excited by the prospect of roughing it in the wilderness with just me, a map, and a compass.

Wait. I don't own a compass.

Not long after my phone buzzes again, I see the sign flashing off to the side of the freeway:

HIGHWAY 330 CLOSED TO ALL TRAFFIC

I zoom past it too quickly to see if there is any more information, but the anxiety flushes through my chest. The Target is the first thing I recognize, so I exit the 210 as soon as I can, then pull into the parking lot, way in the back, far from any of the other cars.

I slam my hand on the steering wheel. *Think, Adrian, think.* I suppose I could call Mom and ask her. Would she tell me?

I'm not ready to talk to her, so I look at my phone again. Right. I could just . . . choose a different route. There has to be more than one way up the mountain.

After forcing the app to avoid Highway 330, I see that it wants me to head up Highway 38, but because of the detours and closures, it'll add two hours to my trip. Two hours will get me in after the snowfall. I switch over to the weather app, and it *says* that snow is still expected to happen in Big Bear, so all I need is enough. Enough to fall, enough to stick, enough that I can dig my fingers into it and make our dream come true.

My dream.

Our dream.

Two hours. I can do that! I mean, I've never driven on a narrow, two-lane highway that climbs up a mountain before, but I am a thembo. This one is for my people.

It's also for Ray—because it *has* to be.

But first: a pit stop. Those are also a necessary part of any road trip, especially if I'm going to survive this climb. I slip on a mask and head for the entrance. I don't know what they feed the Targets out here in the Inland Empire. Steroids? Five meals a day? I've never seen one as enormous as this one. It's two stories, and each story is as big as the one we go to off of Obama Boulevard and La Cienega. I'm overwhelmed instantly and forget what I'm supposed to do.

One step at a time. I rush over to the bathrooms, pausing only to wonder which one gives me the smallest chance of being harassed. I don't know how they treat nonconforming folks like me all the way out here in San Bernardino, but I've not heard great things. So, for the moment, I duck into the men's room, making the trip as quick as possible between peeing and washing my hands. Thankfully, no one else is around; I guess Tuesday afternoons are the best time to come to this Target, as the store is mostly empty.

I have to be quick so I can get back on the road again. I get some Cheez-Its, the world's greatest snacking cracker, and two bottles of water. I'm certain I will have been in and out of a Target in record time, when I am caught in the dreadful snares of a nail polish display. Not just any, but one in my favorite brand that has all these metallic and matte colors that I love.

That we loved.

That *he* loved.

Ugh. Who knew that word tenses would break my heart someday?

I choose a midnight-blue shade and make my way to the self-checkout, but there's a long line and not a single person at the normal checkout stands. Take that, technology! Thwarted by me and my observant behavior. I drop the few items I have on the conveyor belt, and a seated Black woman—her name tag says "Brenda"—immediately picks up the nail polish.

"Oooh, this is a nice color," says Brenda. "I think my baby would like this one."

"Thanks," I say.

"Have you worn it before?" she asks, scanning the water

and dropping it into one of those cheap reusable bags Target sells.

"Um . . . not yet. I just like that brand a lot."

Brenda glances up at me and smiles. "Well, I think you'll look wonderful in it."

That's all she says, other than giving me the total and wishing me a nice day after I pay. I tell her that I hope she does, too, and I mean it. As I walk out of the Target, I feel lighter. More myself. And all it took was a reminder from a total stranger that I am living as I want to.

I have to climb this mountain.

I can't let Ray down.

The phone vibrates.

There's traffic again, this time on the ramp that turns off to California State Route 38. I chug along slowly in Mom's Honda, and sweat is already pouring down my back. The window is down, but without much movement, there's no real air circulating through the car. The AC has been broken for months.

It can't snow today. There's no *way*.

But I keep going, and soon the highway narrows to two lanes and the cars ahead of me start moving. The breeze is nice—still warm and dry, but enough to hit the sweat on my temples and cool me down. I don't know if I'm supposed to do anything special driving uphill; I mostly keep my foot pressed on the gas pedal more than I expect to because of how quickly this highway rises into the mountains. Soon I'm twisting and turning through dense patches of green on my right and the terrifying maw of the valley to my left.

I hate it. It's gorgeous whenever I have a moment to glance over the Inland Empire, but I'm incredibly aware that one wrong turn and I'll join Ray. *If I die here*, I think, *does that mean I have to haunt a highway*? Well, that might be kinda fun. Better than a thrift store.

It hits all at once. I'm far from home. *Really* far. The trip to Joshua Tree a year and a half ago was farther, but I was with Ray's family. I'm all by myself in this Honda, still unsure it even has the power to make it up this mountain, and a million things can go wrong.

They already have. All of them are named Ray.

When the change happens, I don't notice it. It's suddenly . . . different. The low green brush has given way to these tall pine trees that hug the highway, and the air . . . it's actually cool. Like *really* cool. How did that happen? I've been too focused on the road and the taillights of the 4Runner ahead of me, which *never* seems to brake around any of the hairpin turns. I'm dangerously close to being *under* the speed limit at this point, so I steal a glance in my rearview mirror.

Great. There's a whole line of cars behind me.

My heart thumps faster. Faster than I'm driving.

The phone vibrates on the little mount attached to the dashboard. It's her. *Again.*

It's all happening at once, and I'm certain I'm about to burst.

I reach out. I reach *back*.

"Hang up," I tell her. "Mom, just hang up."

"Adrian, *please*," she says. "Where are you?"

"Hang up!" I repeat, my voice rising high. "I'll call right back."

"You promise?" Her words rattle through the phone. Is she crying?

"I promise. But don't answer."

"What?"

"Let it go to voice mail," I explain. "I promise I will call." She's silent for a moment.

"Okay, Adrian," she says. "I'm sorry."

I see the sign as I hang up on her, and I know it's the only reprieve I'll get:

VISTA POINT

An arrow points to the right, and seconds later, I see the turnout. I take it and slide into one of the empty spots, letting out a long breath as I do. I grab my phone off the mount and practically throw myself out of the car.

Vehicles are zooming by. *Still*. How many people had I held up?

"I hope you're laughing at me, Ray," I say aloud, resting my forearms against the driver-side door, my head down.

"Because I feel like the universe's biggest joke."

What am I *doing*? The air might be a lot cooler up here, but this doesn't feel cold enough for snow. I suck in air and choke back a cry, then look up the mountain. I don't even know how much farther I have to go. And there's definitely no snow there. Some clouds in the distance, sure, but . . .

This was a bad idea.

Maybe it's time to admit that.

Then I turn to face the direction my car is headed, and . . . wow. Holy shit. There are so many trees here, and they grow close to one another, like they're friends. Yes. They're friends. I've decided this. And they're all trying to keep one another warm and look out for the others, and then I'm crying because this is exactly the kind of silly, ridiculous idea that I would talk to Ray about, and he should *be* here, but he isn't.

I have to talk to her.

I scroll to Mom's contact page on my phone, and her kind brown eyes look out at me from the photo I saved of her. It's from three years ago, and what I've never told her is that I saved it because that was the day I met Ray. Mom took me to this group meeting at a local church—one we'd never been to because we aren't the churchgoing type of family—so I could meet other kids like me. That's not code for something Mom couldn't really talk to me about. She was being sincere, and even if I'm mad at her, I see the photo I saved of her that I took at dinner that night, and I remember that she tried. Hard.

And that's how I met Ray.

Ray's parents adopted him from Bangladesh. I'm from . . . well, somewhere in Central America. We don't really know. But that was what the group was for, and as I tap on the phone icon to call Mom, I try to keep that group in mind.

She meant well.

So she must *mean* well.

She's adopted, too. She was born in Korea, but two very heterosexual white people adopted her and brought her to a suburb outside Atlanta. It might seem weird to make it a point to call them "heterosexual," but you've never met Barb and Ronald. Or maybe you have, if you've met a couple like them. They are the most heterosexual people I have ever met. Very nice, but Barb feels like a living "Live, Laugh, Love" sign, and the only thing Ronald ever wants to talk to me about is his extensive love of John Deere tractors.

They're cute.

Thankfully, Mom doesn't answer. The call goes to voice mail, which is just the opening two measures of "Stars" from *Les Misérables*, repeating over and over. "This is Anna," she says over the violins. "Leave a message, and I'll get back to you soon."

There's a beep.

I breathe in.

"I'm safe, Mom. I'm almost there. At least I think I am. I

pulled off the highway, so don't worry. I'm not doing anything unsafe.

"I had to leave, Mom. I know you're doing your best. With my pronouns and letting me dress how I want and everything. Ray's parents weren't as good to him. So I'm thankful.

"But you can't say stuff like that to me anymore. I know you're trying hard, and I know your parents are confused sometimes, but . . . I heard you talking to them. Saying that you're adjusting to the fact that I'm not the same person you adopted.

"I mean . . . yes, everyone changes, and maybe you meant that. That I'm just a different person and I'm growing up, and maybe you're a little sad about that. But it sounded like something else. Like I had magically changed into a new being who you didn't recognize anymore just by virtue of being myself.

"I'm still Adrian. Okay? Yes, I'm different, but . . . I'm still Adrian.

"I hope you know that."

I pause. Take in a deep lungful of air.

"I *think* you know that.

"I probably should have asked you if I could take the car, even though you don't work today. Sorry about that. But can you understand that I have to do this? If I don't do it now, I might be far, far away when I go to college in the fall, and then it might never happen at all.

"I don't even know if I'm going to see snow today. The weather says it's supposed to happen in the next twenty minutes, and I see some clouds, but I think I'm going to be disappointed. Which kinda seems fitting, since he isn't here to see it.

"Just . . . let me do this one thing, okay? Then I'll come back home. Just this one thing.

"I love you, Mom."

My phone doesn't buzz when I walk back to the car, nor in the next half hour as I try my best to keep up with the car in front of me on Highway 38. Everyone driving up here must be a local, because they're all taking the curves so effortlessly. I still have the window down, even though it's starting to feel genuinely cold. It's because I can't stop sweating. This highway shouldn't exist. It's an affront to a God I don't even believe in. Like . . . why couldn't they just build a road with less curves? Or maybe something more than a tiny metal guardrail to save me from certain death when I miss a turn and go careening over the edge as poppunk blares from my speakers.

There's a good joke in that somewhere, but I only wince. Thinking about death hits differently now, even when I'm trying to rely on humor.

Maybe Mom was right. This year probably changed me into an entirely new person.

Keeping my eyes focused on the road, I'm trying to look at the densely packed pines. That sensation arrives again:

this looks photoshopped. It simply doesn't look real! I catch an earthy whiff of pine that instantly relaxes me, but I roll up the window shortly after that. The cold seems to drop on me, piercing my skin just like the heat did out in Joshua Tree.

The highway isn't as steep anymore, and I'm starting to see signs of human life. Wooden cabins. Roads that turn off and head deeper into the forest. I slow and pass a cyclist pumping their little spandex legs as fast as they can.

I'm shivering as I drive. Maybe this won't be a pointless trip after all. But I look at the time on the dashboard, and it was supposed to start snowing forty minutes ago.

Did I miss it? Did it already fall and melt away? It probably did, and what a perfect end to this impulsive nightmare of a trip. It was doomed from the start, wasn't it?

There's a town now. Or maybe this is all Big Bear, I don't exactly know. I see a small community store, then a sign for a motel that looms above a flat beige building with red overhangs. It's kinda cute, to be honest, like something you'd see on a postcard.

I twist to the right to tell this to Ray, but it's just his (my) (our) backpack sitting there, and I decide . . . fuck it.

"Where are we, Ray?" I ask. "Is this Big Bear?"

The backpack is silent.

"I just saw a sign for a place called the Lumberjack Café. We must be close."

No response, unsurprisingly.

"It better fucking snow," I tell him. "It's taken me four hours to go like a hundred and twenty miles. Maybe I'll find a hot lumberjack boyfriend."

I laugh, then. It's the laugh of someone who has thought something utterly blasphemous.

"Is it not snowing because you're in hell, Ray? If so, you better save me a seat. They got reruns of *The Golden Girls* down there? I bet they do."

The road forks, but my phone says to stay to the left, and then I see it:

Blue. A massive field of blue.

"Ray, look!" I say, pointing. I can see more of it, past the pine trees and the granite boulders on the side of the road and the tiny gas station.

Big Bear Lake. It has to be that.

My GPS says I'm basically here, but I realize I hadn't entered something specific. I just put in "Big Bear Lake." I slow and move to the side of the road. After some careful researching, I pull off what is now Route 18 and onto Fox Farm Road. I hook a sharp right on Marina Point Drive, and moments later, the crystal-blue water shimmers under the thick white clouds.

"Holy shit," I mutter, pulling my car into an open spot alongside the small park at the shore. Then I'm climbing out, my mouth practically on the ground. This is what I imagine the Pacific Ocean *should* look like. We humans ruined it and made it look like a scuzzy pond in a derelict shopping center. I can see the north shore of the lake, but it stretches so far to the west that it almost seems to go on forever. Green and brown mountain ridges poke up into the skyline, and goose bumps raise all over me. I'm clutching myself to stay warm, but I also know that the sensation is a reaction to what sits before me.

Ray was right. This is fucking awesome.

"I wish you were here," I mutter, and then I stop caring about being a cliché, because maybe clichés exist exactly for this reason. It feels cheesy to cry here on the edge of this lake, but it's the realest thing I've felt since I stormed out of our home and climbed into Mom's Honda.

I wish he was here. Death is senseless and pointless and final, and another cliché rolls around in my head: I'd do anything to have him back.

I got my head buzzed short a couple days ago, so I feel it first on my scalp. It's a sharp prick, and I swat at my head. I think it's an insect that bit me, which also would have been tragically ironic, because of *course* a mosquito or bee would find me in the middle of winter. But then there's another, and it's on my hands, and when I look up, a snowflake lands in my eye.

I whoop in excitement and dance about on the cement path in this tiny park, fully aware that of all possible outcomes, this is perhaps the cheesiest. It's *snowing*. It's snowing, just like we wanted it to, just like I needed it to.

I take out my phone, and the flakes flutter to the ground

softly as I film them. "It's happening," I say.

I move to send it to Ray.

No. There's no point in that.

Because maybe he's here. Maybe this is what I was waiting for.

Nah. That's probably not true. But it's nice to think it is.

I send it to Mom.

Made it, I tell her. I think Ray did, too.

She'll like that.

I watch how slow the snow is falling, and every movie and TV show I've ever seen that depicted it . . . shit . . . I guess it *does* look like that. The flakes are flat, and many of them melt when they hit the ground, but then more and more of the white specks drop down on me, so I hold my arms out. I don't move. Minutes later, there is a thin layer of snow resting on the sleeves of my Paramore hoodie, and I'm like a punk rock scarecrow, warding off all the bad vibes.

"I wish you were here," I say aloud once more.

The snow falls gently on the lake, and the only sounds are the water lapping at the shore. My breath in my throat. My heart pounding in my ears.

Ray should be here, but he's not.

But I'm glad I am.

SHAWL DANCE

BY SUSAN HARNESS

Katy stared at the colorful full-size poster that was pinned to the board in her history class.

> *10th Annual Fort Kyle Powwow!*
> *Fort Kyle Community Center. Saturday and Sunday*
> *9 a.m. to 5 p.m. Contest Powwow, all age groups.*
> *Everyone invited!*

That was this coming weekend!

The poster showed dancers in colorful outfits whose feathers, caught in the static nature of the camera, seemed to sway of their own accord, becoming a vibrant swirl of hue and culture. She ran her hand across the matte finish, her gaze taking in the beautiful brown skin tones that matched her own, the brown eyes that stared back at her.

Katy sighed. No matter how much she wanted to be a part of this, it would never happen. The string that tied her to whatever original culture she'd once been part of had been broken thirteen years ago, when her parents signed the adoption papers for her, the one-year-old Native American baby who needed a home.

Katy always felt as if she stood out, in an uncomfortable way. She hardly knew anyone who looked like her, either at the private high school she attended or in Fort Kyle, Colorado, itself.

The topic of immigration had come up a couple weeks earlier in her history class. "Two questions," Mrs. Clarke had said. "Where did your ancestors come from?"

As Katy listened to the students' answers, it seemed like everyone knew their family history, and most of them had stories handed down from one generation to the next, or they had a relative who had researched a family tree and gifted it to family members.

Several students had ancestors who came from Germany to work the sugar beets in the late 1800s. Some had ancestors from Eastern Europe who arrived at Ellis Island, or Quebec, in the early 1900s to join family members already here. They found jobs in slaughterhouses, butcher shops, or factories in the big cities. A few had family, typically men, who came from Mexico to work in the fields or orchards. One girl said her family was a direct descendant of one of the people on the *Mayflower*; they'd arrived before the United States was even the United States.

Katy's own adoptive parents had ancestors who emigrated from Europe. Her mom's Scots-Irish kin arrived in the early 1700s, settling in the Appalachians; her father's family came from Norway in the early 1800s.

But it was conversations like the one in history class that made her feel so different from the people around her. Talking about where their relatives came from was different from talking about her own heritage, her ancestors, a life and people she had no knowledge of. The only information her birth certificate offered was that her mother was Native American and her father's nationality was unknown. There was no mention of tribe.

Which opened up a ton of questions, intrusive and embarrassing. What does being Native American even mean? That was the question she asked herself the most. And there was no answer. So, that day, a couple of weeks ago, Katy slinked down into her seat and hoped the teacher wouldn't call on her.

Katy returned her attention to the poster. Perhaps this was something that could provide some answers. Maybe this powwow could begin to fill in the gaps. She imagined being invisible there because she looked like everyone else. In Fort Kyle, she wasn't invisible. Sometimes, when she went into a fancy-dress store or attended the ballet performances her parents liked to buy tickets for, she could feel people's eyes rest on her, follow her. She sensed the difference between them: she was brown, they were white. And, she had to admit, there were almost no brown people who entered those spaces. So she stuck out.

But at the powwow no one would stare at her like that, like she didn't belong. She'd just look like everyone else. Unless her parents went with her. Then she would stand out because they would, her dad with his blond hair and blue eyes and her mom with her green eyes and red, curly hair that always seemed wildly out of control even when it was pulled back into a ponytail. Everyone would look at her, wondering why a Native American girl was hanging around two older white people.

She sighed. Could she just exist and have that be okay?

"Hey, kiddo. I was waiting for you in the car."

Katy turned to see her mom leaning against the doorframe of the now-empty classroom.

"Oh, sorry!" she said. "I didn't realize how late it was."

"That's okay." Her mom nodded toward the poster. "Did you want to go?"

"Yeah." Katy paused. "I'd like to."

"I sense a *but* . . ."

Katy turned and walked back to her desk as if to get her notebook. Really, what she didn't want was to see her mom's face as she said her next words. "I'd like to go by myself."

Katy cringed. Even saying it caused her throat to tighten

82

with anxiety, fearing that her mom might be hurt or angry. But when Katy turned around, she breathed a small sigh of relief. Her mom didn't seem upset at all. She *was* quiet, and the quiet was uncomfortable. Katy bit her lower lip as she waited for a response.

Finally, her mom, with that calming smile she could pull out of thin air—she was a social worker, after all—replied. "Honey, I get that." Katy exhaled, not even realizing she'd been holding her breath. Her mom placed her arm around Katy's shoulders. "I've known this day was coming when you would want to experience the world on your own. But I need to think about this, so let's talk about it more tomorrow?"

Katy nodded. There was hope.

The following evening, her mom came up to Katy's room, where Katy lay on her bed doing her homework. After knocking, Mom entered and pulled out the chair at her desk, sat down, and leaned forward, her elbows on her knees. She tilted her head to one side and smiled. "I know you really want to go to the powwow. But I'll be honest, I'm just not comfortable with you going alone."

"Mom! I'm not a child!" Cold fingers of anxiety crept through her. Her invisibility meant everything. She just wanted to blend in, for once, with everyone else. And her parents, by being there, were going to make that impossible.

"No one said you were a child," her mom said with a quiet

smile. "But you're not fully an adult either. Look, here's my concern. You're going to be participating in an event where you don't know anyone, and where I don't know anyone. I can't protect you if something happens."

"Like what?" Katy couldn't keep the exasperation from her voice.

Her mom shrugged. "I don't know. But you're a young woman, and to travel by yourself among so many strangers, that's never a good idea." Katy opened her mouth to voice an argument, but her mom held up a hand and continued. "So, here's an option. Last night I talked with Donna Lone Elk, a Cheyenne woman who works with me. She's been aware of the event, and she said that your interest in attending was exciting. She offered to go with you, to introduce you to the Native American people in Fort Kyle. To introduce you to the culture and to begin helping you find a sense of community." She paused and watched Katy with a steady gaze. "How does that sound?"

Katy weighed the option. It would be more fun to be with someone than just by herself. And to have Donna go with her meant she'd blend in.

"Thanks, Mom! That sounds great. What time will she be here?"

"It starts at nine, so she'll pick you up at eight thirty."

Although Katy wanted to hug her mom the way she used to when something great happened, she hesitated. This thing that was happening? It didn't really include her mom. Her emotions swirled like a whirlwind, and she didn't know when they would settle down.

Or even if they would.

When Donna arrived, Katy had been waiting with a mixture of excitement and anxiousness to have her day begin. She opened the door to a woman who stood taller than she by a few inches, with large dark eyes and a warm smile. Her long black hair, which curved around her face and tumbled over her shoulders and down her back, was reflective in its brightness.

"Katy! It is so nice to meet you," Donna said, pulling her into a gentle hug. "I'm Donna, and I am so honored to go with you to your first powwow. It will be a lot of fun, you'll meet some really nice people, and the Indian tacos are the best!"

"What are Indian tacos?" Katy asked.

"All the fixings of a taco except on fry bread. They're a treat during powwow season."

Donna turned toward Katy's mom. "I'll bring Katy back when it ends, about five thirty." She turned back to Katy. "Ready?"

Katy nodded, turned around, and gave her mom a huge smile and a thumbs-up.

Her mom did the same.

The community center was only fifteen minutes from Katy's house. They'd found a parking spot several rows away from the building. Katy grabbed her purse, and Donna pulled a large shoulder bag from her back seat and led the way.

Weaving their way through the crowd, they found seats a couple rows up in the bleachers. They got settled, and within moments there seemed to be a never-ending line of people who wanted to talk with Donna. Katy was amazed at how many people she seemed to know. Donna had something nice or funny to say, or a touch, a hug, or she'd take someone's hand in hers and not let go for a long time. It was as if the warmth emanating from Donna wrapped itself around each person. Sometimes strangers looked at Katy with interest, with curiosity, and she'd smile back. But sitting here among all these brown faces, she finally felt like she blended in.

While Donna was busy, Katy gazed around the large gymnasium. The six baskets that hung from the ceiling had been pulled up out of the way. In the center, a large oval space had been cleared, bordered by a stage, and surrounded by folding chairs, some that belonged to the center, others that people had brought with them.

Throughout the gym, there were families of grandparents, mothers, fathers, daughters, and sons, some dressed in street clothes, many in colorful outfits that announced they'd be taking part in the dancing. Katy watched as women braided their daughters' or granddaughters' hair, pulling the dark, glossy strands tight against their scalp and deftly weaving the tresses into two French braids that, many times, ended in plaits far below their shoulders. Other women of various ages seemed to have some sort of unfinished project in their lap: a partially beaded piece of leather or a shawl that required long strings of fringe, their fingers continuously busy.

Boys strutted, the colorful feathers of their outfits waving with each step; men stood and talked with one another, sometimes seriously, sometimes sharing a deep laugh. Katy smiled at the energy and the joy that permeated the air around her.

"The costumes are beautiful!" Katy said as she took in the vibrant displays.

Donna leaned close. "We don't call them costumes. Costumes are for theater, playacting. What we do here is what we've done forever. We gather, we drum, we sing, we dance, we give thanks to the Creator for giving us this time of celebration. So, the clothes you see are called outfits, or regalia. They aren't pretend." Although Donna's words were serious, they were softened by her smile. Katy turned away with a smile of her own. Now she knew something about what it meant to be Native American.

People continued to amble by to talk with Donna, and every so often she introduced Katy as the daughter of a distant cousin. The first time it happened, Katy's eyes grew wide. "But I'm not!"

Donna laughed and winked. "We don't know you aren't."

The Native American color guard opened the ceremony. Dressed in military fatigues, men and women marched in step to the drums, holding the flags of their country and their tribal identity in front of them. It was a solemn ceremony of pride and remembrance, and everyone in the audience stood to show their respect for these warriors.

"Welcome, everybody, to the tenth annual Fort Kyle Powwow!" the emcee's voice boomed over the loudspeaker. His role was to oversee the event. He loosened the crowd up with a few jokes, some of which drew laughter, some groans. He then introduced the six drum groups and gave a short lesson on propriety and respect for the space, the culture, and the dancers themselves. Grand Entry was announced by the first drum group, who pounded the central drum around which several young men sat, their voices high and tense in their throat, their eyes closed. Before the dancers even entered through the far door, Katy heard the jingles. Everything here left an impact on her senses.

As the loud, energetic group entered the arena, Donna pointed out the types of dancers and their styles. The movements of the traditional dancers were deliberate, regal. With heads held high and backs straight, they carried a quiet pride. The sound of bells announced the women's jingle and the men's grass dancers, which were more energetic. The women's dresses held many rows of silver cones that clinked in time with their steps. The most dynamic of the dance styles were the men's fancy and the women's fancy shawl, which showed the athleticism, speed, and grace in their footwork. The women, dressed in colorful satin dresses, held their shawls over their shoulders, between their spread hands, giving them the look of butterflies. Katy's breath caught in her throat. If she were a dancer, that's the style she would want to do.

"Those are the contestants," Donna explained. "This is a contest powwow, meaning people are judged for their perfection, how they make and decorate their regalia, the amount of control they have over their movements, their timing for certain dance steps and the sweep of their eagle feather fans. They're also judged by how they hold their bodies, their athleticism, and their footwork." Donna paused. "Winning means money. And in order to win, everything they make and all their movements have to be perfect. Some of these people participate in contests because that's how they make a living; traveling the country is expensive. So what you'll be seeing is some of the best dancing out there."

Learning about these traditions made Katy's heart swell with joy. She felt like part of this community, even if she was just watching from the bleachers. Donna placed her arm around Katy's shoulders and pulled her close. "I never get tired of seeing the pride our people show when representing the best part of who we are. I am so glad you are here to be part of this."

Katy smiled, wondering if that feeling she had in her chest was pride.

She scanned the constant stream of dancers. One person immediately captured her attention—a girl about her age who wore a long white buckskin dress accentuated with intricate beadwork of geometrical designs. Katy, hypnotized by the long fringe that swished with rhythmic grace just inches from the floor, wondered how much the dress weighed. The girl danced with such purpose, standing straight, her arms bent, her elbows thrown back.

Donna followed Katy's gaze. "Now, that's a young woman who will do quite well in the contest if she dances as beautifully and as precisely as the outfit she wears."

As Katy watched the girl, she couldn't help but wonder what her life would have been like if she hadn't been adopted. *Would I be a dancer here? Would I have a beautiful dress, or a shawl? Would I hold my head with such pride?*

She sighed, knowing those questions were unanswerable.

Suddenly, as if sensing that she was being watched, the girl turned and met Katy's gaze. Katy was taken aback by her light-colored eyes, almost golden, so different from the brown eyes she'd become used to seeing. They held each other's gaze for several moments. Katy smiled; the girl did not return that smile. Instead, she faced forward and continued her steps, careful and deliberate, her fringe swaying in time with her feet.

As if on cue, the drums and the dancers stopped at the same time. Silence intervened just for a moment; then the arena was filled with the sound of jingles and talking, a beating drum. This, Katy thought, was the sound of life.

The emcee stepped up to the microphone and made a comment about the thundering pride of the drummers and the dancers. Once more his jokes were met with laughter and good-hearted groans. Then, with a boisterous voice, he announced, "Intertribal! Everybody dance!"

"Let's go," Donna said, rising and wrapping a navy blue shawl around her shoulders. "It's time to introduce you to your heritage. But first you'll need this." From her tote Donna extracted a lavender shawl, its dark purple fringe at least a foot long.

"This is beautiful," Katy breathed as she allowed the strands to drop heavily between her fingers.

"I always have extras. You never know who will need one. That color looks great on you," Donna remarked as they walked to the circle and joined the stream of other dancers.

"Why do I need a shawl? Some people, like those two women over there, aren't wearing one."

"It's a sign of respect for the circle. Some powwows require them, some don't. But I think you shouldn't dance in the circle unless you have one. The women you're talking about? They're not Native. This is probably the first pow-wow they've been to, and they don't know that's what they should do."

"Will someone tell them?"

"No. They'll figure it out. Or not."

While they talked, Katy carefully kept track of how her body moved. Was her back straight? Her head held just so? Were her steps too long, or too short?

"You'll know you're doing it right when the fringe sways in perfect rhythm with your steps." Donna turned to watch Katy's movement. "You're doing a great job," she said with a smile. Katy relaxed.

A male voice interrupted Katy's thoughts. "Hey, how's it going?"

Katy turned to see a young man about her age, dressed in a fancy dance outfit. "Hi! Doing great." She smiled as he fell into step beside her.

"Whew. Dancing is hard work!" he said. "I gotta rest for a minute." He slowed to follow her rhythm and shook out his legs, causing the bells on his ankles to jingle.

Katy turned slightly away and watched him out of the corner of her eye. His face was beautiful. Perfect. He was encompassed within feather plumes of brilliant blue that sprang from a circular holder on his shoulder blades, as well as the small of his back. The feathers swayed and jumped with each step, as if weightless.

"I don't think I've seen you here before," he said, turning toward her and giving her a radiant smile that created a dimple on the cheek closest to her.

It also created a warm feeling in Katy. "This is my first time here."

"To this powwow?"

Katy chuckled, self-conscious in her answer. "Any powwow."

His smile produced butterflies in her stomach. "Well, hey, welcome. What's your name?"

"Katy."

"Katy, it's been nice talking with you. I gotta get warmed up for the contest, but I'll catch up with you later." And he was gone in a frantic movement of blue plumes, his knees pulling his feet high off the ground, his body spinning. Katy realized she hadn't asked his name. But the fact that he even stopped to talk with her was amazing. And he didn't ask anything about her parents. He just assumed she was like everyone else there.

"Oh, and I forgot to tell you about the cute guys," Donna said with a wink.

Katy blushed. A voice to her right surprised her.

"Your name is Katy? I'm Tara."

As they fell into step with one another, Katy wondered why the girl with the golden eyes had stopped to talk with her. And how had she known her name?

As if reading her mind, Tara smiled. "Sorry, I overheard your conversation. I see Alex has noticed you, though." Suddenly, Katy realized that the smile never reached Tara's eyes.

Alex, so that was his name.

Tara spoke in a lofty voice. "The thing is, I know something he doesn't know." She paused and looked away. "You're an apple."

Katy's eyes went wide as her face drained of color, then flushed with embarrassment.

She looked at Tara, whose cool smile chilled Katy even further.

"I've been watching you in this dance circle. You know you dance like a white girl, right? You don't bend your knees." She paused again, then stared directly into Katy's eyes. "So, go back to wherever you came from. You don't belong here."

Katy's step faltered, and her breath stopped as she watched Tara sway away in her beautiful white leather dress, head held high.

Having trouble catching her breath, Katy glanced around to see if anyone saw or overheard the—she couldn't even call it a conversation—attack. Donna, next to her, was in deep conversation with a woman who'd come up beside her. When Katy glanced behind her, the women returned her look, but their faces didn't indicate that they'd heard or seen anything unsettling.

What was she going to do? She didn't want to be here anymore. She didn't want to risk being ambushed by someone else. And she didn't want to face Alex if Tara told him what she was—an apple, whatever that meant. From the tone of Tara's voice, it wasn't a good thing to be.

As if aware of the war going on within Katy, Donna turned toward her, her eyes widening in alarm. She placed her hand on Katy's arm. "Are you okay? Your face is so pale!

You don't look well." Donna began to guide her off the floor. "Let's go back to the bleachers and sit down. I'll grab you some water."

Katy found her voice. "I'm sorry, Donna, but I have to leave. I forgot I have somewhere I need to be." *Away from here*, her thoughts screamed.

"That's okay, I'll drive you. We can leave right now." Donna turned to fold her shawl and place it in the tote while Katy tossed hers on the bench and bolted across the gymnasium. She swore people wore looks of judgment in their unblinking gazes, their downturned mouths, their unsmiling faces, their arms crossed in front of their chests. Katy had soiled this sacred place. She imagined their thoughts: *You're not really one of us. You're just pretending*.

Once outside, Katy pulled fresh air deep into her lungs, and tears of humiliation stung her eyes. When she glanced back, she saw Donna emerge between the doors and frantically scan the lawn. Katy wanted to disappear. She saw the bike path just beyond the hedge and ducked onto it. Here, she was shielded. And her tears flowed freely.

As she walked down the bike path toward home, she replayed the scene over and over again. *I know something Alex doesn't know; you're an apple . . . You dance like a white girl; you don't bend your knees*. Her golden eyes pierced accusingly into Katy's imagination. She sighed and rubbed her forehead. *What a nightmare*. How could she face her mom? She'd been all I-want-to-go-by-myself? So grown-up, but Katy had no idea how to handle this rejection. It cut to her core.

When she arrived home nearly an hour later, her mom was sitting on the porch swing, waiting for her. "Hey, kiddo. What happened? All I know is that Donna called to let me know you'd left in a hurry and looked very upset. She asked me to call her as soon as you got back." She paused and studied her daughter intently. "Are you okay?"

Katy nodded for a moment, but then shook her head, and the tears began all over again.

"Hold on . . . let me call Donna, and then we can talk. Do you want to sit out here or go inside?"

"Sit out here." The outdoors didn't seem so confining.

When her mom went inside, Katy closed her eyes and inhaled deeply. She smelled the sweetness of the linden tree, heard cars roll past, a bird calling.

"I let Donna know," her mom said as she returned with a glass of water. "She wants to talk with you tomorrow. I said you'd call." She paused and looked out onto the empty street. "What happened? Start from the beginning."

Katy told her about the colors, and the sounds, and the beautiful dresses. She told her about the long line of people who stopped to talk with Donna and how Donna would sometimes introduce her as a daughter of a cousin. Katy smiled, remembering the wink and her words, *We don't know you aren't!*

She talked about Donna lending her a shawl and going out onto the dance arena and participating in this amazing experience. But then Katy paused, and her eyes grew sad; her lower lip trembled as her face grew heated. Turning toward her mom, she asked, "What's an apple?"

Her mom's face fell. "Oh, honey. Is that what somebody said to you?"

Katy nodded.

Her mom shook her head in disappointment, her lips drawing a straight line in anger. "It's a slur," she finally said. "It's designed to make someone feel bad about who they are." She paused. "Specifically, it means that person is red on the outside, white on the inside. That they're not Native American, they're really 'white.' But Katy, I want you to look at me. This is important. You *are* Native American. Your heritage flows through your veins, and no one . . . *no* one can question that. Ever." She studied Katy with an intent gaze, then continued. "You have every right to be at that powwow, to participate in that powwow, dance at that powwow if you choose. You are Native American, and your ancestry and your heritage can never be taken away from you."

Katy bowed her head and saw splotches appear where her tears hit the lap of her dark skirt. "But why doesn't it feel like I am?" she asked, the tears running freely down her cheeks. "I don't even know what that means."

Her mom drew her into a hug and rubbed her arm. "It's

complicated," she said quietly. "But it's a complication we can address."

Katy sat, resting her head against her mom's shoulder, feeling as safe as she had when she was a child. She had no idea what her mom meant, saying that this was a complication that could be addressed, but she let it slide away along with the anger and the fear and the embarrassment of that morning.

That evening, while Katy was doing her homework in her room, her mom knocked on the partially opened door. "Can I come in?"

Katy nodded.

Her mom leaned against the doorframe. "Katy, I think it's important that you return to the powwow tomorrow, if for no other reason than to show that you will not be intimidated by anyone. And to prove to yourself that you have a right to actively participate in the culture that is yours. If you want, I can go with you—or Donna can. But I truly believe you need to go."

Katy smiled and nodded. "I'll think about it."

After her mom left, Katy put aside her book and stretched out on her bed. She kept thinking about the word *apple* and her adoption and her right to participate, and it was dizzying, all these emotions swirling. She turned on her side and watched the moon travel from one side of her window to the other, until she finally fell asleep.

"Hey, Katy, Donna's here," her mom called up the stairs.

Katy looked at the clock: eight thirty in the morning. No one said Donna would be by. Katy had not committed to going to the powwow today. She'd not even called her back. The powwow was somewhere she definitely didn't want to be. "Hey, Mom, please tell Donna I'm sick? I just don't want to go."

"Hi, Katy. Donna here. Do you mind if I come up and talk with you?"

"I'm not dressed! I'm not even up!"

"Okay, then come down when you're ready. I'll wait."

Katy groaned. She just wanted Donna to go away so she could go back to sleep. But she gathered up her clothes and went into the bathroom to shower and get ready for the day, whatever it was going to bring.

Donna and her mom sat at the kitchen table in easy conversation as Katy made herself a bowl of cereal. She listened long enough to know that they weren't talking about her, but something having to do with work.

When she finished and got up to rinse her bowl, Donna said, "There's been a change of plans. We won't be going to the powwow this morning."

"Okay," Katy answered, confused.

"I'd like to take you to a panel discussion at the university that some of our elders put together in honor of the powwow. I think you'll hear important stories about our heritage, *your* heritage, and all the ways our claims to that heritage have been interrupted. Are you up for that? It'll last about an hour or so. Then I can bring you home."

Katy sighed and faced Donna. "So you know?" she asked. "About what happened yesterday?"

Donna nodded. "Your mom told me. I hate to say this, but you're not the first person in our Native community that has experienced being shamed by another Native. It's called lateral violence, when we try to shame other people in our community because we feel so ugly inside. It's as if we put our pain on someone else's shoulders. But pain doesn't transfer; it just grows. Now, instead of one person feeling pain, two people are. And the darkness spreads. I think these people at the university have important things to say. To all of us. Want to join me?"

Katy thought for a moment and nodded. As long as it wasn't the powwow, she'd be okay.

Donna smiled and studied her. "You are one strong young woman, Katy. I'm not sure you even know the strength you have in you, but I see it shining through right now. Let's go."

When they arrived at the lecture room, there were several rows of people already there, and few empty chairs. Four people of different ages sat at a table in the front, facing the audience. One man was an elder who wore a Pendleton vest, his long, thin braids hanging to his stomach. Two middle-aged women wore jeans and nice tops. Each wore beaded earrings, and one wore a bracelet of turquoise, the other a bracelet of metal upon which figures were carved. The youngest woman was not much older than Katy, and she wore a long skirt adorned with ribbons and a white peasant blouse.

Katy watched as they talked with one another, their shared laughter rolling across the floor toward the audience. Its sound made her smile.

"There's a spot," Donna said, walking toward two empty seats. Katy stared at the person who occupied one of the chairs next to them. It was Alex! He waved and motioned for them to sit beside him.

Joy and dread argued within Katy. Had Tara told Alex about her being a pretend Indian? She looked intently at his face, but he gave no sign of anything other than his happiness to see her. She took her seat next to him and suddenly became self-conscious, unsure of what to say.

She didn't have to worry. He began the conversation. "Hey, I looked for you," he said, his voice quiet, his gaze steady. "But I didn't see you after we talked." He smiled; there was that dimple. "I was going to buy you an Indian taco!"

"Oh, I had to leave. I'm sorry. I would have loved to share that taco."

"Well, maybe next time," he said, flashing a grin.

The elder man on the panel stood up, holding an eagle feather between his fingers. He introduced himself as

Albert LaPlant and welcomed everyone, asking them to join him in prayer.

"Creator," he said, his voice deep and rich. "Thank you for bringing us together for healing, for strength, for our stories, and to share our lives, for giving us a chance to understand one another. Please help the young ones hear; please help the old ones tell our truths. Thank you." He sat down, and the woman next to him began to speak.

"Good morning. My name is Evelyn Stillwater, and we are so happy you all are here. As you see, we have people of different ages on this panel. That's important, because our culture has been assaulted, our people have been assaulted, over centuries. We carry scars deep within us, and those scars have become part of our DNA, so our next generation carries them as well. It is important for us to talk about our experiences, and it is healing for us to know that you are listening, hearing, those stories. Each of us will speak about different assaults we've experienced or seen or learned about. I'd first like to introduce Liz Denver."

All applauded for the youngest woman on the panel.

"Good morning," she said, "and thank you for coming. As you can see, I'm one of the youngest people here. I'm in my midtwenties. I grew up in a border town, just outside a reservation in South Dakota. My mom is white, my dad is Lakota. They didn't want to raise me on the reservation, but they felt it would be good to be nearby, to keep me in touch with family. The border towns are ugly. They are filled with many white people who despise who we are; they are filled with people in our Indigenous community who despise who they are. There's a lot of anger, hurt, and hatred in these towns.

"Going to school was tough because I felt pressure from both whites and Natives, a feeling that I didn't belong. If I got good grades, Natives would say I was acting too white, acting better than everyone else. If I spoke my own language, white students, or even adults, would say I was nothing but a dirty Indian. I was expected to fight all kinds of people. Most times I could settle things with words, but sometimes I would just have to stick up for myself.

"Border towns aren't going to go away. So, as I grew up, I kept wondering how I could make them better, healthier. And to do that, I needed to go to college. Until I reached college, I thought the animosity I experienced was normal. Until one of my professors required me to read *Custer Died for Your Sins* by Vine Deloria, Jr., and it opened my eyes to a history I didn't even know existed. And that's the history I want our next generation to hear, to know.

"I'm currently studying for final exams for my education administration degree. I want to see what I can do to heal the wounds that the reservation border leaves on all of us. I hope to begin a job next fall at the school I went to." She smiled with shy pride. "Thank you for listening. Now I'd like to present Evelyn Stillwater."

Again, there was applause for both women. Katy

considered Liz's words and realized that the racism didn't occur just in the border towns; she'd experienced it herself here in Fort Kyle!

Katy remembered going into a store with a friend, the same store her mom shopped at for some of Katy's clothes. As the girls looked through the racks and sifted through the folded shirts, Katy noticed that an employee was never very far from her, seemingly busy folding and fluffing and hanging clothes. A quick glance showed that Katy's friend was wandering around unnoticed. At first Katy wondered if she was imagining things, and she watched the employee out of the corner of her eye, moving when Katy moved, stopping when Katy stopped. Thinking back now, maybe the employee was concerned that the teenagers were going to rip her off. Except only one of the teens, Katy, seemed to be under surveillance. Was it racism? If it wasn't, why did it feel like it was?

Katy's attention was pulled back to the present as a silver-haired woman took the mic. Evelyn's voice was strong, despite her elderly appearance. "My people come from the mountains. But what stayed in my mind and in my heart happened east of here." She talked about ruts, deep trails left by wagons and by people on foot, which scarred the landscape. "The first set of ruts I saw was over in Nebraska, when tens of thousands of people crossed the Great Plains in what they called Manifest Destiny—the idea that white settlers were entitled to lay claim to this so-called empty land." Evelyn paused. "It wasn't empty. We lived here, many tribes lived here. We lived on it, died on it, buried our people in it, buried our children's umbilical cords so their spirit would be deep in the soil, eternally part of this land. But I never thought about the number of people who came until I saw wagon ruts carved five feet into limestone."

Evelyn paused again and took a sip of water. "The second set of ruts I saw was on the Trail of Tears, where over sixty thousand Choctaw, Chickasaw, Cherokee, Creek, and Seminole people were relocated from their southeastern lands and sent to Oklahoma Territory. More than four thousand Cherokee died from that forced twelve-hundred-mile walk. I've heard that on parts of the trail, the ruts from that walk are three feet deep.

"All those ruts are scars on our soul. Thank you for listening. Now I'd like to introduce Claire Standing Bear."

Again, applause. Katy imagined deep grooves in a limestone hill and the thousands, maybe hundreds of thousands of feet that created those grooves in the rock. She wanted to see it for herself. It contained a part of her history. Her eyes opened wide; she'd never thought of history as being *her* history; it just was. Now she realized it was a history that belonged to other people. What had happened to *hers*?

Claire, a woman in her forties, took the mic and stood quietly for a moment, looking around at the group. When she finally spoke, her voice contained a quiet strength. "Has anyone here been to the Haskell School, in Lawrence, Kansas?" A few people raised their hands. "You should go there sometime. It was an Indian school." Claire looked up and gave a wry smile. "Well, I guess it's still an Indian school; it's now called Haskell Indian Nations University. But back when it was created, in the late 1800s, it was Haskell Indian Industrial Training School—a boarding school."

Claire stepped out from behind the table and moved toward the audience. "So when you think of boarding schools, you think of those big white buildings on the East Coast where rich kids go to learn to be leaders, right? Haskell didn't train leaders; it trained workers. My great-great-grandfather went there. He was forced to go. The stories that have been passed down to my brothers and sisters and me make us angry. He was just a little kid when he arrived. The school administrators shaved his head, cut his braids! You know, we don't cut our hair unless someone very close to us has died. They burned his leather clothing and gave him cotton clothes to wear. That's why he was always so cold in the winter. Cotton just lets the cold seep into your bones; leather is a good insulator.

"Then the administrators gave him a white name; he was called Charlie. His true name was lost forever. They beat him for talking in his own language. He had friends who ran away from the school because of their beatings, and if they were found, they were brought back and beaten really bad. The school didn't have enough coal to keep it warm in the winter. It had no shade, so it baked in the summer. All the kids slept in one large room, sometimes sharing beds, towels, toothbrushes. Diseases like tuberculosis killed a lot of kids." Claire paused and scanned the room. "When you think of those fancy boarding schools, how many of them have a cemetery on their grounds?" The room was silent. "None. But the Native American boarding schools did. They have a lot of unmarked graves. Evidently, it was embarrassing that so many kids were dying on school grounds. Administrations just stopped keeping track."

Somebody raised their hand and asked, "Didn't they keep records that tell how many died?"

Claire shook her head. "They lost a lot of the early records in a fire. We have no idea how many are buried in that little cemetery or beyond. If you go, be sure to go to the little museum there. There are letters that children and parents wrote to one another that were never delivered. Some were found in their original envelopes. Kids wrote, pleading for their parents to come get them. Parents wrote to say how proud they were of the children. Both people remained in darkness." Claire paused again, her eyes shiny with unshed tears. "I've been to that cemetery. I feel the souls of those children." She wiped the tears away. "Thank you for listening."

Katy swallowed and wiped her own tears. Had her first family gone through such heartache? Had her first family's people been moved across the country by the military?

Had they been forced to become something other than who they were? *Why don't I know these things?* Katy wondered angrily.

Just two rows in front of her, a Native American woman stood up and clapped. "It's important for us to hear your words. Too many of us don't know what happened to us. We don't know why we feel the way we feel. I read somewhere that the U.S. military declared over one thousand wars on American Indians. One thousand wars. Think of all our men, young and old, our women, our children who died. Think of the villages that were destroyed. Think of the humiliation our people went through as they were moved from our homelands to lands far away, many times at gunpoint." She paused, and tears streamed down her face. "Thank you for telling us, all of us, the truth."

The entire audience rose then, and the applause was thunderous. The room was noisy with conversations that began after the talk. Donna stepped away to join one of the groups. Katy sat and thought about all she'd heard and how it felt to hear her history—angry that this was the first time she'd heard any of it.

She waited until Claire was free, then walked up to stand in front of her. Claire smiled in greeting and waited quietly for Katy to speak. "There's something else that happened to us," Katy said after a few moments. "I'm adopted. I don't know who my parents are, or the tribe I come from. All I know is that I'm Native American. My parents adopted me when I was a year old. I don't know the reason.

"I went to the powwow, and that is the first time I was around people who looked like me. I get tired of the questions people ask me: Why don't I look like my parents? Why don't I know who my real parents are? Why don't I know my tribe? Why don't I know my culture? There's nothing I can say. A girl in the powwow circle yesterday called me an apple."

A tear slid out of the corner of one eye, and Katy wiped it away with her fingers. "I don't even know what it means to be American Indian. I've never heard these stories you have all told. Why haven't I heard them before?"

Claire nodded, smiled, but remained silent.

Katy paused. "My parents are good people. They are kind and understanding. They try to protect me, but there's not a lot they can do when someone asks me questions or calls me names." She swallowed and continued. "I go to a good school, and I've never heard these stories." She smiled through her tears. "I'm sorry. I've never told anyone what all this feels like. It feels like I'm in a storm and I'm disintegrating into pieces of me." She looked at Claire. "Does that make sense?"

Claire stood up and walked around the table. "Can I hug you?" she asked as she extended her arms. Katy nodded and let herself relax in the safety of someone strong.

"I'm so sorry this is happening to you," Claire said as she rubbed Katy's back. "But you always have a community here, with us. You can talk to us about anything, ask us questions, learn the Indigenous ways. We'll teach you. We'll also teach your parents, so they can support you. It doesn't matter who raises you, you have a Native American heritage. You are part of a culture that is all of us."

Katy stepped away from the embrace. "Thank you so much, Claire." She laughed self-consciously. "I should introduce myself—I'm Katy. I'm just trying to find out who I am, and what that means. Thank you so much for helping me."

Alex's voice, loud and boisterous, entered the conversation. "Oh, I see you've met my auntie!" Alex stood beside Katy and looked her earnestly. "She's a good person. I think you were led to her. I'm really glad." He paused and glanced at his watch.

"Hey, if you still want, we can go to the powwow and get an Indian taco!"

"Sounds like a plan."

Katy smiled as they walked through the hallway. She didn't want to get her hopes up too high, but maybe this was what "being Native American" meant, feeling both joy and pain and holding them together in her heart.

"*Thank you, Creator,*" she whispered as she stepped into the sunshine.

WHITE PEOPLE

BY MATTHEW SALESSES

The one thing we liked about the town where we lived was our house, which was a farmhouse set back behind the park where the town had created a reservoir by damming up the river. The grounds of the reservoir were all old farmland, so the park seemed like an extension of our backyard, like one long plot of land, at least to me. The town disagreed, and sent official letters to remind us that we did not have free rein over public space, but by then the reservoir was already a part of my imaginative landscape. Along the back of the park was a small woods which must have served as a windbreak, and that separated the old farmland from a smaller area covered in sand dunes. No one knew how those dunes had formed—glaciers was the usual explanation for any unusual landforms in the area—but town history had it that they had been expanded first through bad farming decisions and then by an attempt to turn the land into something like a giant sandpit for children. When the latter effort failed, the dunes were taken over as an unofficial firing range, the kind of thing that can happen only in a small town.

Nearly everyone in town had guns, and the dunes provided a semi-secluded but also semi-open landscape to try out a shotgun or rifle before a hunting trip or to fire off a few rounds from a handgun stolen from a parent. Spent bullet casings were scattered across the sand, and it became my habit to collect these casings, which glittered with leftover danger. Occasionally I found duds with the bullets still attached, which I brought back to the house and tried to explode by dropping chunks of granite on them or by striking two together.

My point is that my parents gave me a lot of freedom to wander and play on my own, until my father was fired. After that, everything changed. He wasn't able to find another job (not for lack of effort—he applied everywhere and called in every favor he could), and we would have had to move back to Hartford if my mother hadn't taken over the family decisions, expanding her realm from me and the house to how we spent and earned money. It was as if she had drawn a line in the sand, and that line was our property—she refused to give it up. It represented something more to her.

After months of my father's failed attempts to land a job, she decided that the only resource we had was the land itself, and she started a chicken farm, with the plan to distribute organic eggs to local restaurants. It was a reckless idea, with little chance of success, but none of us knew that then. My mother's uncle in Korea had run a successful chicken farm, so it seemed like something we could invest our belief in.

At ten, I thought the farm was the best thing to ever happen to me. First, a giant tent showed up, which my mother bought online and made my father assemble in the yard—a tent maybe half the size of the house, meant for community activities, which my mother planned to use as a coop—and then she came home with five hundred chicks in the back of the SUV. My father couldn't believe it—he thought my mother had lost her mind—but he didn't have any right to complain. His way had failed; now we were trying hers. Even I could tell that the power had shifted. Whenever he seemed about to criticize her, one look from my mother would shut him up.

I fell in love. Five hundred baby birds, vulnerable yellow puffballs, dependent on me for life. It was a welcome break from school, where I was lonely and bullied and had to fight for any respect from the other kids. Not only had I been a new student, someone from out of town, but I was also one of only two Asians in my grade, and the only one who was adopted. The other was a Japanese girl, Anna Honda, the kind who put the *model* in model minority—small, pretty, shy, girlish, and probably a genius. That we were the only two made us as much rivals as friends, though perhaps Anna was more of a rival to me than I was to her. She might have been happy to fade into the background, but if one of us had to be known as "the Asian girl," I wanted it to be me. I would rather that than "the adopted girl." Or maybe I was just jealous that Anna fit the type. I didn't get the best grades, I wasn't the most polite, I was mouthy and boyish and wild, and I refused to take anything lying down. Yet I wanted to be the model Asian girl, even if that model was bad.

On the farm, I could forget about that part of my identity. My mother and I raised the chicks carefully, like the last hope they were, even feeding them out of our hands at first, administering liquid vaccines with an eyedropper, one by one. They grew quickly, though my mother explained that—just as I wasn't old enough yet to bleed—they wouldn't lay eggs until week sixteen. In the meantime, we tightened our belts. What money we spent went almost wholly to further investments. My mother spent hours online, watching farming videos. We got a machine to turn plants into chicken feed. We learned that many farms fed their hens sawdust, many farms kept their chickens in cages—what we could offer were eggs someone had cared for. With the tent as the "coop," we were able to move the chickens each day from one patch of grass to another, so they always had new food to eat, new ground to scratch.

My mother went around to the neighboring towns and got every Asian restaurant in a fifty-mile radius to agree to buy eggs from us as soon as they came, by promising better eggs at the same price they were already paying. They had nothing to lose. Soon strangers of various Asian ethnicities were stopping by the farm to look at the chickens or talk with my parents: Chinese and Vietnamese at first, then Filipino, Indian, Thai, Cambodian, Pakistani. If we could get our numbers up to around a thousand hens, my mother calculated, we would be okay.

When the chickens were fourteen weeks old, though, eight fell over dead in the night. The next night, twelve more. My mother was frantic. Each chick was an investment not only of money but of energy, care, hope. My father, who by that time was coming around, called the veterinarian. The vet knew all about us. Small-town gossip. He knew about the chicken farm and that my father had lost his job. My mother gestured for my father to put the call on speaker.

"Will you even be able to afford the fees?" the vet asked. "Do you have insurance? Will you sell the land once the farm fails?"

"It's not going to fail," my father said.

"You're lowering its value, you know."

"It's not going to fail," my father said again, raising his voice.

I was surprised. It was the first time I had ever heard him defend the farm like that. Before, he had acted like it didn't matter if it failed, like what was the difference?

He stared at the phone as if glaring into someone's eyes. It was anger, I realized, which gave him that belief in us, that confidence, though he seemed to be angrier about the gossip of the farm than about losing his job. I couldn't get my child's brain around this puzzle. It didn't make sense to me. It was a question I would often ask myself afterward, why criticizing the farm made him angrier, especially since at first he didn't care for it. As if, as soon as the vet said we could not succeed, my father made up his mind to do so for the first time.

"I heard Vaughan Farm is pretty pissed off," the vet said. "You're taking their business."

My mother covered her mouth. Vaughan was the one big farm nearby and the source of most local produce (at the supermarket, all you could get were national brands and Vaughan). Their farm was two towns over and took up a lot of land, a proper dairy outfit. But it had been around long enough that it used older, crueler practices. That was how we planned to distinguish ourselves. We had actually driven over there to check them out, and the only livestock outside were cows—the chickens were all locked away in a long green metal coop that looked like an army barracks.

"Vaughan's my biggest client," the vet said. "I wouldn't want to ruin that relationship."

"Of course you wouldn't," my father said. "And we wouldn't tell anyone."

The vet laughed once, and hung up.

Besides our one local vet, the nearest veterinary offices were in Hartford. It was unlikely anyone there would drive out of the city for a client of our small size. We would have to take a few chickens into a clinic instead. The biggest problem, however, was that we weren't experienced enough to know which birds to take. We couldn't tell which were the ones in the worst shape—the hens that died had displayed no outward signs of illness. Maybe someone more experienced than we were could have told the difference. To our eyes, there was nothing separating the chickens fated to live from those fated to die.

We couldn't do anything, my father said, but wait. "Let's take care of them the best we can and have faith."

"Faith," my mother cautioned, "may not be enough to save our chickens."

"Let's have faith in ourselves," said my father.

It was like he had become a different person. He smiled and squeezed my mother's hand. It occurred to me that it had been a while since I last saw them touch. I wanted to trust this new, faithful father.

My mother stared at her hand in his, then came to a decision and shook him off.

We went back to work, putting in extra effort to keep the chickens happy, moving the tent to the far end of the

117

property in case it had been on a bad patch of grass, making sure to shovel up every drop of manure as quickly as it fell. That night, my father said he would stay up and watch over the sleeping chickens. He said it was strange that they died only at night. I wanted to stay up too—I hadn't thought about this, though my mother's unsurprised expression said that it had already crossed her mind—but my father said he would go alone. He was going to take a gun.

I hadn't ever seen a gun around the house, or seen my parents shooting one, and they had never even talked about guns, so I didn't know we owned one. I had actually wished many times that we did own a gun so that I could try out some of the duds I'd collected from the dunes—I had a whole box hidden in my closet, the way other girls collected charms for charm bracelets or little plastic foods with plastic faces. The bullets were part of my imaginative landscape, which never truly felt real. If anything, I often felt as if, to most of the town, the world I lived in did not exist. I wanted to make it exist. If my father was like me, he might have hidden his gun in the same place I hid my bullets, a box in the back of the closet. I wanted to look for it right away.

Only my mother's reaction brought up any notion of the danger involved. She bit the insides of her bottom lip and said that a gun existed for only one reason, to kill. As soon as you touched a gun, you were saying you were willing to kill something.

Up until that moment I had been thinking of a gun as something more like an appliance, an oven that could turn cupcake batter into cupcakes, probably because I had never seen one in real life, only what came out of one.

My father nodded.

That night, after I did my small amount of homework and went to bed, I listened for my father in the yard outside my window. I must have recognized, on some level, the incongruity of taking a gun to kill a virus, because I imagined viruses swooping in like vampire bats, creatures my father had chosen to face alone. It was the kind of bravery white knights showed in books, the kind I wanted to have in school.

I imagined finding the gun and sneaking it into school, with it in one pocket and the bullets I'd collected in the other. During our active shooter drills, they always said a good guy with a gun would stop a bad guy with a gun. How safe I would feel with a gun in my pocket, if one of the white kids called me Chink or Jap. No more than a few days earlier, one of the white boys had told me that Japs like me had started the last world war, and I hadn't even known what he was talking about, only that I wasn't Japanese. The next day, I took a couple of bullets to school to give to Anna, who would have to protect herself if what the boy said was true. It was an act, I thought, of solidarity. Anna pulled me into the bathroom and said I could get in trouble for bringing bullets to school, as if I was the bad guy. I didn't get her: she played only with dolls and stuffed animals; she always wore a ribbon in her hair. "Don't your parents teach you anything?" she asked. She explained to me about the last world war and how there might be another soon, with the climate crisis getting worse—how entire nations might have to move from one place to another. "Japan is an island," she said. "It's like a sitting duck. Korea's a peninsula."

"I don't know anybody in Japan," I said.

She rolled her eyes. "Don't be such a white person," she whispered.

That was always how we talked about white people, in a whisper, since no one seemed to like it when you said the word *white*.

"Or is it because," she asked, "you're adopted?"

I had to hold myself back from hitting her.

When I told my parents what Anna had said about war— but not what she had said about adoption—my mother said that in World War II, the Japanese had made us fight and die for them and had used our bodies, women's bodies . . . it took me a moment to realize the *we* meant Koreans—the *our*, Korean women. She never acted like my father and I were not Korean, because we were adopted. I felt strangely relieved to be included in the victims. The rest of what my mother said barely registered.

"That's in the past," my father said. "It doesn't apply here. Here we're all the same to white people, and we have to stick together."

My father had said this many times. Many times I had been mistaken for Anna and she for me.

But my mother said the past did apply, that the kind of thing she was talking about didn't go away in America just because in America, everyone Asian suffers.

Now my father was out in the yard with a gun. I imagined people in the shadows, white soldiers and Japanese soldiers swooping down, and him having to make a choice: Which of them were making the chickens sick? What would he choose? I listened for the gunshots I sometimes heard from the dunes as soft pops.

A gun existed for one reason, my mother had said: to kill. Except for the chickens, I had never seen anything die. It seemed to take a long time for me to fall asleep, but I didn't hear anything. Or rather, I heard the same sounds I always heard, the sound of wind and the rustling leaves and occasionally the coo of a snoring hen.

When I woke, my father had laid out rice and banchan for breakfast.

"Nothing happened," he said. "All the chickens lived."

My mother put her head in her hands. Her shoulders shook with relief.

It was a miracle.

My mother spilled tears. Not for a long time had I seen her cry. My father and I were silent. Finally, she got up to wash her face. When she returned to the table, we ate a long, quiet breakfast. Usually my parents kept up a stream of chatter, reminding me to do this or that. That morning, my father could barely keep his eyes open. The only thing that kept him there was food. He shoveled down two bowls of rice, one after the other, as if the night had sucked all the energy from him. My mother silently refilled his bowl. We had agreed to eat less until the farm brought in revenue, but she didn't scold him. As soon as he was done eating, he went to bed.

It was the same that night. Again my father stayed up with the chickens. Again they all lived. Maybe the disease had simply run its course, I thought; maybe they had just been lonely. My father kept staying up with them until the alternating schedule became normal, and he traded our company for theirs.

HAUNT ME, THEN

BY MEME COLLIER

Before Hazel sees spirits, she smells them. They possess a faint but distinct scent—dried flowers, burnt rosemary, black pepper, fruit on the verge of overripening in the sun. And the air tingles with energy wherever they linger, like a lightning storm gathering on the horizon, or a static shock to the fingertips.

The only way most people can detect the presence of spirits, unless picture frames drop from the walls or coffee mugs hurtle across the kitchen, is the unsettling sense that something is off. Hazel can never tell at first glance if she'll step through an entryway and smell fire and ash, feel a low thrumming, like the vibration of a bee's wings disturbing the air. Sometimes condemned shacks are as empty as they look. And sometimes houses like Merle Westover's—a two-story with mustard-yellow wood siding, white trim, and a narrow front porch lined with azalea bushes—are haunted.

As Hazel looks up at the house from behind the steering wheel, she shakes her head. "I'll never get over how normal these places look."

Beside her, her brother Jamie waves his hand in dismissal. "There's no such thing as normal. You know that, Haze. Remember the Benson situation? Their gigantic mansion looked like it came right off HGTV, and holy shit, I think that made our top ten most fucked up cases, easy."

When Hazel gets out of the car and closes the door behind her, she finds the previously occupied passenger seat empty. In an instant, Jamie's disappeared from the car and materialized at the bottom of the steps leading up to the porch, waiting for her.

"I think you'd better stay out here," Hazel says.

"Aw, come on, seriously? I can help you. I'll kick that ghost's ass to the ninth circle."

She doesn't bother to correct him. Jamie already knows that truly evil entities are few and far between, that most spirits are ordinary people still lingering on Earth, and any fallout is more due to confusion or lack of control than malevolent intent. "Appreciate the support, but Ms. Westover's got enough on her plate with just one spirit in her house."

"I don't know what you're talking about. I'm the

friendliest Casper you've ever seen."

And despite his dark hair standing up in haphazard spikes as if he were caught in a windstorm, the torn jeans and hand-me-down bomber jacket, the tattoos and smattering of piercings over which their parents would've lost it had they ever seen them before his passing—there's an almost childlike air about him. Hazel can see it, the part of her brother that reassured her when they were kids, told her that no matter how much she sometimes felt like an outsider growing up, she wasn't alone.

"But . . . yeah," Jamie goes on. "Probably not the best idea."

"Probably not." Hazel opens the driver's door again and turns the key to the first notch in the ignition. "Here, I'll leave the radio on for you."

She turns the dial, bypassing country, pop, gospel, heavy metal without pause until she settles on something she knows Jamie, ever the music snob, won't complain about. As the DJ announces a new release by The Killers, Jamie's suddenly back in the car, slumping down with the seat pushed back all the way, and propping his boots one over the other on the dashboard. "I'll live, I guess. You know, ironically."

Her brother is funny as always, but this time, Hazel can't bring herself to laugh.

Once inside the house, she's glad that she didn't let Jamie join her. Merle watches her walk around without protest, but she's clearly on edge, as if Hazel's the last prospective buyer of a house nearing foreclosure. And Hazel's young age and even more youthful looks don't help. "I promise, I know what I'm doing," she assures Merle. What she doesn't say is that she started college this year, which is expensive, and she needs Merle almost as much as Merle needs her.

"Can you . . . Do you see anything?" Merle crosses her arms, wrinkling the tiny flowers on her blouse. Her eyes are iron, but Hazel doesn't miss the way her shoulders hunch inward.

"How long ago was the passing?" Hazel asks.

Merle's fingers tighten on the sleeve of her sweater. "Two months."

"Spirits don't always manifest, and if they do, it takes a lot of energy. That can mean time." Or passion—anger, love, guilt. Hazel knows from research and experience that something must serve as a catalyst to drive the energy into a fervor. At this point, though, Merle's nephew probably doesn't have enough power on reserve to do more than rattle a few pipes.

Hazel pushes open the door to the boy's room, revealing a bed covered in red, black, and gray; a desk; a TV; posters of Linkin Park and the Grateful Dead and *Fight Club*; a piece of art that resembles dripping ink. The bed is made, the books on the desk are stacked, a PlayStation controller rests at the base of the TV.

"What's his name?"

Merle leans heavily against the doorframe, as if the floor has suddenly tilted. "Cody."

"Thank you." Hazel walks slowly around the room. "Cody, my name is Hazel. Can you hear me?" His presence radiates like heat from a furnace, more intense than before, but there is no movement, no sound. Even the ceiling fan is still. "Cody? Show us a sign that you're here."

After a few moments, Merle says, "He's been slamming doors, making loud footsteps. Acting like a moody teenager."

"We'll give the house a thorough cleansing—burn some sage and incense, ring a bell, light a few candles. And you could dust, vacuum, and mop for good measure," Hazel says. "Cody is a young spirit. You might not hear anything more from him after that."

Merle lets out a huff, but Hazel recognizes from practice the sigh underlying the sound. There's a sadness to that sigh, a longing. Hazel knows the feeling well.

"Seems like I'm always cleaning up after somebody," Merle says.

Jamie first appeared three weeks earlier, nearly six months after his death, with the scent of smoke, cinnamon, and summer grass wafting through the air. He came at three in the morning, when Hazel woke from another dream about her birth family. Those dreams never failed to leave her feeling empty, but with an inexplicable, inextricable tangle of thoughts and feelings hanging heavy in her chest. And Jamie, for all his bravado and jokes and snark, had always had a knack for knowing when Hazel needed him. He wasn't like her. He'd never let her down, even now.

In her dreams, she'd been flying over the landscape of rural China—mountain ridges like camels' backs steeped in fog, stair-stepped rice terraces covered in spring water, the sunlight turning them into a patchwork of stained glass. She'd soared until she reached a village nestled in one of the valleys, and there, she found them—her parents.

Afterward, Hazel was never able to remember the details of the dreams; it was like trying to keep water from slipping through cupped hands. She didn't know these people's names. She couldn't understand them when they spoke. But when she saw them, she had no doubt as to who they were. She just knew. And for the duration of her dream, she would simply watch them, take in the missing years in the sun-hewn lines of their faces, in the depths of their eyes. It made her heart ache. And then she would wake, alone in her apartment in Savannah, Georgia, USA.

Except not this time. Hazel had sat up straight in her bed, shaking with cold. That was unusual for Savannah in March, to say the least. She blinked; blue moonlight was streaming in through the window near the far wall and falling across a silhouette.

"Heya, Hazel," Jamie said. His eyes were gleaming obsidian in the darkness. "It's been a while."

Hazel blinked again. "Jamie? How—What are you doing here?"

"Jeez, don't get too excited now," he said, grinning. "You'll make me get all emotional."

Hazel was at a loss for words. Dealing with spirits was her job, for Christ's sake, and here she was, responding like a scratched record. "Jamie, do you remember—you do realize—"

"I'm dead? Yeah, I know."

She shook her head. "You shouldn't be here."

"I get it," Jamie said, shrugging. "I'm not keeping polite hours, and I didn't exactly knock, but—"

"No, I mean you shouldn't *be here*. I opened all the windows after your funeral, unlocked all the doors, and covered all the mirrors. I did everything to make sure you could move on. This shouldn't be possible."

"But here I am." And it was true—he moved like flesh and blood, looked more alive, in fact, than the last time Hazel had seen him, when his pupils were little more than pin-holes due to a cocktail of drugs and drink. "Is that so bad?"

No, she wanted to say. She did miss him—how could she not, when he was the only one who'd understood her for so many years, in ways that their parents never even tried and her girlfriend—well, ex-girlfriend now—couldn't quite reach? But Hazel was dealing with his death, no matter what they said, and she'd buried him half a year ago. Yet here he was. Hazel ran a hand through her hair. "I'm sorry, but I can't do this now. Please. Just go."

When she looked up, Jamie was gone, and the moonlight streaming in through her window formed a blue pool on her bedroom floor instead.

For three days, he stayed away. And then early the next morning, before the heat and humidity had risen to envelop Savannah like a blanket, Jamie was back, marveling at the complete lack of paintings or pictures in Hazel's apartment, saying it hardly looked as if anyone lived there at all.

Hazel had been adopted first, from a city nestled along the Yangtze River, with a population ten times that of Atlanta's, where she was raised. She was not quite a year old, underweight, but otherwise fairly healthy.

Jamie was nearly two when their parents brought him home from South Korea. He had a full head of thick, downy hair and a cleft lip on his left side. There was minimal scarring post repair, thanks to the work of a top-tier plastic surgeon.

But long before that, on the other side of the world, Jared Newman and Rachel Gray, in their freshman year of college, had met through a Christian campus fellowship. Before the end of senior year, they were married, and three years later, when many of their friends had had their first baby or even their second, Jared and Rachel remained childless. They went to a doctor, then another for a second opinion, but ultimately decided not to pursue costly fertility treatments. If God wanted them to have a baby, then by His will, they would have a baby.

Time marched on. They had all but given up on the hope of having a family until one spring when their church held an international missions conference and there was a panel of couples who had adopted from other countries. This was an option the Newmans had never considered, but the more they prayed over it, the more it seemed like the Lord was leading them down this path. They had wanted children for so long now, and there were so many orphans in the world who would grow up without a home or guidance, all important factors for having a full and righteous life. It was a perfect match.

A friend of a friend they met at the conference had adopted a baby girl from China, and she was the cutest, most beautiful toddler they'd ever seen, just like a little doll. China offered primarily girls, and the Newmans ideally wanted one of each gender, so they looked to South Korea for a boy. And that was that—God's plans for all four of them had finally come together, and now their family was complete.

This is the story they told Hazel and Jamie—an impressionistic painting of words bathed in bright colors and missing quite a few of the sharper details. At first Hazel didn't mind the gaps, but then came the ghosts.

She could never make an exact science of her gift, her curse, but she now believed that puberty had something to do with it, because her ability to interact with spirits didn't truly come into its own until she herself came of age. As a small child, she'd occasionally see something flit across the corner of her vision, or she'd hear footsteps late at night from the attic above her bedroom, but around the time she turned twelve, everything changed. She couldn't deny their presence. And they were aware of hers.

That was the push that first sent her down the rabbit hole in search of answers about her past. She couldn't help but wonder if her birth parents, whoever they were, could communicate with the dead as well. The single computer Hazel could access at home was the family's old desktop, a whirring behemoth that was slow to start and not much faster to run. But its poor functionality wasn't the only reason Hazel needed another method of researching. Anything that could be considered part of the occult was strictly taboo in the Newman household; Hazel and Jamie weren't even allowed to trick-or-treat, because their parents viewed Halloween as borderline satanic. Moreover, Hazel was pretty sure there would be hurt feelings at the very least if they discovered she was trying to find her birth parents.

To play it safe, she went to the library. That was how she learned about the one-child policy, how this forced many families to bear the pain of giving up their children. Hazel had always thought that maybe her birth parents couldn't afford to keep her, or that they preferred a boy. The idea that they might have wanted her all along, that there were grandparents and siblings who had been missing her all these years—it was almost too much to bear. She worried that more knowledge, more emotions involved, might only complicate her life further rather than offer helpful information. So she decided instead to focus on what she did know—that she could see ghosts, and she needed to learn what to do about it.

Meanwhile, Jamie was doing his own digging, for entirely different reasons. From the very beginning, he had always wanted to know the "why"—why was the sky blue, why did he have to go to school every day, why did everyone have to go to church every week, why did his birth parents give him away? For years, he believed that the cleft lip had classified him as special needs, and that served as his answer to "why." He didn't discover until later, when he made a secret Facebook account during junior high and joined a couple of online adoptee groups, that many birth mothers wanted to keep their babies. He had no idea that for a long time, there was a law in place that such children were granted citizenship only if their birth certificate listed a known Korean father.

Jamie was angry. He blamed their parents, who were briefly flirting with the idea of adopting a third child, from India, in anticipation of facing an empty nest in the next few years. "It's like we're collector's items picked up while traveling abroad," he'd said. "Or maybe a fucking Taste of Asia sampler." He blamed Korea and China. For quite some time, he cursed humanity as a whole.

No one knew how to handle his newly kindled rage—not Hazel, not their parents, not Jamie himself. So Hazel did what she could. She told him about the fire burning inside her, the secret she'd kept from every living soul until that moment.

Hazel told him about the ghosts. How she could speak to them, how they'd come to pour out their stories while she listened, how she realized she could work with them until they felt ready to move on, and then she and the spirit could both find rest. She relayed the history of Philip, a three-year-old who'd lived in the house before their family bought it. He'd drowned accidentally, tragically, in the backyard pool. Philip had not realized he'd died; he only knew that his family had, for reasons unknown to him, grown very sad and quiet and then left him behind.

"So—" Hazel said when she was done explaining it all to her brother.

"So what?"

Her gaze cut to Philip, who was sitting in front of her with his legs crossed, his blond curls shining, stuck close to his scalp from the wetness. "Do you believe me?"

"Of course I do," Jamie said without a beat of hesitation. "You're my sister."

Hazel didn't realize she'd been holding her breath until she let it out, and the tension rising in her chest dissipated along with the exhaled air. "Thank you."

"You don't need to thank me. You and me, we've gotta stick together. Right?"

She took him in—the tousled hair sticking up in the back, his bright smile, the scrunch of his eyes. "Right."

Contrary to Hazel's prediction, they do hear more from Cody—or rather, they hear more from Merle. Three weeks after Hazel's first visit, Merle calls again. "At first it seemed like the cleaning—cleansing, whatever it's called—worked, and then he started up again a few days ago. I thought he'd stop if I ignored him, but it just got . . . louder."

"I'll be there this afternoon," Hazel says before hanging up. As she slips her phone into her messenger bag, Jamie asks, "Our friend's causing problems again, huh?"

"Apparently so. It's strange. I didn't think he'd have the energy to overcome the cleansing."

"Must've been a tough bastard, huh?" There's a glint of fondness in his eyes, tempered by a hint of sadness. It's so very *Jamie*, that look of his, and the wave of grief that washes over her upon seeing it is nearly visceral.

"Yes, I would say so."

"Well." Jamie straightens from where he's been leaning against the wall. He doesn't need the support, but old habits die hard, even more so when it comes to spirits. "Shall we carry on? Or am I joining the team this time?"

"Jamie . . ."

"Hazel," he says, his voice low. "I know you're a badass,

but even fearless leaders like yourself could use some backup. Let me help you."

It isn't a good idea. Hazel doesn't feel quite right bringing Jamie in on the case without Merle's knowledge, and she can't exactly explain that her dead brother is here to assist. But Jamie has had years of experience in helping her with jobs and listening to her stories. He knows what he's getting into. And she misses having him come along, misses his grounding presence by her side, his ability to charm strangers in a matter of seconds and smooth the edges of their wariness and their grief.

Hazel sighs. "Fine. But once you get him to appear, I'm doing the talking."

"Deal." Jamie grins, clapping his hands together. "Now, come on, Scooby-Doo. We've got a mystery to solve."

But after backtracking to Merle's house, it doesn't take Hazel long to realize that Merle isn't about to give up any answers.

"I didn't have this much upset going on at the apartment I used to live in, and above my head, there were four children running around unsupervised," Merle says, throwing her hands toward the ceiling.

"I'm sure this must be disturbing to you for multiple reasons," Hazel says, then, gently, goes on. "Ms. Westover. I know this may be difficult to discuss, but given that the cleansing didn't seem to have much effect, I have to ask . . . Is there any reason Cody would be upset with you?"

"And why is it that you 'have to ask,' exactly?"

"It's just—residual emotions are often intensified for spirits, but they usually stem from somewhere. Even if it's small."

"Our relationship wasn't perfect," Merle says, crossing her arms. "But Cody is—was—my nephew, and I love him."

Jamie tuts as he shakes his head. "This poor lady is so deep in denial that I don't think a bulldozer could dig her way out."

"Of course," Hazel says to Merle, ignoring her brother. "Well. Why don't we focus on that, then? Maybe you can try concentrating on a happy memory that was important to both of you. It might help Cody find the closure he needs to move on."

"All right," Merle agrees.

Hazel goes out to her car to fetch the necessary supplies. She takes out a large white candle from her bag, one that will attract good energy and gather it, amplify it before reflecting it back into the surrounding environment. As she rummages around the back seat for a bundle of matches, Jamie asks over her shoulder, "So you really think this is gonna work? The power of positive thinking, and boom, problem solved?"

"No," she says. "Clearly, there's more to the story than what Merle is telling us. But she'll say it when she's ready, or she won't. I'm not here to help only the dead, you know that."

What Hazel doesn't mention is that the sense of guilt emanating from Merle in waves is almost as strong as her grief. She knows what it's like to carry regret that you can barely speak of. Not once since Jamie's return had they talked about the past—not when he appeared in the middle of movie night, or when they walked in the park after her classes or drove to take care of a haunting. Instead, they laughed over Keanu Reeves's acting, judged owners by their dogs, debated the accuracy of *Poltergeist* compared to the real thing. The same goes for the future; neither of them have breathed a word about Jamie leaving or Hazel asking him to go—like she's done with so many others before him to try to free them from the pain of lingering, of holding on for too long.

If it weren't for her brother's invisibility to everyone else, it'd be as if nothing had changed since they were little kids, when they were still close and Jamie was alive and himself and whole. But Hazel still dreams of Jamie's death. In her vision, there are train tracks, but no train. The iron of the rails is cold; the wind tastes bitter on her tongue. The sky swirls blue and inky black like a Van Gogh painting devoid of stars. She knows that this is where Jamie died, high and alone and so cold, his lashes clumped together with frost, but the only hint of his presence is a fleeting flash of gold darting across her mind's eye. She hears the train's horn racing upward in volume like a teakettle brought to boil, and then she wakes in her bed to the hum of the air conditioner and the feeling that the train is about to barrel through her window.

The third and final call that Hazel receives from Merle sounds like a clip from a real-life murder mystery or a medical show—all garbled sentences that don't quite make full sense, fuzzy audio quality.

"Something's wrong. He— I don't—"

"What's wrong?" Hazel presses the phone closer to her ear.

"I don't know. I just—please. I need your help."

"I'm on my way right now."

"I'm sorry. But I . . . I don't know what to do." And Merle does sound lost, much younger than her years.

"You don't have to apologize," Hazel says. "I'll be there."

Thirteen minutes and two bypassed red lights later, Hazel and Jamie are knocking at Merle's front door. It swings inward, and Hazel is hit full force with chaos, a feeling she can only describe as ink swirls come alive, teeming and seething and writhing in on each other. There's the heavy scent of burning pine. And then she sees the mottled red bruise on the right side of Merle's face, curling along her temple and creeping down her cheek. Jamie lets out a low whistle.

"What happened?" Hazel asks. "Cody . . . did he . . ."

"I felt this push while I was carrying the laundry downstairs, and then—" Merle gestures to her face. "It happened so quickly."

"I'm sorry," Hazel says as she enters the house. "I won't leave until we've got a hold on this, okay?"

"Thank you."

Jamie follows them into the living room. "Remember, Hazel," he says, "I can't exactly play bad cop here. So I think that role is up to you."

Merle sits on a stuffed armchair and motions toward the love seat.

"Ms. Westover," Hazel begins, "I hate to press you, but given the circumstances, I really need to know more about what might have happened between you and Cody."

Merle worries at the little golden cross hanging from her neck. "Yes, yes. You're right." She takes a long breath and then goes on, "Cody's father and I—well . . . We grew up in a broken home, and Cal swore he'd never be like our daddy, which he wasn't, until he got hold of a bottle. I found him a counselor, took him to AA, but he just couldn't stop drinking. One night he beat that boy 'til he was black-and-blue, so I— I reported him to the police." Merle closes her eyes. "I got my own brother arrested, and the look on Cody's face . . . I can see it even now, the hurt and fear. The betrayal."

"You did the right thing," Hazel says. "You helped your brother as best you could, and you protected your nephew."

"I told myself that, at the beginning. Took Cody in and tried to finish raising him right. But no matter what I said, what I did . . ." Merle shakes her head. "We all knew that Cal had quite a few demons living inside his head. But he was also the boy's daddy, and Cody loved him for it. He had a hard time reconciling those two truths. Something like that, it doesn't let you go."

Hazel glances at Jamie, right beside her, who has grown unusually quiet. He's jiggling his leg up and down and staring at a neat stack of coasters on the coffee table. As she watches him, she thinks of the first cracks, the beginning of the chasm that yawned dark and wide between them as the years went on, as Jamie lashed out against their parents and couldn't understand why Hazel didn't do the same.

Hazel remembers him pacing across the living room rug one night while their parents were out. "They're suffocating us, Haze! They've been doing it all our lives—hell, they were doing it before we even came to this country. Why aren't you on my side here?"

"I *am* on your side, Jamie, always. But they're our parents."

"So they get a free pass?"

"No, but they do love us. They think they're doing the right thing."

Jamie stopped, looked at her. "Which makes it even worse."

Then came the drugs. Jamie smoking weed in the woods behind their school's old baseball field, skipping class because he'd been out on a bender the night before, ferrying heroin from his dealer to the group of their classmates who drove Lexus sedans and Mercedes-Benz convertibles. She thinks of the knock-down, drag-out fights between him and their parents, how they grew progressively in frequency and intensity over the years, rising to a crescendo until finally the wave came crashing down and Jamie stormed out of the house for the last time while their mother sat on the bottom step, crying as she watched him leave.

"You're right," Hazel says to Merle. "Things like this, they don't just let you go." She stands, her bag of supplies in hand. "I'm going to try to summon Cody. That way you can talk to him and hopefully get him to move on peacefully."

Merle nods. "All right."

As Hazel takes out plastic sandwich bags, each one filled with a different ingredient for the incense—verbena, saffron, pepper, muskflower, sweetgrass—Jamie calls out, "Cody, are you here?"

Hazel strikes a match and sets the mixture alight. The incense flares like a sparking log, and then a young man with red-tinged hair, his image blurred around the edges, appears in the entrance to Merle's living room.

"Hello, Cody," Hazel says, and Merle's gaze jerks to her before sweeping across the room like the beacon of a lighthouse. "My name is—"

But Cody isn't looking at Hazel. "Who are you? What are you doing here?" he asks, taking a step in Jamie's direction. "Get out of my house."

Jamie holds up both hands, palms outward. "Look, man, we just want to talk—"

"Get out!" Cody yells, his voice reaching a preternatural volume. The lights go out with the sound of a live wire zapping a bug; wind tears through the room with near-hurricane force, and then the lights return and Jamie is gone.

Fire flashes through Hazel's veins, fire so hot it burns like ice. "No. Jamie—Jamie!" She cannot think. She's banished so many spirits, laid dozens to rest, but this situation is totally and completely different. "Ms. Westover, your nephew—please—"

"What do I do?" Merle's eyes are wide, wild, almost neon in their blueness.

Cody looks as if he's made of static, channels crossed and jumbled. The bulb in one of the table lamps blows. "Reach out to him," Hazel says. "He's got to calm down."

Merle grasps the golden cross resting beneath the *V* of her collarbones. "Cody. Listen to me, please."

The static flickers, angry and electric.

"Try again," Hazel says, although all she's thinking is *Jamie, Jamie, where are you?*

"It's me, Cody. I'm here. I'm right here," Merle says.

Cody's form stills, sharpens, like the view through a camera lens coming into focus. "Aunt Merle?"

"I'm sorry." Merle's voice barely wavers, but tears fall down her face, trickle along her jaw. "I should've done better by you."

"I don't . . . I didn't realize." Cody looks around, taking in the state of the room before turning to Hazel. "There's just this anger inside of me, and I— It freaks me the fuck out. I can't control it. I swear I didn't mean to hurt her."

"She knows, and she's here to help you," Hazel says. "We both are."

"How?"

"I'll guide you forward. Onward. It's time for you to find some rest."

"But what about my aunt?" Cody asks. "I left her—it was my fault, and if I go now . . . she'll be alone."

Alone. Hazel has been alone for so long that she senses the weight of her solitude only in the quiet before she falls asleep, in those first few minutes after she wakes. Yet she knows that it's like a mark on your forehead, your heart, your place of dwelling—a mark that can't be so easily washed away, even with time. "I wish I could fix it. But your aunt's a survivor."

"Yeah. Yeah, she is," he says. "Look, about my dad . . . he wasn't always like that, you know? I mean, he used to save up money every year and we'd go to the Iron Bowl. The parking was shitty, and our seats were way up in the nose-bleed section, but we didn't care." Cody crosses his arms over his body, hugging himself, and he suddenly reminds Hazel of Merle during that first visit. "But I get it, why she did that. I do. Can you tell her that for me?"

"I will." Hazel holds out her arm and says, "Here, take my hand."

Cody places his hand in hers. Hazel feels a flare of fire, of bottle-rocket pain and violence the color of wine before the sensation shifts to the brush of something cool and weightless across her skin. She reaches for Merle's hand with her free one, and Cody follows Hazel's lead, completing the circle. Merle starts in shock as Cody's spirit touches her palm.

"This house will always be your home," Hazel says, her voice calm, firm, "but you must move on from it. Go in peace, Cody Westover. We wish you well."

Merle's lips move soundlessly. Cody speaks, his words as quiet as a TV with the volume turned down, and then he is gone.

Tears run down Merle's cheeks like rain. She lets out a single, shuddering sob, and it's like the bottom falling out of a darkly clouded sky. Although Hazel wants nothing more than to tear out of the house, to search for Jamie and shout his name, she guides Merle to the sofa. Merle half sits, half falls down onto it and puts her head in her hands.

"I'm so sorry, Ms. Westover," Hazel says. "Can I get you some tissues?"

Merle points in the general direction of the left side of the house. "Bathroom . . . It's down the hall."

"I'll be right back." Hazel goes first to the front door and opens it. Her car sits parked by the curb. It's empty. And although she didn't really expect otherwise, it still hits her with the gravity she felt when her parents got the call

145

about Jamie and the policewoman said—so kindly that it hurt—"I know this is hard right now, but when you feel ready, we need you to come identify his body."

Who was Hazel kidding? As if she'd ever be ready.

It had been two years since her brother left home. Two whole years of radio silence, of Hazel pouring herself into communicating with spirits on behalf of others, focusing on using her ability to help them, to find purpose in her calling, her loneliness. And then Jamie showed up at her apartment right before she was about to leave for chemistry class one Tuesday morning. He'd come to see her, he said, but there was something very clearly off about him. The jerky and jittery way he moved, the stilted rhythm of his words, the spacey look in his eyes—all of it was wrong. When he didn't come back from the bathroom, that was when she found him ransacking the medicine cabinet.

"Haze, I'm sorry—" Jamie began, shoving both hands in his pockets to hide their contents.

What she felt in that moment was more than betrayal. It was—a loss of faith. Even when her father said again and again that Jamie wouldn't come back and her mother stopped talking about him, Hazel had always fervently believed that he would return. But not this way. Not like this. No, this was every bad thing their parents had ever assumed about him or feared he would become. This wasn't her brother.

She couldn't bear to look at him, so she'd averted her gaze to the mirror above the sink instead, at her reflection, which appeared far more resolute than she felt. "You need to leave." And when he didn't react, she held open the door.

This is one of the moments Hazel regrets the most. She wishes she'd said instead, *I don't care what you say—I'm going to get you help.* She wishes that she wasn't so fucking young. If only she'd never made him go.

Usually, Hazel doesn't mind eating out, seeing a movie, going for a walk or a shopping trip by herself. She's become accustomed to her own company since moving out of her parents' house; grown to enjoy it, even. But now, after Jamie's return and disappearance yet again, she really feels it, the isolation, like something physical pressing in on her from all sides. It's amazing, she thinks, how a person's absence can affect you even more than their presence. How what you've lost can more sharply define you than what you have.

When Hazel enters her apartment, it's quiet, so quiet that she can hear herself breathe. For a long moment she pauses there in the hallway and lets the silence wrap around her. She stares at the sunlight coming in through the glass above her front door, watches it make shifting shadow patterns through the trees outside and onto the floorboards below.

"I'm sorry," she says to the silence.

The leaves dance. Dark, light, and then—Hazel feels the

wind, as if it were coming right through her walls. There's a quiet rustling, like the flutter of a bird's wings. She turns around.

"Jamie." Hazel breathes his name as if she were saying a prayer. "I thought . . ."

"So did I, for a second. Who would've guessed that one angsty dude could almost do me in?" Jamie says, scratching the back of his head. Then, quietly, "You know, I thought about not coming back."

Her brother was always the kind of person who could fill an entire room with his presence, but he suddenly looks quite small standing there alone in the doorway, as if he were someone returning to their hometown after many years away, and he's a bit lost now among the new storefronts and people and streets. But Hazel isn't lost at all; in this moment she can see so clearly in him the boy she used to know, her brother, her best friend. And she forgets about what she always tells the people she tries to help, that peace can come in letting go, in moving forward. That may not be entirely wrong, but for now, the two of them need to find their own kind of peace. And that will have to be enough.

"I understand why," she says. "But I'm glad you did." She gestures toward the recesses of her apartment. "So . . . would you like to come in?"

Jamie smiles, the sun reflecting gold in his eyes. "I'd like that."

LOVE IS NOT ENOUGH

BY LISA WOOL-RIM SJÖBLOM

PING!

"HI! HOPE IT'S OKAY TO CONTACT YOU DIRECTLY. I SAW YOUR POST IN THE GROUP AND JUST WANT TO SAY THANK YOU! I WANTED TO SAY SOMETHING AS WELL BUT WAS TOO AFRAID OF ALL THE HATRED YOU GET WHEN YOU CONTRADICT ADOPTIVE PARENTS IN THESE GROUPS. THANKS AGAIN! /ANA CILIA"

"HI! THANKS FOR YOUR DM. I JUST GOT SO MAD!"

"I WAS BORN IN KOREA, ADOPTED AS A BABY."

"I'M ADOPTED FROM COLOMBIA, WHERE ARE YOU FROM?"

"I WAS A BABY TOO AND HAVE MISSED MY FAMILY EVER SINCE."

"PEOPLE DON'T UNDERSTAND HOW YOU CAN MISS PEOPLE YOU'VE NEVER MET!"

"ME TOO. BUT NO ONE WANTS TO LINK IT TO THE ADOPTION. THEY THINK IT'S A 'TEENAGE PHASE.'"

"I'VE BEEN GRIEVING MY WHOLE LIFE. I'M DEALING WITH SEVERE DEPRESSION."

"I KNOW! I'M ALWAYS BEING TOLD THAT I'M UNGRATEFUL AND SPOILED!"

OREO

BY SHANNON GIBNEY

Louisa Halsted knew that she wasn't Black enough, but she wasn't going to let that stop her from trying.

She joined the Black Student Union, tried to broker her math skills into a treasurer position, lost her bid, and settled for parliamentarian—the whitest position on the slate, according to her peers, and the most futile, according to her. At the meetings, everyone talked over each other, and there were tons of side conversations going on while a little bit of work got done. They petitioned the library for more books by Black authors and got them. They planned their annual Black History Month banquet, which featured dry chicken and endless speeches by Black elders in ill-fitting suits and gowns who urged them all to stay in school, not fight, graduate, and attend an HBCU. This year they had successfully organized to hire a fly DJ for a banquet after-party, which everyone was excited about. Not bad for a measly sophomore.

But Louie, with her curly blond hair and green eyes, her yellow skin and tiny body, stuck out in all the wrong ways. Her hair would not be tamed into a cute bob, like all the other Black girls were wearing. "Afro," Lance Palmer and his crew would call her in the halls, and now also at the dance. "Why you tryna play like you down when you *ain't*?" And she wanted to melt into the wall. Although the wall wouldn't take her either.

She locked herself in the bathroom late at night, practicing Black English, which she realized all too late was a key marker of blackness—something she had never had access to in her white household. "I'mma slap the black offa ya," she would say softly into the mirror. This was something she had seen in a movie, but had never heard an actual real-life Black person say. "We 'bout to light up this mother-fucker," she said out of the side of her mouth. She'd noticed that swear words sounded different, even more powerful to her ears, in Black English. "She don't know shit," she said next. And then, a side eye and a disdainful frown for the imaginary white girl on the other side of the mirror: "Yeah, thanks, Katie. You a real G, ain't chu?"

Then she would shake her head and laugh at how ludicrous she sounded, the longing to hear herself in the language so strong. She was a mixed Black girl adopted into a white family who felt unseen by the white kids and unaccepted by the Black ones. And it seemed like she was the only one in all of Newport News, Virginia.

When Louie wanted to distract herself from feeling like an outsider, she turned to literature. While her peers jostled and flirted and ran into each other in the halls between classes and lunch, she would be propped up against a wall, reading *The Underground Railroad*, or *Sula*, or *Killing the Black Body*. On the bus, too, she propped her knees up on the seat in front of her, her head below it, hiding in a book. Reading Baldwin and Hurston, she had the feeling of conversing with an old friend who *knew* she was Black and didn't need any performance or proof of belonging. She had just read, "I believe that the fact of the juxtaposition of the white and black races has created a massive psycho-existential complex. I hope by analyzing it to destroy it," in *Black Skin, White Masks*, when Nia Edwards, the coolest girl in school, sat down beside her. Louie was so surprised, she dropped the book on the floor.

"What is it with this Tragic Mulatto situation, anyhow?" Nia said dramatically. Her butt was only halfway on the seat because Louie was in the middle, taking up most of the space. Nia pushed her left hip into Louie's. "Are you really just gonna hide behind books for your whole high school career?"

Louie pushed herself up and moved toward the window so that Nia could get herself on the seat properly. She

gazed at Nia's long, straightened hair and her finely man-
icured nails. With her almond brown skin, luminous eyes,
and *don't give a shit* attitude, she was definitely in the "in"
crowd at school, even though she seemed to be a loner. In
fact, Louie couldn't remember a single time she had seen
Nia with a friend.

"Wha— What are you doing here?" Louie stammered.
She heard how ridiculous the words sounded as soon as she
spoke them, and she flushed red.

Nia laughed. "What do you mean? I ride this bus home
every day, same as you." She slung her bag off her shoulder
and placed it on the floor between her legs. "It's a free country," she said. "At least, that's what I hear."

What in the world did Nia Edwards want to do with *her*?
Like two-thirds of the bus was empty. She had plenty of
places she could sit. Plenty better than beside the weird
mixed "wannabe" girl.

The bus engine revved up, and the driver shut the
doors. They were about to leave. Nia looked straight
ahead, and Louie could think of nothing to say, so she
leaned her head against the window and opened her book
again.

Nia glanced over. "Why you reading *that*, anyway?" she
asked.

Louie snorted before she could stop herself. "This?" She
held up her copy of *Black Skin, White Masks*. "It's a classic!"
Her nerd cred—basically synonymous with whiteness in

the eyes of some of the Black kids—would rise astronomically after this conversation, but she didn't care. Fanon had captivated her imagination with his treatise on the colonization of the Black mind.

Now it was Nia's turn to snort. "What it is, is *boring*."

Louie gasped. Before this moment, she had never wanted to fight someone. How could anyone even *suggest* that Fanon was anything less than breathtakingly brilliant?

The bus turned left on Grant. Just a few more stops and they would be at Everest and Nineteenth, Louie's stop.

Nia laughed. "Whoa, I guess the Tragic Mulatto ain't so tragic after all," she said, eyeing Louie playfully. "Sharing her unpopular thoughts on literature and everything. Speaking up for herself."

Louie could not decide if she was the source of a joke or sharing one with Nia. "Tragic Mulatto?"

Nia sighed. "Yeah, you know the trope: mixed Black girl who doesn't fit in with the white kids or the Black ones? Doomed to live in the in-between space forever. Never to find her people." She said the last line melodramatically, with her hand to her forehead. Both girls laughed.

"No, I never heard of that," said Louie. She would look it up tonight.

"Nella Larsen? *Passing*? *The Autobiography of an Ex-Colored Man*?"

Louie shook her head.

Nia frowned and looked straight ahead. And then it felt

awkward again. "Clearly, you're reading the wrong books," she said.

Louie's brow furrowed. She was far more used to the coarse hallway insults about her hair or her "flat butt" than being upbraided about her reading habits. It was the most interesting conversation she'd had in months, but she wasn't exactly sure if she was *enjoying* it.

Without warning, Nia leaned over and whispered in Louie's ear. "Yo, check this out." She beckoned toward her bag on the floor, a wide and open smile plastered across her face.

Louie leaned over, eyebrows raised.

Nia bent down and brought out a thick, dog-eared paperback copy of *Anna Karenina*. "You wanna read some *real* literature, the Russians are where it's at," she said. "Finished *Notes from Underground* last week. That shit was dope as hell. Never read anything like it."

The bus pulled up to a corner. Louie looked out the window. They were at her stop. She had been so busy talking with Nia that she hadn't even noticed how close they were. She frantically grabbed at her backpack, unzipped the zipper, and stuffed her book inside. Then she rose and smiled half-heartedly at Nia.

"Hurry up, Oreo! We ain't got all day," someone yelled from the back of the bus.

Louie's face burned, and she pushed past Nia, out into the aisle.

"You can go ahead and fuck all the way off!" Nia shouted back at them.

"Language!" the bus driver shouted.

Nia sighed. "It's so tiresome, being surrounded by Neanderthals all the time," she said, just loud enough for Louie to hear.

No one said anything else as she made her way out of the bus. When she heard the doors shut and the brakes shudder behind her, she allowed herself to smile.

"You can't begin a paper with a thesis statement," Nia said firmly, scrolling through Louie's paper on *The Round House* on her iPad. It was two months later, and the girls were sitting on the third floor of St. Clair High School, waiting for American Lit to start.

Louie harrumphed. "Oh hooey," she said. "You can do anything you want, if you do it well."

Nia gave her the Black Girl Side Eye and frowned. "Hooey? That some kinda white folk slang for *bullshit*?"

Louie laughed, but inside she was cringing. By now, Nia had been over to her house—to study and to see her impressive library (which now included *Notes from Underground*)—and Louie had been proud of herself for not freaking out too much. Or trying to hide just how white her white family was. Or how white *she* was. It was weird. She felt so comfortable around Nia when they talked about books and ideas, but she couldn't seem to shake the feeling that one day Nia would decide she was actually too white to hang with and drop her. They had also hung out at Nia's house a few times, and her parents were warm and welcoming. None of Louie's insecurities were piqued.

Louie sighed. "I'll look at it again, I guess." She watched as Janessa Keller sauntered down the hallway in her ripped jeans and tight red top that stopped just below her breasts, showing off her even tighter tummy. Louie may have been able to write somewhat convincingly on strategies toward freedom in ethnic literature, but she would never, ever be the cute girl. It was ridiculous for her to even care about such things, she knew, but some days it got to her.

"Why you eyeing that heifer?" Nia asked, closing the iPad.

Louie's face flushed; Nia was so good at observing people and discerning their true motivations. It was quite a skill, but also unnerving when she turned her attentions on Louie. "I—I think she's nice," Louie stammered.

"Janessa is a lot of things, but nice?" Nia shook her head. "That ain't one of 'em."

"She calls me over to sit with her crew sometimes at lunch," Louie said.

"So she can ask you for help in Spanish, next period," Nia snapped. "And notice your own use of the word *sometimes*. If someone wants to just be your friend *sometimes*, then that ain't too nice at all."

Louie felt an anger brewing in the pit of her stomach, but

she pushed it down. "Last week she told me I should wear green eyeliner, to highlight my eyes."

Nia shook her head. "That's a terrible idea. What does she know about your eyes, anyway?"

Louie scooched a bit away from her friend. Nia's bluntness sometimes felt like barbs. "She was trying to help me."

Nia laughed. "Listen, Louie. Girls like that don't help anyone, okay? Unless there's more helping in it for them than us."

Louie's stomach fluttered. "Us?" she asked.

Nia grinned. "Yeah us, dummy. The Black and Proud Nerds." She gathered her bag and books for next period. "The Oreos," she said softly.

Louie felt her stomach relax, and she laughed. Then her eyes widened. "But they don't call you that, do they?"

Nia sighed. "You think you're the only one who's *too white* up in this joint? That only pretty little mixed girls get called Oreo?"

Yes, that's exactly what I thought. Louie studied Nia, with her high cheekbones, deep mocha skin, and braids that had recently been put in and flowed all the way down her back. In the short time they had been friends, Louie had spent a lot of time trying to measure herself up to Nia, who represented a kind of blackness she could never be. She had never once thought about what it might be like to actually *be* Nia, a brilliant Black girl who dug Russian novels and couldn't help but talk back to those who threw stale insults her way. A person who could never tolerate simplistic definitions of blackness.

Nia stood up to walk to chemistry. "See you after seventh period?"

Still feeling chagrined, Louie nodded slowly. "See you then."

A few months later, the Black Student Union meeting was sparsely populated by the usual characters: Kendrick Brand with his starched pressed pants and exacting attitude, Lance and his raucous friends, and Janessa and her fashion crew. Louie and Nia sat toward the back of the room by the open window so they could better smell the spring wind. It was only a matter of time before school let out, and they would be free for two whole months.

"So, with the money from the Sweethearts Dance, we can supplement the savings toward our trip to the African American History Museum next fall," Louie said excitedly.

A collective whoop went up around the room, followed by clapping.

As treasurer, Kendrick passed around a sheet of paper with the current balance of the BSU savings account: $2,566.13. A veritable fortune to them—definitely the most money the BSU had ever had.

"Yo, you think we can raise more and stay in the city overnight or something?" Lance asked. "You know, get in a little . . . what they call that again? *Extracurricular* activity." He leaned over Nia lasciviously, and she pushed him away.

Louie laughed. "Yeah . . . I think we all know there's no way that's happening."

Lance play-frowned at Nia. "Girl, you know I'd be good to you. Way, waaaayyy too good to you."

The whole room hooted.

"Boy, please." Nia swatted him away.

Louie had noticed that Nia was less annoyed with him than she pretended to be. And who could blame her? Lance was not exactly bookish, but he was hot, witty, and—Nia's favorite—funny.

Louie cleared her throat. "Actually . . ."

The side conversations were ramping up now. Janessa and Paula and Nikki were discussing a store they wanted to visit in DC, Kendrick was saying that they should put the money into the scholarship fund, and Lance was pontificating on his *love prowess* to the whole room.

Nia looked at her sideways and shrugged. *What can you do?* seemed to be the message.

Louie stood up. "Actually!" she yelled.

Janessa and Paula and Nikki turned to her, their eyebrows rising in surprise. Kendrick sneezed. And Lance just laughed. "Well, will you look at that! The white Black girl done found her voice!"

"Fuck you, Lance," Nia snapped.

Louie put her hand on her friend's shoulder. "No, it's

174

fine," she said, the calmness of her voice surprising even her. "He's not wrong. And also, Nia's right, Lance. You can fuck off."

Everyone in the room just blinked at her for what felt like a solid minute. Maybe the longest minute of her life. Louie felt her skin redden, completely exposed for all her foibles, all her ridiculous desires to *be Black* (whatever that was), all her whiteness on display and beyond her control to hide. But also, she realized suddenly, all of it came down to one singular desire, and that was *to belong*. That was what she wanted all along. And yes, that had something to do with blackness. But maybe not everything. Belonging, she had discovered through her friendship with Nia, could take many forms.

"So, Nia and I were thinking that a creative and productive way to use any money left over after the museum trip might be to create like, a Living Black Studies group or something," she said, trying to keep her voice steady.

She had everyone's attention, and it made her feel both powerful and scared.

"What does that mean?" Janessa asked.

"It means that we would maybe invite a guest speaker in—someone from the city's Monuments and Buildings Commission, for example. Ask them to talk about the James Monroe statue at the square, and what can be done to take it down."

"Racist ass motherfucker," Lance said under his breath.

Louie nodded. "Right. This is 2023, for God's sake! Why are we still venerating these racist pigs?"

There were assertions around the room.

Energized, Louie went on. "Then we were also thinking of including readings on the topic that the speaker is discussing. Like for this, it might be on the racist history of monuments, buildings, and even schools in Virginia."

More nodding from her peers.

"And we could even start a blog or something, to post our writings and what we're learning and everything."

A collective groan went up. "Girl, we ain't tryna write nothing!" said Cam. "We already got enough homework in this motherfucker."

Louie sat down, feeling defeated but also buoyed by how far she had managed to get on selling their plan.

Nia stood up. "You don't have to write anything if you don't wanna. Maybe your medium is film, maybe you're a sound artist and want to do an interview with someone in the community that you think people should know about. Maybe you took some dope photos at a rally or something. The blog could be a place we could share all of that."

Cody was nodding, slowly. Other kids looked thoughtful.

"You making some good points now, Sis," Janessa said, pointing one long blood red talon at Nia. And her crew was also nodding in agreement. "That *do* sound fly."

Clearly excited, Nia went on. "How can we expand what blackness means, culturally, so that it becomes a potential site of freedom rather than a confining category? How can we make sure that when we say 'blackness,' we are talking about every kind of Black experience, not just the ones the white power structure has deemed acceptable? That's what we're really interested in getting at with this project."

Louie clapped, then jumped up. "Bravo, my friend!" she shouted. "Exactly!"

Nia cringed, but managed a half-smile back.

And with that, the energy in the room completely deflated.

"You Negresses always talking some kinda high-falutent shit . . ." Lance mumbled.

Janessa and Nikki and Paula went back to discussing the high boots they wanted to buy, and Kendrick snorted.

"Anyway. It's nice to see there's so much initial interest," Louie said, recovering herself.

Then, out of nowhere, Cam's slow drawl. "Nah, I see where you going wid it," he said. "I get made fun of by my boys 'cause I like fucking caving. They be telling me, 'Ain't no Black people can even say spelunking, much less do it.' But I'm like, 'Nigga, if I'm motherfucking *spelunking*, than obviously, a Black man be doin' it."

Cody and Lance looked at Cam like he was a stranger for a minute, then burst out laughing. "Nigga, you one crazy motherfucker!" Lance exclaimed, laughing. "Niggas ain't want nothing to do with caves. Everybody know that. Maybe for hiding in them during slavery times, but

177

since then? Nah, Fam. Nah."

Cam grinned, but there was definitely some tension behind it that Louie could recognize. "No, everybody *don't* know that. Niggas can do whatever niggas wanna do." He looked around the room. "Am I right?"

The air was electric as Cam searched for affirmation in each individual. Janessa slowly met his eyes and nodded, as did Nikki. Paula just looked down. Kendrick nodded, and so did Ebony.

Nia winked at Louie and whispered, "We got 'em!"

"Okay, as parliamentarian, I'm tabling discussion of the Living Black Studies project, expanding blackness, and even spelunking till our next meeting in May!" said Louie. "Come next time with your ideas and questions, as well as what you are willing to contribute." She looked each of her peers in the eye. "Meeting adjourned."

Nia and Louie leaped up and hugged, doing a circular jig together.

"Oreos can get it done!" Nia exclaimed.

"Viva las Oreos!" Louie said, pumping her fist in the air.

Janessa laughed.

"Y'all the weirdest ass Black girls I ever known," said Lance.

"And that," said Louie, "is why you love us."

Lance frowned for a moment. Then he smiled. "You right."

TRUFFLES (OR DON'T WORRY, THE DOG WILL BE FINE)

BY ERIC SMITH

I'm in the barn again. Why do we even *have* a barn?

Thick stalks of hay dig into my thighs from the bale I'm sitting on, pinching at my skin no matter how much I shift my weight. My jeans might be thick, but my skin has never been. I know that much about myself. Heart on my sleeve and all that . . . I'm living my life like an emo song mistakenly dropped on a country music playlist.

I close my eyes, inhaling and exhaling, the simultaneously sweet and stale and wet smell of the farm enveloping me. The straw, the earth, the autumn leaves, and the lingering scent of burning barrels full of them somewhere in the distance. The smell is comforting, even as I'm wildly aware of the fact that I fit in here just about as well as this barn does.

I don't.

My parents farm blueberries. Yet we've got this barn with stables and hay, as if horses are one day going to sprout up out of the soil. Uncle Morris has a barn on his property, and Dad just had to get one of his own. At least, that's the story Mom tells whenever she has someone come by to clean the thing. It mostly sits empty.

Why is there even hay in here?

I grip the bale of hay, hot tears streaming down my cheeks.

It's all just . . . playing pretend. The barn. The stables with no horses. The hay that no one is going to eat, save for the mice that probably live in it. None of it fits, but it feels like it's supposed to. Like I'm supposed to. Like everyone *wants* me to while simultaneously pointing me out. The adopted brown kid with the white country family. I couldn't be a needle in a haystack if I tried. I'm like a pitchfork someone tossed in there—obvious, different, and jutting upward.

The hay jabs into my palms, and I let go, shaking my hands as I grit my teeth.

I exhale.

This Thanksgiving was supposed to be *different*. The last one before I leave for college next year. Before I'm across the country in Oregon, in a place where traveling back to South Jersey for the holidays is a costly impossibility. No more awkward, quick looks from cousins as they grow old enough to understand, or whispered chatter among aunts and uncles who are old enough to know better. No more unspoken questions that color the eyes of every new friend or boyfriend or girlfriend who arrives on the scene, just quick enough to disappoint me and leave their name forgotten at the next get-together.

Doesn't matter how fresh the damn cranberries are around here. I'm not coming back, and I sure as hell have no plans to spend another Christmas or Easter or St. Patrick's Day at Aunt Melinda's cranberry bog a few miles down the road.

"It's a farm!" she insists.

It's a red fucking swamp, Melinda.

I just wanted a good Thanksgiving.

Just one.

"He's in here!"

Startled, I lean back, almost falling off the hay bale. Dad squeezes his way through the narrow opening in the heavy barn doors, prying them open a bit more for Mom.

The two of them look panicked. And nothing like me. Dad has the gait and muscle of Bruce Willis in his early movies, complete with the shiny bald head, though Mom is definitely not someone who needs saving. Tall and lean and strong, a retired ballerina who now teaches Pilates to bored husbands and wives in the farming community, she probably could have kicked that door open herself.

"Dylan, Jesus," Dad says, walking toward me, sounding a little out of breath. "You can't just take off and—"

"You said there wasn't going to be anyone new this year."

I stand up, crossing my arms, trying to hold back all the emotions brewing. It's bad enough I have to deal with this when we travel for the holidays, visiting aunts and uncles in homes in bigger cities, with streetlights instead of fireflies. This is *our* home.

"I know. I'm sorry," he says, "but I can't predict surprise guests!" He looks to my mom, who shrugs, shaking her head at him. "How was I supposed to know Kevin had some new girlfriend?" he asks.

"You could have been stricter on the invitations," she suggests. "Family only, and all."

"Stricter?" Dad laughs. "It's Thanksgiving! The invitation is just a text saying, 'Hey it's at our house this year.' This isn't a wedding." He turns to me, a smile warming his face. It's impossible to be angry at that smile.

"Come here, champ." He waves at me. "What did she say? What happened?"

I shake my head as her words replay in my head.

It's so nice your relatives let the help have Thanksgiving with you.

"Don't worry about it," I say.

I don't want to repeat it. I'm not mad about being

mistaken for one of the many people hired to work on the farm with us. It's the fact that someone like this random new girlfriend—and other people who have visited us and given me strange, what-are-you-doing-here looks—thinks I don't belong *because* of it. But I don't want Dad kicking anyone out, or Mom verbally berating the girlfriend. I mean, I do. But I don't. Because that'll just be another thing everyone whispers about me.

I reluctantly walk over, and Dad reaches out, grabbing me into a hug with him and Mom.

"I'm sorry," he says, giving me an extra squeeze. "I'll go tell that little shit to never bring a date around again. With his taste in girls, he should perhaps consider dying alone."

"Oh my God, Dad." I laugh and push him away.

"What?" He smiles, feigning ignorance. "Too much?"

"You're *always* too much," Mom says, rolling her eyes and then looking toward the door for a beat. She squints her eyes, like she's listening, and turns back. "Did you hear that?"

"Hear what—" Dad starts.

"Shh." Mom goes to the barn door and peeks outside. "Everyone is out in front of the house."

"What?" I walk over to her with Dad, who struggles with pushing the door all the way open until Mom does exactly what I know she can do and gives it a good kick. It swings open wide, and Dad immediately looks at her with hearts in his eyes. Gross.

The whole family is gathered in front of our house, a car parked in the driveway, the headlights still on, motor running. I can hear everyone babbling excitedly from here, even as far off as we are. It's Uncle Aaron's car.

"Come on . . . something's happened."

Dad hurries out of the barn, Mom following. They both break into a small jog, their breath in trails of white from the chilly November air. I don't hear any screaming or crying. I'm guessing no one is *dead*, so I trail behind, my feet crunching against the brown grass and fallen twigs and leaves. The air is sharp and crisp, like the fountain drink Sprite at a fast-food restaurant.

As I get closer, I realize that mixed in with all the muttering and excited chatter that's been going on is . . . laughter? And a lot of it. A couple *oohs* and *awws* surprise me. I spot Kevin and his girlfriend, Samantha. He makes eye contact with me for just a second, but in that quick glance I can see how wildly embarrassed he is, like if he doesn't look at me for too long, all this might disappear. Samantha's eyes flit up at me and also dart away. I hate this game.

You did something embarrassing, just apologize for it and move on.

"Dylan, come here, check it out."

Dad's smile could drown out the headlights of Uncle Aaron's car, which is parked nearby, exhaust pluming up into the air. I inch up next to my father and see Uncle Aaron holding a little quivering lump of fur.

It's a puppy.

But something isn't right. It's not a dog you pick up at a pet store or see on television. Not a cute puppy that would be bopping around in a TikTok video. No, his fur is matted all over the place, and one eye is sealed shut. The other, light blue, looks around frantically, squinting at the bright lights of everyone's phones that are currently taking photos and videos, flashes from soon-to-be-terrible photos interrupting the black of the night.

The eye settles on me for a minute, and the puppy's paws stretch forward.

I reach out, and the dog whines a bit as I pet his head, fur hardened, like it's stuck there. With a yelp, the little one darts back, and I see there's a little nip missing from his ear.

I can feel the expression on my face crumbling.

And Uncle Aaron must see it.

"I found him on the side of the road on the way here," he says. "Who knows how long he was out there."

"Made me sit in the back!" a voice exclaims. I look, and it's his wife. Everyone in my family laughs.

I can't take my eyes off the dog. "Where . . . where was . . ."

"He was by himself." Uncle Aaron shrugs. "He might be one of those Australian shepherd dogs. See the eyes? Well, eye. I'm gonna warm him up and take him into town. There's a clinic over in Trenton that's still open on the holiday and—"

"Can I have him?"

The words tumble out of my mouth before I can think.

"Oh, um. . ." Uncle Aaron looks at me and then over at my parents, who look like deer in headlights. A wave of silence has washed over the crowd of eager family members, everyone afraid to say the wrong thing. Uncle Aaron's car is still running, the hum of the engine interrupting the quiet, the lights cutting a beam through the settling country fog around our house.

Something about this dog. This puppy. It has me feeling fit to fall apart.

"I mean . . . it's up to . . . your mom and daaaad?" It's a reply and a question. I think I hear Mom audibly wince.

"Just putting that all on us, huh, Aaron?" Dad grumbles. He turns to me. "You're leaving us in a year, you know. You're gonna leave us with a year-old maybe-shepherd dog?"

I press. "He can keep you company while I'm gone."

"You don't have to sell me on it, sweetheart. Let's keep him." Mom beams, reaching over to give the puppy a little scratch under his chin. The one eye closes, and I swear I can see his tiny body sigh.

Uncle Aaron hands the trembling bundle of fur to me. I hold him close to my chest and feel him shaking.

"Lotta trauma there," Uncle Aaron says. "Gonna need some work."

I almost say *same*. Almost.

"You sure this is how you want to spend your Thanksgiving break?" Dad asks. "Your entire winter break? You'll probably have to stay behind for Christmas and miss going to Aunt Casey's—"

I glance up at him with a smirk.

"Yeah, okay," he huffs.

The puppy stops shaking for a moment, nuzzling into my sweater.

"It's okay," I whisper. "I've got you."

Kevin's girlfriend bounds on over, across everyone in the family.

"Oh my goodness, he's so cute! Can I hold him—"

The puppy reels around and nips at her hand.

"Ow!"

I will defend this dog with my life.

The Monday after Thanksgiving weekend, I am hustling off the school bus and running down the road toward home. I barely even say goodbye to Carmen and Lewis, who live on neighboring farms and take the same hour-long bus to and from school with me.

I glance at my phone and reread my text exchange with Dad.

Dad: Hey, is today an early dismissal day?
Me: No, why?

Dad: Oh nothing, just . . . your dog is being weird. You'll see.

Me: What?! What's going on?

And then nothing. Phone service at the farm is terrible. My heart pounds in my chest as the farm comes into view, our little house tucked around tall pine trees, sprawling acres of dirt with bare shrubs lined by a white fence on the other side. Farther in the distance are the woods.

The small patch of woods where my dad and his best friends take his truffle pigs.

I will never, ever understand it. You don't eat truffles that you find in New Jersey. Nowhere in the *world* does anyone import "South Jersey truffles." A delicacy that is not; the South Jersey truffle sounds like a horrible dance move or maybe an urban legend monster. But Dad and his pals went to Italy one time in their twenties, and that was it. It's a tradition they all bond over, wandering the woods with the truffle pigs, who dig up truffles that we can't eat.

The pigs eat them, so that's nice for them, I guess.

When I reach the front door to our house, I hear him yell for me over by the animals.

I run toward the small buildings attached to our house, where Mom raises her chickens and Dad keeps the pigs. It's not a farm for animals. We grow blueberries. Half the place is for tourists to pick their own blueberries, and the rest Mom and Dad sell to grocery stores or make into jellies and jams.

And yet. We've got the barn. Dad's got his truffle pigs. Mom's got chickens that have feathers that look like the dresses celebrities wear to the Met Gala.

I round the corner of our home, and there's the smell of the animals. The chickens and the pigs, their food and their . . . leavings. It's not great. And when I peek into the sty, one of Dad's truffle pigs is sprawled out on a layer of mud, some piglets eagerly nursing and oinking loudly.

This is a new development. I don't think I knew that one of the pigs was pregnant.

"When did she have babies—" I start.

"Shh," Dad says, getting up from the floor. He steps toward me, wraps an arm around my shoulder, and nods back at the pig. "Look closer."

I squint.

And then I see it.

The puppy, my puppy, is in the mix with the piglets, squirming his way in between wriggling pink bodies, a splotch of black and brown cardigan sticking out terribly. I immediately lunge forward, but Dad pulls me back.

"It's okay," he says, and I try to relax. "There's a warm bottle in there. He just seemed so sad without you around, and I was carrying him about the farm when mama here had the piglets. He just . . . went for it."

"It's cute, but won't . . . don't pigs . . . won't she . . ."

"Oh my God, she's not going to *eat* him," Dad says, laughing. And then he stops abruptly. "Wait, is that a thing?"

"Jesus, Dad." Sometimes, I swear, he acts like he doesn't know anything about working on a farm, yet he owns one. I lean in toward the sty and the sow and reach for the pup . . . when the pig snuffs loudly and glares at me. She nudges the pup gingerly with her snout, pushing him back up against her, and lies back down in the mud with a slap.

"Huh." I glance back at Dad and sit down on the cold earth. "Well, I don't want him out here alone with her."

"Wouldn't dream of it," he says, sitting next to me. "Have you thought of a name yet?"

Sitting here, nestled up with the truffle-sniffing pigs, I suddenly think I have.

Six weeks after piglets are born, you can start training them to sniff out truffles.

Dad does not know how to do this.

Dad *thinks* he knows how to do this.

Mom leans against the railing on the porch overlooking the field that leads to the woods in back of our house, sipping a cup of tea a little too loudly. Plumes of steam rise up from the cup. Winter in South Jersey is no joke, the ground out there is hard and frostbitten, the deck slick and a little slippery from frozen dew.

Truffles whines in my arms, squirming around.

"Does he need a walk?" Mom asks as Dad shouts orders at the piglets in the field. They are scampering around everywhere, and he looks like a preschool teacher trying to herd a bunch of wayward toddlers.

"No. I took him out," I say. "I don't know what's . . ." He squirms harder, whining. "I really don't get what's going on with him."

Suddenly Dad shouts, diving after a piglet. He misses and hits the hard ground with a smack, and Mom shrinks back.

Truffles squirms wildly in my arms. "Okay, fine," I grumble, putting him down.

The little pup runs so fast down the deck stairs that he stumbles on the last few, tumbling into the frozen grass. I hurry after him as he takes off into the field toward Dad and the piglets. He stops there, bouncing around with the pigs, wrestling with them.

Dad is still sitting on the ground. "Huh," he says, watching Truffles play with the piglets. "Think he wants to train with the piglets?"

"Define *train*." I cross my arms.

"Listen, I'm gonna figure it out—" He dives again to try to capture a piglet, and he misses. "Ugh. You'll see."

The piglets hurry across the thawing field toward the wood, stopping to dig up buried sponges that are soaked with truffle oil along the way. They are focused and determined.

191

Truffles rolls around on the ground and looks up at me, tilting his head to the side.

"Come on, buddy," I say, nudging him off his back. I try to push him along after his piglet brothers and sisters, but he skirts back, pressing into my hand. "You're gonna get left behind." I pick him up and look into his eyes. Those soft blue eyes that blew up my heart on Thanksgiving. "You can do this."

I want him to fit in with his family. The piglets that wrestle with him on the grass, that snuggled him up at night when he needed warmth, needed a bottle.

He tilts his head again and licks my face.

"Why won't you do this?" I ask.

What happens when I leave? When I pack it up and head to college on the opposite coast, leaving him behind with Mom and Dad and all those shitty relatives and their awful dating choices. Who will make him feel like he belongs, if not his piglet siblings?

"Hey."

I turn around, and there's Dad, hands on his hips. He's got a piece of wheat between his teeth, and I have no idea where he got it from. Everything is dead right now. He must catch me squinting at it, because he smiles a little.

"It's fake. Part of the look. Took it out of your mom's potpourri wreath." He smacks his lips and takes the reed out of his mouth. "Tastes pretty bad, come to think of it."

We watch one of the piglets sniffing around at the ground

before the little thing starts digging eagerly.

"Found something?" I ask, nodding.

"Maybe." Dad shrugs. "Hey, you know it sometimes takes like twenty years for a truffle to grow to the point where you can harvest it?"

"Really?" I ask.

"Yep. Takes a long time before it even knows what it is."

He looks at me for a beat and then back up toward the piglets and the woods.

"You know, this whole farming thing . . ." He sighs, flicking the stick away. "Not my first career choice, and sometimes I still feel like I'm playing pretend. But your grandparents were thrilled when I married a farm girl. I could continue the legacy. Growing blueberries or cranberries, maybe peaches. But I always thought I'd—"

"I know, go work as a park ranger in the big city." I grin. Around here, big city means Philadelphia. He nudges me a little with his shoulder, and Truffles squirms around.

"Listen, some of us are just . . . born to do certain things really well. This whole thing, the land and all that . . . that's me. It's who I am even if a part of me wishes it wasn't. That part of me who thinks about Italy and truffle hunting in the woods." He looks up toward the patch of trees and at the piglets stumbling around everywhere.

"You think I don't know that if me and your mom cut down the trees over here, we could probably make more money with the farm? Plant more bushes for idiot tourists looking to spend fifty dollars so they can take home three dollars' worth of berries?" He grins, and I laugh. "I keep it because it keeps a little of that silly dream alive. Adults can play pretend too, you know."

I glance up at him, and he's staring at the trees a bit wistfully. A piglet scampers by, and I wonder if he's going to make a lunge for it.

He looks like he might try.

He looks like he might cry.

"But you shouldn't have to," he adds, looking down at me, and he's definitely crying.

"Dad—"

Truffles squirms in my arms.

"Look, I've had to play pretend most of my life, Dylan." He clears his throat. "And I don't want that for you. I know we don't talk about . . . you know, adoption stuff all that often. We should. But we don't. I know, though, that you try really hard to fit in with everyone all the time. Mom's family, my family."

He looks at Truffles.

"Dylan, you can't *make* him fit in with his . . . well, his chosen family there," Dad says. "Same way we can't make you fit in with all of ours. And that's okay. It's okay to not fit in. And when you head off to college this fall, I want you to be you. Not what you think you have to be."

The piglets sniffle and snort around, the truffle oil sponges buried under the dried-up grass.

Truffles looks up. Both of his ears lean back. He sniffs at the air, and for a moment, it feels like time stops.

"Think he's caught the scent of one?" Dad asks, his voice gone soft.

"Maybe." I slowly bend down, placing him on the earth. His little feet dig at the soil, and I glance up at my dad.

"It's okay to let go," he says. "He'll figure it out."

And I do.

Truffles bounds for the woods, and my dad holds me.

CATCH

BY NICOLE CHUNG

The candy shop was our first stop when Julie came to visit. My cousin always said that the saltwater taffy alone would be worth the trip. On her first morning in Catchers Bay, we spent a long time examining the plastic containers of taffy that lined a full half-wall of the candy shop, discussing the relative merits of vanilla, chocolate, and peanut-butter flavors, hand-selecting every piece that went into our communal white paper bag. While Susan, the owner of the candy shop, printed out our receipt, I fished out a piece of red- and-white-striped peppermint taffy and Julie helped herself to a deep magenta chunk of raspberry ripple.

"Are you girls planning to enter the contest?" Susan asked, pointing to a flyer posted on the bulletin board behind her. "They just tagged fifty crabs and released them into the bay. If you catch one, you win five hundred dollars. Get your picture in the paper, too."

I could think of a lot of things I might do with five hundred dollars, but the whole thing sounded like too much work to me. "There must be a *million* crabs out there." I shoved a crumpled white waxed paper wrapper into my pocket, already going back for my second piece—bright pink, with a strong, sweet strawberry scent. "How is anyone going to catch one of fifty?"

Our village used to sustain itself by shipping seafood and timber all over the region; now people here also relied on the dollars that flowed in during the summer months, when visitors from bigger, bluer inland towns arrived with money to spend. The contest must be to boost tourist excitement, I thought—just like the spring craft fair, the Fourth of July fireworks extravaganza, the fall harvest festival, and the winter lights display. But a crabbing contest sounded like the seaside version of searching for a needle in a haystack. All the tagged crabs could be out to sea by now.

I looked at Julie, expecting to see her nodding in agreement. Instead, her hazel eyes were wide, her face alight with the same excitement I saw every time she visited and got her first glimpse of the Pacific in a year or more. "I bet we can do it, Anna," she said.

"Um, Jules, I don't really know if it'd be your thing. Anyway, this is supposed to be your vacation?"

Julie lived in Ohio, where her mom and mine had grown

up. Her parents sent her out nearly every summer to visit my parents and me on the Oregon coast. Usually she stayed for a week or two, but this year we'd both pleaded, and her parents said she could visit for an entire month. I was always surprised that she never got bored here—our provincial seaside town was a place I frequently dreamed of escaping. But Julie loved her yearly visits, even though she had to take two or three planes and then sit through the three-and-a-half-hour car trip from the closest airport. She was enthralled by our quiet harbor and dramatic sand dunes, the old-growth forest, the river that sprouted from some distant point in the mountains and emptied into the sea near Catchers Bay. "You don't know how lucky you are," she'd told me once. "It's like you live in a postcard."

I knew my mom and dad were happy to host Julie any-time—they had always wanted me to have a sibling, but it had taken most of their savings to adopt me when I was a baby, and it wasn't something they had been able to do again. Julie and I were the youngest cousins on our side of the family, just a few weeks apart in age, and we'd always been close. Aside from my parents, she was the first person in our family to know that I was bi. When we were little, we were pen pals. Now that we were both about to turn fifteen, our snail-mail correspondence had given way to a never-ending text thread. I sent her drawings from the fantasy graphic novel I was working on, and she told me about her volleyball team. She was the one who'd introduced me to

K-pop on one of her visits, and I couldn't help but think about how strange it was that my white cousin was the only reason I knew any Korean words at all.

Her older sister, Lauren, came along with her a few summers. I never knew what to make of Lauren. She made fun of me for reading all the time, calling me a nerd (but also took my books without asking); she complained that our house was small, the beach was boring, and there was nothing to do in our town. Defusing conflicts with Lauren was a delicate tightrope walk of rotating strategies: Sometimes Julie would grab my hand and we'd walk away. Sometimes she would hold her ground and argue back. Sometimes she would appeal to her sister, urge her to apologize, try to get her to stay and hang out with us instead of disappearing for hours. Julie's efforts rarely seemed to pay off, but she never stopped trying. She seemed like the older sister, even though she was two years younger than Lauren.

Though my parents still offered to host both my cousins every summer, Lauren hadn't come with Julie this year, partly because she had just moved to another town with her dad. I didn't know why Aunt Stephanie—my mom's sister—and her husband had divorced a few years ago, or why he'd recently decided to move, or why Lauren was going with him while Julie stayed behind. Even if Julie and Lauren didn't always get along, even if they were only separated by a few hours of highway, I thought it must be so strange to go from seeing your sister every single day to hardly seeing her at all. My parents had suggested that we not pry, just let Julie bring it up if she wanted to. So far, she hadn't, but then she had just arrived.

The two of us drifted home from the candy shop at a leisurely pace, watching fishing boats pass each other in the bay. We soon turned onto the road that led to my parents' gray house on the point, gravel and broken white shells crunching beneath our sneakers. Most of the few thousand residents of our town lived within a few miles of the bay, in houses and manufactured homes and RVs nestled between the harbor and the hills. My mom and dad moved here, to my father's hometown, not long after my adoption, which is why Catchers Bay is the only home I can remember. Before that, they were both in college in the Portland area, where they met and got married and eventually adopted me. When Dad's dad, my grandpa, got sick, they came here to help take care of him. Now Dad taught fourth grade at the village elementary school, while Mom taught middle school math in a town fifteen minutes up the road. Dad told me that nowadays, most children of Catchers Bay fishermen, like him, had little choice but to flee or find new careers, or both. Many locals, including my late grandfather, lamented this, believing that environmentalists ("tree huggers," Grandpa had called them) were trying to destroy the fishing industry, but Dad said it was just a fact that many fish populations had declined due to overfishing and climate change.

My parents stayed because, they said, they had "roots" here, which I took to mean that they knew and got along with most everyone. As the only Korean kid in town, though, I had never fit in here the way they did. There was a Thai family that ran a small restaurant—their kids were much younger than me, but I liked seeing them when we ate there or stopped by for takeout—and an older lady who I thought was Korean ran one of the stands at the farmers market. Sometimes I'd see people, families of color, during the busy summer tourist season, and I might even spot the occasional Asian adoptee like me with their white parents. But my friends and teachers and nearly everyone else I knew who lived here year-round were white.

I knew the familiar white spaces and white faces as well as I knew everything in this town, from the creaking docks to the stinging salt air to the way the color of the waves changed from hour to hour, season to season. The other residents were used to me, too. Sure, a few kids called me names, a few adults looked at me a bit suspiciously—but I was still the granddaughter and daughter of men known by everyone in town. While others who looked like me might be assumed to be foreigners, I was different. I was allowed.

No one would have guessed that Julie and I were cousins just by looking at us as we walked home side by side. They didn't know all our inside jokes or see our frequent conspiratorial glances. I knew that Julie wasn't my sister—she already had a sister. I knew that we weren't even biologically related. But I'd long thought of her as such a kindred spirit that even I sometimes forgot how different we looked. I had been a little worried that as we got older, she'd become more like Lauren—too "cool" to want to hang out and have fun with me, her awkward, bookish cousin who was decidedly *un*cool and lived in the absolute middle of nowhere. But she always seemed so glad to be here. Every time we saw each other, it was as if we'd never been apart.

"So, what do you think about the contest?" she asked as we lounged in rocking chairs on my parents' front porch. "Could we just give it a try?"

I held back a sigh. What was the harm? I could show her the ropes. Julie would probably tire of it soon enough. "Okay," I said. "I'll show you what to do tomorrow."

When I woke up the next morning, I wasn't surprised to see my cousin still asleep on the futon in my room, where she always slept when she came to visit. Julie had never been an early riser.

Mom was already gone, off to teach summer school, but I found Dad in the kitchen, flipping pancakes.

"Morning, Anna," he said. With his brown summer beard and flannel shirt, he looked very much like the fisherman's son he was—at least, more than he did when he went to school clean-shaven and in button-downs. "How about you scramble some eggs?"

I started a pan heating and beat the eggs with a bit of

milk, salt, and pepper in a bowl. Dad opened the oven to check on the broiling bacon.

"I've got the lunch shift at the diner today, so you girls will be on your own," he said.

During the summertime my parents sometimes worked part-time at local shops or restaurants to help keep our family afloat. Dad, who did most of the cooking in our family, was a better-than-average backup diner chef.

"We'll be fine," I said. "Julie wants to try crabbing today, so we'll pack some sandwiches to bring with us."

Julie had filled my parents in on our—her—plans the night before. Dad glanced over at me, looking amused. "Good for her. Never a bad time to learn something new."

"I guess," I said. "But we could catch and eat seafood without doing the whole contest thing. I don't really understand why she wants to do this."

"She's never done anything like it before. Maybe she just thinks it will be fun to try."

Julie appeared, still looking sleepy, as we were setting food on the table. After breakfast, the three of us went out to the shed and fetched one of our family's ring-shaped crab traps. We didn't have our own dock, but there was a small one close by, at the edge of the harbor before the turn onto our road. Dad snagged a frozen turkey leg from our freezer and said it would do for our first day's bait.

At first, of course, Julie needed my help to do everything—she'd been crabbing with us only once or twice before, and my dad and I had done most of the work. I thought she might give up the whole idea when it was time to secure the bait to the trap, but after watching me do it, she got the hang of it.

The two of us spent most of the day sitting on the sun-warmed planks of the dock, playing games on our phones, taking photos to send to our friends, diligently reapplying sunscreen so we wouldn't burn. Julie checked every crab she caught for a telltale plastic tag. I taught her how to pick them up to avoid getting pinched—though she did wind up with a few bandaged fingers, and often preferred to nudge them over the edge of the dock with her sneaker instead. Every hour or so, she would grab the thick rope and haul the ring out of the depths to check her catch. Even wearing work gloves, this was hard to do—the trap was often weighed down by crabs, the rope freezing cold from the bay. Julie's arms looked about as scrawny as mine, but she was determined, and stronger than I'd realized.

My cousin started keeping a trap in the water from morning until evening. Softhearted and determined not to keep more than we would eat, she threw back most of what she netted. But regulation-size crabs kept finding their way into my parents' big stainless-steel cooking pot.

Sometimes Julie could be convinced to take an afternoon or a day off—we rode our bikes to the beach, hiked the lighthouse trail, went to the outlet mall with my mom, and made many more trips to the candy shop and the ice cream parlor. But she insisted on keeping to her schedule at the dock as much as possible, frequently running down to check the trap. My patience with her began to flag, as did my parents' eagerness to seek out new crab recipes. When I asked Julie if she thought the prize money was really worth all the time she was spending, she grinned and said that I didn't appreciate *the thrill of the hunt*.

One Saturday morning, while my mom and I waited for her to get dressed so we could all go to town to buy groceries—and more crab bait—I couldn't help but vent a little. "She's *never* going to catch one. Can't she see that it's, like, a hopeless quest?"

Mom looked up from the book she was reading, and I was suddenly struck by just how strong the resemblance was between her and Julie. Julie also looked like *her* mom, I guess—or all of them looked like each other: three peas in a pod, with their light brown hair, pale freckled skin, and ever-changing hazel eyes. If everyone in town hadn't known me since I was a baby, they might imagine that my parents were Julie's, not mine. Thinking about this gave me a little pang for some reason, but I pushed it aside.

"Just let her have this, honey," Mom said. "Goodness knows she could use the distraction."

My cousin had not grown up as I had, I reminded myself. Her parents were city people. Not outdoorsy. Little though I seemed to fit in here, from childhood I had been taught the working rituals of my father's family: how to read the tides, set traps and cast fishing lines, clean the day's catch. For me, such experiences had long since been drained of any novelty or excitement. Now, I considered the traditions and the life I'd inherited—did I belong here after all? At least, more than I had realized?

I loved the ocean, the forests, the nearby mountains as much as anyone else in my family. But I knew I'd leave at the earliest opportunity. And for that reason, oddly enough, I could almost understand Julie's obsession. For her, visits to our tiny coastal town gave her a chance to try on another life. As an adopted kid who sometimes felt like I had stepped into a stranger's life, I supposed I could see the appeal of that.

"Has Julie mentioned her dad or Lauren at all?" Mom asked me.

I realized that she was concerned about Julie, and I wondered what Aunt Stephanie had told her.

"No," I said. It was the truth. Nor had Julie talked to her sister since arriving, as far as I knew, though her dad had called her a couple of times. I understood why Mom was asking me, but I didn't want to talk about my cousin when she wasn't there, like a grown-up would.

Though Julie hadn't said a word to me about Lauren or her dad, I knew that didn't mean she wasn't thinking about them. I'd almost asked her, a few times, how she felt about them moving away. But I hadn't, not even with all the opportunities I'd had sitting with her on the dock, hoping for a miracle to land in our net. Was I being cowardly, or failing Julie somehow? I'd always felt so close to my cousin, been able to relate to her without even trying. She made me feel as though I belonged in our family—which wasn't true of all my relatives, even though I loved them.

But I had no experience with what she was going through right now and I realized that I was afraid of doing or saying the wrong thing and hurting her. Maybe just spending time with her, letting her spend a few weeks trying to do the impossible, was enough. Maybe Mom was right, and all Julie needed was something else to think about for a little while.

One evening in the last week of Julie's visit, Mom and I were making peanut butter cookies when Dad came in on a gust of cool, damp air. "Sorry. I'm later than I thought I'd be. The diner was busy," he said. "Should I start working on dinner?"

"I thought we'd just get pizza tonight," Mom told him, sliding another tray of cookies into the oven. "I already ordered it. Anna, where's Julie?"

"Three guesses," I said, unable to suppress a small eye roll.

"Better walk down to the dock and get her. The pizza will be here any minute."

I left the house in short sleeves. I should have known better; I was chilly by the time I came to the mouth of the harbor. Julie used to be surprised that even in the full sunlight of a late June afternoon, the wind here could pick up and make you shiver—where she was from, summers were hot and humid, no matter the time of day. On her first trip out to see us, she'd had to borrow pants and hoodies from me because all she had in her suitcase were shorts and tank tops.

The dock came into view, stretching out into the dark waters of the bay. I saw a slight, skinny girl standing alone in the distance, just a few feet back from the water. Instead of cupping my hands to my mouth and hollering, I walked out to join my cousin. A trap rested at her feet, empty of crabs, the bait picked nearly clean. I nudged her shoulder. "Ready for dinner?"

"In a minute. Look at this."

She held out the white plastic bucket she had carried back and forth between the house and the harbor for days now. Peering inside, I saw the small round eyes of a single Dungeness crab staring up at me. I angled the bucket to get a closer look, momentarily distracted by the irate snapping claws of my cousin's captive, and then I saw it: a small yellow tag secured around its right claw.

"You did it," I breathed. Fifty tagged crabs in the bay—in the entire Pacific Ocean—and my cousin had actually caught one of them. It felt like a miracle.

"What do you think they're going to do with her?" Julie asked.

"I don't know." I honestly hadn't thought about it. I reached a hand into the bucket, spreading my thumb and pinkie wide to try to span the crab's shell. It was mammoth, at least seven inches across, eager to be free of its plastic prison. It began to scrabble in the bucket, opening and closing its claws with menacing little *clacks*, and I yanked my hand away to safety. "They'll probably check the tag to verify it and take a picture or something," I guessed. "And then . . . I guess . . . maybe someone will eat it?"

"Her. It's a her. I checked." Days ago, I'd been the one to flip a crab over and show Julie how to determine whether it was male or female, based on its abdomen. She fingered the small plastic tag. "I don't even really *like* crab," she said a bit guiltily.

"Well, maybe that's because you've been eating it, it's all we've been eating for weeks now."

I looked over at my cousin, ready to laugh, and saw that her eyes were shining with tears.

"I want to let her go," she told me.

"What?" I knew that Julie was upset, but I couldn't begin to understand why she would let her prize go. "You worked so hard! What about the money?"

"Look at her," she said, her voice wavering. "She didn't ask to be singled out. She's just . . . stuck."

I knew it was Julie's choice to give up her chance at fleeting local fame and five hundred dollars. Still, I didn't want her effort, her great achievement, to go undocumented. I fished in my back pocket for my phone, aimed it down into Julie's bucket, and snapped a picture.

"There," I said, after I'd sent it to her. "At least *we'll* remember what you did."

Together, the two of us managed to remove the tag using the shears from my dad's tackle box. Julie pocketed it before dropping the crab back into her harbor home. Within half a second we'd lost sight of her beneath the dark surface of the water.

As we walked back to the house, Julie carrying the trap and me the empty bucket, she mentioned her sister for the first time all month. "I think Lauren would have loved this."

I wasn't sure, as Lauren made fun of nearly everything we did, but there was nothing for me to do except nod. It occurred to me that as well as I knew Julie, Lauren was still a mystery to me. And maybe she had changed since the last time I saw her.

"You should text her," I said. "You can send her the pictures and tell her how you won this bizarre contest and no one else will ever know."

We turned down the road to the house, where my parents were waiting with pizza and peanut butter cookies. Julie drew in a deep breath, then exhaled slowly. "It's strange without her here," she admitted. "It's strange without her at home. She moved with Dad to go to a new school—Mom and Dad said that she's been unhappy and needs a fresh start. I hope she likes it there. I love her, and I miss her, but the truth is, I also feel . . . I don't know . . . like there was this worry, this weight I was always carrying. And now I'm not?"

The guilty look was back in her eyes. I knew that I hadn't gone through anything like what my cousin was going through. But, as an adoptee, I did know how it felt to miss someone who was always supposed to be there with you and wasn't. I knew what it meant to love people you couldn't always understand, to have questions about your home life that you couldn't answer, to constantly feel as though you had to explain your family to others. I knew how it felt to wonder if there was something more you could have done, something more you could have *been*, to keep your whole family together.

I also knew that nothing that had happened in either of our families was my fault. Or Julie's. And it wasn't Lauren's, either—for the first time I realized that her attitude might have been a means of trying to make sure that she had her family's attention. I hoped Lauren would be happier in her new home, with her new start. I hoped it *was* what she needed.

If Lauren had been with us this summer, Julie's days would have been filled with keeping tabs on her, arguing with her, making apologies and explanations for her. There would have been no time for something as strange, as silly and wholesome as our town crabbing contest. Maybe that

211

was why Julie had been so consumed by it—maybe it was the first time in a while that she'd had the luxury to think about something so frivolous. Now she had managed something that seemed impossible, at least from where I stood, and she'd done it for no one but herself.

"I'm proud of you," I said. "And I'm sorry I got kind of annoyed with you about the contest. I think it's amazing that you actually won, even if no one ever knows but us."

"Thanks," she said with a smile. "You can make it up to me with some more saltwater taffy, first thing after breakfast tomorrow. And then we can ride bikes to the beach."

Suddenly she shook her head and laughed—a short, disbelieving bark that made me think of the seals in the harbor. I realized it was one of the only times I'd heard her laugh this visit. "Lauren is trying to convince our dad to get her a motorcycle," she said. "He'll never say yes."

"Maybe *you* should ask for a motorcycle," I said, stowing the trap and bucket in the shed. "Once we're old enough to drive."

This time her laughter was long and loud as we walked toward the house. "Sure. I'll tell them all it's *my* turn to rebel."

Julie took one more picture before we went inside, a selfie of us standing together in my yard, the sunset blazing behind us. She held it up for me to inspect.

One of her arms was draped around my shoulders. My skin was a rich, light golden brown, the way it always got when I tanned in the summer, and my short dark hair faded a bit into the twilight around us. Julie was half a head shorter, freckles still visible in the gathering dusk, her eyes crinkling in the corners as she smiled. Her face was so much like my mother's. Mine was like no one else I knew. Looking at us, you wouldn't have known that we were family. That was all right, I thought.

Julie and I knew.

ALMOST CLOSE ENOUGH

BY STEFANY VALENTINE

My favorite time to gaze up at Yue was on nights when she didn't look like a glowing pearl in the night sky. In the darkness of the universe, it was easy to overlook something hidden by Earth's shadow. But from my bedroom window, Yue's city lights shined the brightest. She had a way of tricking people into thinking they were staring at a constellation of stars. And so, I made a wish upon those stars.

Take me home.

It'd been over a decade since the last time I'd set foot on Earth's moon. Since the first lunar settlers decided to make it their home, Earthlings no longer referred to the moon as a simple floating rock meant to illuminate Earth's night. She was Yue now—an orbiting mass with various countries, cultures, and languages of her own. What was it like to revisit my Yuen nation of Novidom? To swim in Novish lakes? To breathe Novish air? To feel the sun's rays from anywhere other than Earth?

"Soara?" Mom's voice fluttered from the doorway. "Was Kaylee going to pick you up, or did you want me to drop you off at the movies?"

The warmth of Yue's city lights caressed my cheek as I peered back at Mom. "The movies are three blocks away. I was going to walk. If that's okay."

Mom glanced out my bedroom window. Instead of looking up at the clear sky, she peered down at the streets. Yes, the movies were within walking distance. But she never liked the idea of me going out at night. Especially since we'd moved to Edmonton, Colorado—a place famous for its trees and the beasts that lived within them.

"I'll take my bike," I insisted. "And I'll ping my location when I get to the theater."

Mom pinched her lips together. She glanced down at my vacuumed carpet—at my organized desk, at my perfectly made bed. Tonight was special. I needed to present the side of me she needed to see in order to get what I truly wanted.

"Are you sure you don't want me to drop you off?"

I smiled reassuringly. "No need to emit carbons when I can take my bike."

That was a factor Mom couldn't argue with. Earth would forever be at war with its greenhouse gases. In fact, if it wasn't for the changing climate, humans never would've settled on Yue. And they never would've created colonies that orbited Earth's atmosphere just to escape its own pollution. And now that the planet was returning to its Green Zone, Earthlings did whatever it took to restore their air.

Mom sighed. Despite my point, she still would've rather dropped me off at the movies than let me go by myself. "Fine. But if you don't ping me in twenty minutes, I'm going to drive down every street looking for you. And I will've emitted more carbons doing that than dropping you off directly."

I kissed her cheek. "I guess that means I'd better get going. Oh, do you think you could give me some extra cash? I wanted to get some snacks for Kaylee since she paid for my lunch yesterday."

After digging in her pocket, Mom handed me a twenty. The face of America's first female president smiled up at me. It wasn't as much money as I'd hoped for, but I supposed this was enough for now.

I thanked Mom before bounding down the stairs. Pictures of our family lined the walls. No matter how many times I walked these halls, there was never a moment I didn't feel the differences between me and my adopted parents.

I was Yuen. They were Colonists. No, we weren't Earthlings. But just because we came from Earth's upper atmospheres didn't make our backgrounds identical.

As members of the human race, Earthlings, Colonists,

and Yuens all looked alike. And yet we were also very good at discriminating against one another. Years ago, humans judged each other in terms of where they lived in relation to the sun. And now we judged each other when it came to where we lived in relation to gravity.

Earthlings, with their short frames and proportionate limbs, were still the standard of beauty within our orbit. Colonists lived on artificial planets that floated around the thermosphere. But the centripetal force used to create synthetic gravity made their legs longer than the legs of Earthlings. As for Yuens, we couldn't hide in a crowd of Earthlings. Our infamously long necks made it impossible to deny where we were born.

If I was destined to be raised by parents who weren't Yuen, I suppose I would've wanted to be adopted by Colonists. Their culture is similar to mine. We appreciate astrology, share a palate for soy-based proteins, and possess a physiology that only we understood. My parents and I look enough alike for Earthlings to think we are biologically related, but I know we aren't. And that makes all the difference. Being Yuen and being raised by Colonists is almost close enough to being home. And yet, it never is.

I laced my shoes up, then pulled my bike off the porch. The thing about being Yuen on Earth meant that everything was designed for a body that wasn't mine. Including my bike. But Dad had done everything to make it more accommodating. He designed a special seat that allowed me to pedal without my legs cramping up. So that's what I did all the way to the theater.

I chained my bike, then dropped a pin for my mother's sake. And as long as I didn't drop another pin, this would be the only location Mom knew I was at. She responded immediately with a heart emoticon. My mom loved me so much. Would she still love me if she knew the real reason I wanted to meet Kaylee at the movies?

I walked to the back of the building where no lights were shining. In the darkness, the warmth of the solar system called to me. I gazed up at Yue, and my chest ached. My adopted parents felt this way about their home on the Aldrin Colony, too. Every time they saw it drift through the thermosphere, they pointed and said, "Of infinity I am." It was a mantra—a sacred phrase Aldrin Colonists used to remind themselves that one day of struggle was nothing compared to the universe's infinite time.

Did Yue have a mantra too? Did Novidom? I'd grown up here on Earth for so long that I didn't have any memories of who I was as a Novish Yuen. Aside from my given name and the fact that my parents had taken me in as a refugee of the ongoing wars on Yue, I didn't remember much about my childhood.

"Punctual as always, Giraffe Girl." Kaylee appeared at my side. "You never miss a drop."

I said nothing as I handed Kaylee the twenty Mom had given me. She snatched it up, then held it to her face.

"Are you kidding me? Twenty?"

"It's all I have."

Kaylee whistled. "You do realize you Yuens have a different metabolism than us Earthlings, right? Twenty dollars' worth of hay isn't even going to get you high for an hour."

I didn't repeat myself.

"Ahh, you're lucky I like you, Giraffe Girl. Tell you what, you give me this twenty and I'll give you a little something else."

Kaylee tucked the twenty inside her jacket and pulled out a small bag. She tossed it to me, but I wasn't quick enough to catch it. Great. Way to feed into the stereotype that Yuens were just clumsy Earthlings on stilts.

"What is this?" I asked, picking up the bag from the ground. Inside was a white pill the size of my fingernail.

Kaylee smiled and wiggled her brows as if to build suspense. "They're calling it . . . moondust."

"Pass." I spat the word out, handing the bag back to Kaylee. I'd become numb to some derogatory terms like Giraffe Girl and even Treetop. But moondust was one of those terms that itched my throat. Mostly because it addressed the political conflicts between Middle Kingdom and Novidom on Yue.

"Come on, Soara. I need you to try it," Kaylee insisted.

Oh. So I was Soara now that she needed something from me?

"Look, I got a huge stash from my supplier and I need to

get rid of it, okay?" she said. "The high is all right, but it's supposed to work better for you Yuen types."

"I'm just looking to relax." And escape from the perpetual sense of being ostracized on Earth. But I wasn't going to tell Kaylee that. "All I want is hay."

Kaylee rolled her eyes. She reached into her pocket and pulled out another small bag. The pungent odor of dehydrated hay wafted in the air. To my innocent parents, it probably smelled like forest embers. To me, it smelled like secrets I needed to keep from them.

"Fine. Here." Kaylee opened the bag and cut the contents in half. My heart sank. She wasn't kidding about the amount. "But keep the moondust, all right? It's supposed to be some good stuff. Gives you euphoria with a splash of hallucinogenic. Tell your Yuen friends about it, eh? I need to sell it all."

I gave her a weak smile. She didn't realize that as my hay dealer, she was the closest thing to a friend that I had.

The forest behind the theater was the perfect place to dose. It was quiet, and I loved the smell of sticky pine sap on damp earth. A rock jutted out from the middle of a clearing. This was my favorite place to sit and stare up at the night sky. Every now and then, a colony drifted overhead. Sometimes I'd see Yue. But right now, she was hidden behind the tree line.

I pulled out my bag of hay. This was hardly enough to get

medicated on. But I had two hours to kill—the length of a movie my parents thought I'd be watching. Doing meds at home wasn't as liberating as doing them beneath the stars. Mom and Dad did their best to make my time on Earth feel like home. But they didn't realize that home wasn't synonymous with life on the colonies. It was hard enough being Yuen on Earth. But it was even harder when my parents did things, said things, or cooked things that were Colonist, thinking that it brought me the same amount of nostalgia that it brought them.

Medicating was the closest I got to figuring out who *I* was. It shut out the voices telling me that I was too tall, too alien, too anything other than me. I was a Yuen girl being raised by Colonist parents on a planet that neither of us called home. But if every aspect of my existence was built on telling me that I *wasn't*, when would it start telling me that I *was*?

This hay was not going to be enough to answer the torrent of questions whirling inside me. But taking the pill on top of smoking the hay might be. I sighed as I stared at it sitting like an elongated pearl in the palm of my hand. Was the high worth this pill's derogatory name?

I glanced at the pathetic amount of hay one last time.

Then I dry swallowed the pill.

I should've asked Kaylee how long it would take for the pill to kick in. Cross-fading hay with this new medicine probably wasn't a good idea. But if I was going to make the most of the next two hours, I might as well double up on meds. What's the worst that could happen?

I rolled the hay, then lit it with a lighter I kept hidden on this rock. Smoke itched my throat, but I kept it in my lungs until the relaxation kicked in. When I exhaled, my blood fizzled, forcing my limbs to cave to the fullness of their weight. Finally, a moment of silence.

Then a twig snapped. Was it a beast? Or a ranger patrolling the trees for juveniles like me? I pulled the roll from my lips and fanned the air. It wasn't unheard of for girls my age to experiment with medication like this, but being caught with a pollution-generating substance was not worth the disappointment it would bring to my parents. Especially since Dad's job was cleaning Earth's ozone.

Another twig snapped.

"Hello?" A boy's voice called to me.

I exhaled with relief. It was probably just another teenager who'd gotten lost in the woods. After all, I wasn't the only one who used this place as an escape.

"Who's there?" I called.

A pale face emerged from behind a fir tree. His milky skin glowed in the low lighting, reflecting the stars like a moon.

He was Yuen. What was someone like him doing in the tiny town of Edmonton, of all places?

The boy crept closer. Silvery hair like mine wisped over his elongated face. It fell to his shoulders in that androgenous style everyone at school was obsessed with. But it didn't fit us Yuens, given the length of our necks. Which was why I kept my hair cropped to the scalp. The only thing I grew out were my bangs. They covered my forehead, cutting the length of my face in half and making me look more Earthling. Hopefully.

"Oh," he said when he saw me. "Hi. Have you seen a dog run through here? He's a collie mix. Goes by the name Sam. Or Dipshit. Depends on the context, I guess."

"Um, no. I haven't. But if you head the other way, you'll reach the movie theater. You can ask around there, I guess."

The boy stopped in front of me. From my seat atop the rock, his eyes were aligned with mine. They were perfectly round but tapered downward at the tear ducts. I didn't know if that was considered beautiful. What were Yuen beauty standards anyway?

The boy smiled at me, thin lips tightening to reveal square canines. "Smells like hay, doesn't it?"

I kept my expression reserved. "I'm not sure what hay smells like, so I wouldn't know."

His cheeks dimpled when he smirked. "Riiiiight. You're just sitting here on a Friday night *not* smoking hay."

"Correct. I came out here to enjoy the stars."

He held his hands up. "Hey, I'm not one to judge. I like to enjoy a roll from time to time. All I'm saying is that we should own up to who we are."

"I wasn't smoking."

"Great." The boy beamed. "Then you're sober enough to help me find my dog."

I glowered at him, but he kept smiling. He knew the predicament he'd just put me in. And he wanted me to know that he knew.

I weighed my options. On the one hand, I could've admitted that I was smoking. He didn't go to my school, so who was he going to tell? On the other hand, maybe a piece of me wanted to help him find his pet. The Yuens who lived on Earth were mostly located in bigger cities. Not here in a blink-and-you'd-miss-it town. Was he new here? Was he adopted too, or were his parents biological? The curiosity swelled inside me.

"Sure." I stood up and discreetly slipped my roll inside my pocket. "I'll help you find your dog."

The boy blinked, as if not expecting this from me. I supposed now it was my turn to grin.

I hopped down from the rock. On level ground, this boy was only a few inches taller than me. I rarely ever meet anyone who could see the top of my head. Warmth blossomed over my cheeks.

"My name's Rith. And you?"

"Soara," I volunteered.

Rith's eyes flashed with recognition. "What is that? Colonial?"

"Yeah." I glanced down at the decaying leaves around me. My parents had given me that name when I was adopted, because a Colonial name was easier to pronounce than my Novish one.

Rith eyed me up and down. He followed the length of my body up to my eyes. I shifted back and folded my arms over my stomach. My clothes may've hidden my frame, but beneath his gaze, it was like he could see through them.

"You don't look Colonial," Rith concluded. "If I had to guess, I'd say you were Yuen. Novish, specifically."

Not many people understood Yue enough to name its countries, let alone a small island like Novidom. But this boy was Yuen too, so I supposed he could name more than just the large nations like Middle Kingdom, the United Lunar Republic, and other countries that constantly made headlines on Earth.

"You want to know how I know?" Rith leaned in, and that smile sprung across his lips once more.

"Because you're Yuen?"

"Because I'm Novish, too."

I shook my head, unable to wrap my mind around the fact that for the first time in my adolescence, I'd met someone like me. I was a desert waiting for a rainstorm. And here he was.

"Now"—Rith pulled his gaze off me to scan the trees— "where did that scamp run off to?"

In two strides, Rith disappeared back into the tree line. How was it possible for anyone to move that fast?

"Wait!" I called, racing after him. "Where are you going?"

"Well, I've got to find my dog." Rith chuckled. "I can't just stand here all night chatting about Novidom."

I could.

"What, um, what are you doing here? In Edmonton, I mean?"

"I live here," Rith said. "Obviously."

I nearly tripped over a log. How did he live in Edmonton and yet our paths had never crossed? But more importantly—he looked my age. If he was seventeen, why hadn't I seen him in school?

"How long have you been here? Why Edmonton?"

Rith chuckled. "What is this—an interview? And why else would I be here?"

Edmonton was a town of tree farmers and solar engineers. We lived here because Dad had gotten his degree in solar harvesting. It'd always been his dream to live on Earth and help the planet restore its atmosphere. And what better place to do that than in a rural town covered in trees, like this one?

"Are you . . ." I didn't want to ask. I didn't want him to say no. But my soul ached for a yes. "Are you adopted?"

Rith stopped, and I froze beside him. He lifted his gaze to the thick branches above, as if searching for inspiration or patience. Or both.

"Seventeen years ago, Novidom raged with political war." His voice was melodic, as if he were speaking to himself. "The Middle Kingdom said that Novidom was theirs.

Novidom said it no longer recognized itself as a territory of the Middle Kingdom. The United Lunar Republic was on the brink of world war with the Middle Kingdom—yada, yada. It wasn't safe to be a child in that region."

So he was one of the refugees who made it out of Novidom after the revolution. Just like me.

"I was a child, and I lived on the thirteenth floor of an apartment." Rith chuckled to himself. "I was just learning how to say my numbers, so that was all I could count up to in Novish. Thirteen. What about you, Soara? Do you remember anything from Novidom?"

Rith turned to me and waited for my response. I stared into his round eyes and tried to remember. My memories were tucked deep inside, but I couldn't call on them. Congestion built inside my skull as if my brain had been replaced by a fog. Or maybe the pill was kicking in; the corners of my vision swayed like mirage lines.

I shook my head. "I don't remember. I was just a kid back then."

"Oh," Rith said. Then he glanced into the trees as if something had caught his attention. Not only was my vision fizzling, but Rith sounded like a daydream singing to me from the end of a tunnel. "Well, I still need to find my dog."

I followed behind him, trying to seem sincere in helping him find Sam. But all I wanted to do was listen to more stories about Rith's time in Novidom. And figure out how to walk straight when the trees started dancing.

I tested my voice. "So . . . what else do you remember?"

Rith gave me half his attention while searching for Sam. "What else do you want to know?"

"Everything."

I wanted all of it—the good and the bad. What did his young mind remember about Novidom? What was it like to look up at the sky and see Earth? Did he have siblings? What was it like to have biological parents? To see into faces that perfectly resembled his own? Did Rith remember what it was like to sit on the couch and read a book while his father worked at the computer? Did he help his mother pick out locations for winter vacations or share family recipes? Because I'd always wanted those sweet nothings. And maybe if I listened to him, I could live vicariously through his moments.

Rith stopped searching for his dog to look at me. Though I'd said only one word, it was as if he understood me at my core.

"Okay. I don't have much time. But I'll share what I do remember. Close your eyes."

I shut them and giggled as euphoria crept in. *Stay sober, Soara.* "Why?"

"Because I want you to picture everything I'm saying."

The pill might've peaked at that moment. Instead of seeing darkness, my vision swirled with a kaleidoscope of colors. Geometric lines swayed in cadence with the sound of rustling branches. Rith spoke, and the colors latched onto his voice. Like an artist organizing oil on a canvas, Rith painted pictures in my mind.

"My last normal day on Novidom started like any other . . ."

He didn't have to say much more. With the medicine in my system, I saw it all. Kaylee was right. This pill was made for me. It seemed to find all the suppressed memories I had of Yue and bring them up to the surface.

"That morning, we were eating fanfan . . ."

I shouldn't've been able to remember what fanfan was. Aside from my Novish name, memories of Yue had all but faded to black. And yet, as Rith spoke, a bowl of white grains appeared before me. The steam tickled my face. This meal was sweetened with syrup and seasoned with crushed peppercorn and sun-dried lunar cactus. Even the jelly of cactus juice and the squish of steamed rice between my teeth felt like it was real life.

This must've been what Kaylee's pill was capable of. I could perfectly live through Rith's story and use my forgotten memories to fill in the details.

Rith's voice faded into the background, yet it was loud enough to guide this vision. Apparently I'd become his childhood self. I knelt on the floor of his crammed apartment. The picture was so clear, I felt the warmth of the sun beaming in from the window and heard the TV playing in the room behind me. The Minister of Novidom was addressing something about the Middle Kingdom's advances. She was encouraging people to stock up on water and clean air while they could.

Rith had a mother. A father. He lived with aunts, uncles, and a cousin. That was the culture of Novidom. We were a community. As a small island on Yue, helping each other succeed was the only way to thrive.

Rith's father kissed his mother on his way to work. He wore a thick robe that protected him from the sun. Yue's atmosphere was still developing. It meant that solar rays were just as deadly as the cold vacuum of space.

Rith's dad left, and I didn't think anything of it. He was only four rotations old at the time. His relatives worked while his mom stayed home to watch Rith and his cousin. And they thanked her for raising them. Children were the future of Yue.

"Can we play outside?" I asked in Rith's voice once my version of him had devoured the fanfan.

Rith's mom glanced at the TV with a worried expression but nodded anyway. She dressed Rith and his cousin in thick ponchos. They weren't as heavy as his dad's robes, but were dense enough to protect us without crushing our developing bones. Mom opened the front door. Rith's cousin and I burst into the hallway. Some part of me knew that seeing who got to the elevator first was a daily ritual practiced by Rith and his cousin.

"Tan'ya Fi!" Rith's cousin's name burst from my lips. He was older than Rith by one rotation, which meant he was faster. And Rith hated it. It wasn't fair that he could be so quick. "Slow down!"

Tan'ya Fi reached the elevators and slammed the button. Rith pushed him in the shoulder because he never got there first.

"Absolutely not," Mom scolded. She crouched and held Rith's arms so that I had no choice but to look at her. Rith was just about to cry when the elevator door dinged.

A father and son stepped out. They were the new family that moved onto our floor. Rith had seen them only a couple of times while they were arranging their apartment. Like him, they lived with extended family.

The new neighbors had a boy Rith's age. His long silver hair was matted in the back. He had large gray eyes. It seemed as if he was always searching for something. I'd seen those eyes before—but where? The moment the boy stepped out of the elevator with his father, I forgot that Rith had gotten into trouble for pushing Tan'ya Fi.

"Hello! Want to play with us?" Rith's voice came out of my mouth.

The boy looked to his father, but his father tugged him down the hall. That must've been a no. They walked away as Rith's mom guided us inside the elevator. Not once did the boy look away, even when the elevator doors slid shut.

Tan'ya Fi and I played on the playground of our apartment complex. Sometimes we ran around. Other times, we'd lay on our backs to catch our breaths. That was when we'd stare up at the black sky. Stars were visible even during the day. Earth was fascinating because it never looked the same. Sometimes I saw more land than water. Other times, all I saw were clouds. What was life on Earth like? As a child, Rith didn't think he'd ever know.

Crafts flew overhead. There'd been many of them gathering in the city lately. I wasn't sure what that was about. All I knew was that Rith's relatives talked about it a lot. It seemed to make them anxious.

A new shadow fell over me. I turned to see who was there. A pair of round gray eyes gazed down at me.

"Hello." It was the new boy who'd moved into Rith's complex. "Can you help me find my dog?"

Rith sprung to his feet. His mom had taught him to be a helper. And this boy was interesting to me. The longer I stared at his freckled cheeks, the more I wondered where I'd seen his face before.

Rith and the boy searched around the complex for his pet. Apparently he'd been playing with his dog by the street when it ran off. Rith wasn't allowed to walk across the street by himself. He needed to hold someone's hand before crossing. But his mom wasn't around. Even Tan'ya Fi was still at the playground. Rith didn't feel like going back, so he took the boy's hand, and we crossed the street together.

I wasn't sure how long we searched. We'd wandered down several streets calling out his dog's name, yet no animals came running our way. The heat of the day wore on. The neighbor and Rith decided to take a break from it in a ditch. They crouched beneath a bridge as a stream trickled at their feet. The boy hugged his knees and stared down at the water. He seemed so sad.

"It's okay," Rith said, patting his back. "Let's look at the fish instead."

We peered into the water, and our reflections stared back at us. But this body I was in wasn't what I'd thought it was. I had a pair of icy blue eyes. My silvery hair ran in curls down my cheeks, and freckles dotted my forehead. I looked like my dad. I was pretty. I had a mother who'd said so.

But something wasn't making sense. The more I tried to focus, the more my vision bubbled, as if I were looking at everything from underwater. Was this a memory? A dream? Why was this reality starting to fade like ice melting all around me?

"Are you my friend?" The boy's voice was enough to snap me back into the moment.

"I don't know," I replied. "I don't think you ever told me your name."

He looked at me with gray eyes as deep as the rocks beneath the water's surface. "My name's Ya'lak Hen Rith. And you?"

I didn't get a chance to reply because a tumultuous quake split the ground. Heat singed the air. A cloud of smoke and fire irrupted over the skyline. If we hadn't been under a bridge when the Middle Kingdom dropped its first bomb on Novidom, I don't think Ya'lak Hen Rith and I would've made it out alive.

One Week Later

I'd been staring at the same math equation for ten minutes, waiting for the clock to count down. Statistics was usually my favorite class. No matter where I was, numbers were the same on Earth as they were on Yue and the colonies. But this Friday afternoon was special. Instead of planning an escape to the woods for a second dose of meds, I was prepared to spend my time doing something more fulfilling.

Finally, the bell rang. Everyone stood up to leave. I packed my papers into my bag and allowed my peers to walk around me. Still, a classmate bumped into my shoulder.

"Do you see her forehead?" she whispered to her friend.

Her friend giggled. "Oh my gods, I could park my bike on that thing."

I touched the clip pulling my bangs out of my face. And smiled. Comments like these weren't anything new. But I was. And this time, I was grateful to have my large forehead noticed. My biological parents had blessed me with this body. And though they'd died in the bombing of Novidom thirteen Yuen rotations ago, they were still alive through me. And the commentary of my narrow-minded classmates had no power over the honor of carrying Yuen blood.

It'd been a week since I awoke alone and confused in the woods. It took me a while to realize that Ya'lak Hen Rith hadn't truly walked the forest with me that night. The pill had awakened my own memories and forced me to recall the boy from down the hall. I'd created a seventeen-year-old version of him to guide me through my own memories. And if it wasn't for that experience, things at home might've never changed.

I'd biked back to my worry-stricken parents, and after they questioned me on why I hadn't come home that night, I came clean to them about dosing. At first I thought they'd punish me for keeping secrets from them, but instead of seeking discipline, they sought to understand. My lying wasn't the real problem. I was sneaking away to medicate because I didn't have a safe space to process my sense of not belonging at home. And once they realized that, the dynamic of our household shifted for the better.

My parents weren't disappointed in me, but in themselves. Mom hadn't realized I felt so alone. Dad wished I'd talked to him about this sooner. We discussed ways to bring more Novish culture into our house and agreed to monthly family counseling sessions. But the therapy wasn't what made me want to race home. At least not today.

Kaylee bumped into me on my way to the bus stop. She waited until we were alone before speaking. "You ready for more moondust?"

I was a full head taller, but I straightened my shoulders to smile down at her. "No. I'm good."

"What? You didn't like it?"

"It's not that I didn't enjoy it," I said, coming to an intersection in our school hallway. "It's that I have better things to do with my time."

"Soara, I need to sell my stash," Kaylee insisted. "You're the only Yuen I know. Help me out. For old times' sake."

I headed to the bus stop while Kaylee took a left. "I'm sure you'll figure something out."

The bus driver dropped me off in front of my house, and I raced inside. The smell of sweet syrup and spices greeted me at the door. Mom was in the kitchen laying out the ingredients we'd gathered from last night's grocery run. Dad was bent over a Novish cookbook.

Ever since that evening in the woods, I'd been craving a bowl of fanfan. But reconnecting myself to my childhood dish was just the beginning. I wanted to know what Yuen clothing was called, what Yuen politics were. I wanted to learn everything I could because I knew that Ya'lak Hen Rith was also living life as an orphaned refugee somewhere in Earth's orbit. If our paths ever crossed, I wanted him to know that he wasn't as forgotten as I'd thought I was.

Mom and I steamed white grain. Dad and I mixed the sweet syrup with spices. I stirred the fanfan until everything had combined. Mom added pea beans in her bowl. It was a childhood snack she'd grown up with on the Aldrin Colony. Her dish was salty and crunchy. Mine tasted like nostalgia. Dad was the tiebreaker.

"I think I prefer Soara's," he said, his spoon still in his mouth. "But just to be sure, let me take another bite."

I yanked my bowl back before he could steal some more. "Stop eating my food!"

"Stop giving me food to eat." Dad laughed, jabbing his spoon at me.

I giggled, then surrendered my fanfan. It wasn't hard to make, so I started another dish. Besides, I liked knowing that from now on, I'd be able to eat fanfan whenever I wanted.

"Hey, I've been thinking," I said as Dad sampled more of Mom's dish. "Do you guys remember my birth name?"

"Noc'Si A Lun," Mom said. She even put an accent where it belonged. An Earthling wouldn't have known to do that. "Of course we remember. Why do you ask?"

"Do you think I could start going by that name from now on? I'm proud of my heritage, and I think I'm ready to start acting like it."

Mom studied me for a moment before she put her bowl down. "Well, sure you can! But don't you think people will put you down because your name is more beautiful than theirs?"

I chuckled to myself. "Yes. I'm sure. And I'm okay with that."

Of course my peers would roll their eyes when I corrected their pronunciation of my name. And I'd grow numb to their protests, as I had with "Giraffe Girl." But my name was sacred to me. It was my mantra, tying me to my birthplace. And if Ya'lak Hen Rith was somewhere out there, perhaps hearing my name would remind him of the first place we'd called home.

SEXY

BY JENNY HEIJUN WILLS

I don't stop until I notice I'm a block past the metro station and have to go back. Ugly-crying in public is so humiliating, but I can't stop. Glimpsing my reflection in a storefront window near Yonge and Bloor, I see teary mascara lines stream down my face. Awesome.

She's such a thirsty nobody! Why would he even go for her? Me love you long time! Their vicious words and gross mock accents drown out the noise of downtown rush-hour traffic.

It's impossible to know what's worse. That my asshole boyfriend, who it turns out is just as immature and shitty as every other guy at school, abandoned me, leaving me to face those hyenas alone. Or that my best friend—my only friend, really—hates me so much that she would hang out with those scavengers and not only validate their cruel torture but, like, instigate it.

I've never felt more alone. Which is a real feat. Because my entire life has been about loneliness. Well, that, while also being overwhelmingly crowded.

I slink down the metro station steps, wiping my nose and mascara-stung eyes on the back of my mitten. I look down and see thirty-seven notifications on my phone. Half are from Ainsley, my *ex*-best friend, and half from Drew, the world's biggest coward. I'm on fire with shame and regret. And overcome by an urge to chuck my iPhone into the cavernous black hole from where, according to the sign, the train will burst forth in two minutes. I want to throw away my entire social lifeline and all the contacts in it, so that I, Hannah Russo-Hartman, just vanish off the face of the earth. Again.

Three Days Earlier

It's the strangest thing. Someone likes me. Like, *likes* me. Maybe even loves me. Someone who told me I have the softest skin, the prettiest hair, the sexiest eyes. Me! The never-recipient of DMs from mystery admirers or invitations to a semiformal, or even a pity glance when the entire class had to do mandatory swim classes back in ninth grade. A girl so invisible the teacher didn't even notice my two-week absence last term when I had the chicken pox.

That same girl now has a serious boyfriend of nearly four months who literally everyone at school agrees is objectively hot, brilliant, and cool. And believe it or not, he texts her in the middle of the night, so when she wakes up, it's to long, winding confessions of his adoration, his attraction, his addiction to her. *"I was reading these notes about, you know, that famous novel I was telling you about, and I couldn't stop thinking about you. . ."* he texted last night around two. *"At first, I thought, this Valmont guy is so screwed up. A real sociopath. But these last few weeks with you, I get it. I mean, I actually get the lengths a guy is willing to go in the name of love. The risks he's willing to take. But what is love? That's what Laclos was getting at, right? Is it infatuation? And is infatuation madness? And what can we as a society accept in the name of . . ."*

The message went on forever. He has total dad energy sometimes, which I tease him about. Like, he actually uses punctuation in his texts like an old man. And I still have no idea what he was talking about, even after googling some of the weirder words. But it makes me feel fizzy all over when he talks to me like that. Like he wants to forge this deep connection with me. Sees me as his equal. As his peer.

A part of me wants to publish Drew's romantic love-texts and say to everyone, *See! I am good enough, and in fact, contrary to what you all told me since middle school, I can get a boyfriend. All YOU judgmental fake-ass bitches can literally fuck off.* And while I'm at it, I'd add, *And moms, I know you mean well. But your advice that I should wait until college to date because that's when I'll blossom into my true self is total BS.*

I wish I could say all that stuff. I wish I could post selfies of us together, announce our relationship across all my social media, and maybe even get a tattoo of his name.

But I don't.

Sure, technically, I *can't* get Drew's name tattooed without permission from one of my moms, and that's as long a shot as either of them agreeing to me backpacking across Asia after graduation in eight months, like Ainsley and I have secretly been planning since tenth grade. Drew jokes that he'll sign the permission form for me, but I just roll my eyes. Besides, I'm only half serious about the tattoo. It's that other stuff. Like publicly announcing our relationship and whatever? I don't even do that.

It's because, even though I'm super excited about how things are going and I've never felt so loved before, so *seen*, this weird part of me doesn't want anyone to know. My parents, people at school, or friends at Tae Kwon Do. Even Ainsley. Especially Ainsley. I can't explain it. But there's something that makes me want to keep Drew a secret, even from my best friend in the universe.

It's different from feeling embarrassed. It's just that these days, I can't look anyone in the eye anymore. I try to tell myself that this is normal, this is what typical teenage sexual awaking is, or whatever. He's my first boyfriend, so it makes sense that I'm a bit awkward. But deep down, I know there's something else going on.

Maybe it's that he's more experienced. He's probably had tons of girlfriends before me, but I'm afraid to ask. I don't want to seem jealous or immature.

I wish I had an older sister or, like, a therapist to talk to about this stuff. But my moms, while they warn me that they'll send me to a therapist whenever I pull an attitude on them, are secretly afraid of the emotions that will be unleashed if I actually start to see one. At least that's my take on their weird, empty threats.

Anyhow, it's a professional development day, so we have the day off from school and I'm lying flat on the area rug in my room. I'm bored. The one person I wish would text—or pick me up to hang out—can't, because he has to work. Plus, I'm supposed to be working on university applications, but I'm too lovesick to focus. Instead, I scroll Instagram and TikTok until my head throbs.

Out of curiosity, I search "#FirstLoveAnxiety" and this video pops up. It's by one of those accounts where a college-age person with superlong acrylic nails gives actually pretty good advice from the passenger seat of their friend's car.

I press play. "We protect the most precious and vulnerable things in our lives by hiding them from the people we know. There was this study done that says that people conceal the things that matter most to them to avoid the judgments of others that might ruin their experiences . . ."

The person accentuates their points by flourishing their hands, flicking and flashing their bedazzled nails. I let the video loop at least ten times before I sit up, and it's like the world around me suddenly makes sense.

This is exactly how I feel about my relationship with Drew. Like, our connection is beyond words, and there's nothing I can say or do to make anyone understand how unique it is. It's like one of those tiny bunnies my moms and I found in the woodpile last spring that they said we should leave alone in case their mother came back and smelled us on her babies. My moms said we'd taint the bunnies if we were in contact with them, and their mother would abandon them and they'd be orphans. I guess the main takeaway is that newborn, innocent, and cute things can be ruined by people who interfere.

Anyway, getting back to Drew . . . The only loose variable in my new philosophical clarity is Ainsley. I want to share my new thoughts with her, tell her everything in fact, but lately she's been super clingy and then mad when I don't respond to her neediness. Obviously, she can tell I'm keeping something from her. Even though Drew and I have been talking for a while now, we only made it official last month. Like, an entire month I've been acting more and more distant from Ainsley. So it's partly my fault. Drew made me swear not to tell a soul. "It's sexier that way," he promised. "Like Romeo and Juliet." And it's not like he has a girlfriend or anything, and he has way more experience than me, so I agreed.

But keeping this secret from Ainsley . . . it's like hot-cold every day and it's gotten to the point where I'm avoiding her texts. I feel guilty. We've got this huge term assignment due on the history of the Canadian parliamentary system, and we're supposed to be working in pairs, but I keep canceling on her whenever we plan to get together. Each time she reaches out, this uncanny feeling comes over me and I become one of those baby bunnies, trying to remain still, trying not to blink, to breathe, because maybe, if no one actually sees me, they'll just leave me alone.

I sound like a total contradiction, right? Complaining that I'm invisible one minute, that no one notices me, but then freaking out about my secret being exposed. Maybe I've been like that my whole life. Knowing some things are impossible to be kept private, but wishing they could be. Which makes me desperate to control how people actually see me. Or wanting to be noticed for the *right* reasons and not because I'm a loser reject.

My phone vibrates, and I get a notification that Ainsley is trying to FaceTime me. I let it ring without picking up. I can't tell her about Drew yet. But armed with TikTok wisdom and a new sense of validation, I promise myself I'll tell her after the weekend. On Monday. Even though he made me promise to keep our relationship a secret.

"For now, ma belle," he whispered into my neck while we were half talking about the future, half making out in the back of his Corolla a couple of weeks into our relationship. I withdrew for a second, froze, afraid this had all been an elaborate prank or that he was embarrassed by me and wanted to keep me hidden. Like I was unworthy. Not cool enough, or experienced enough, or pretty enough.

I saw my reflection in the side mirror. I didn't get what he sees in me, with my tragically uncurlable hair, barely there eyelashes, and fish lips. Especially when he has those dreamy, wolflike grayish-blue eyes, a wavy mop of perfectly tousled black hair, and is tall and athletic, compared with me, who is short and skinny.

But he pulled me back to him, lightly brushing his lips against mine, the corners of his mouth curling into a sexy smile. "It makes it more exciting . . ." His breath on my ear and his Quebecois accent—a leftover from spending the first ten years of his life living in Montreal—sent shivers down my back. So I emptied my head of those doubting thoughts and sighed deeply with my entire body and accepted being a kinda-mistress, for the time being.

"When are you planning on telling me what the hell is going on?"

I'm stunned by Ainsley's anger when she accosts me at my locker before homeroom. But even though she is putting on a big show of indignation, I can see how much I've hurt her. Her green eyes shine with almost tears.

"What are you talking about?"

Ainsley's entire body is clenched. Her emerald eyes flash with a rage like I haven't seen since we were ten and some kid called me a name that went totally over my head (I still don't know what it was—it wasn't one of the obvious slurs) and Ainsley rushed to my side, told him he was a racist trash bag of a nonhuman. Her face turned so red her freckles disappeared. And her hair had flown around her head like it was made of flames she could control to destroy her enemies—like Anne of Green Gables meets Medusa. We've been best friends ever since.

I immediately regret trying to gaslight her. She hates me now. I'm the one at risk of being turned to stone. And I totally deserve it for being so weird and letting a guy come between us, especially these last few weeks since Drew and I became an official couple. For letting Drew convince me to keep a secret from my best friend.

My face must look sad, because Ainsley's expression softens. She sniffs. "You've just been super absent lately. Did I do something wrong?"

Now's my chance. Maybe she'll understand.

"No! Of course not! I just . . . can we talk after school? I'll come over. My parents are going to some art gallery fundraiser tonight."

Ainsley visibly relaxes. "Yeah, sure . . . meet me at my locker after physics?"

"Yes!" I nearly shout at her, relieved to be able to stall for a few more hours. "I can't wait!"

With an empty smile plastered on my face, I reach into my locker, grab random notebooks without checking if they're the ones I actually need for first period, and leave her standing there while I try to calmly walk away.

I can't concentrate on anything in AP French, as per usual. I gaze out the window so I don't accidentally look in Drew's direction and expose our secret. I'm so nervous about what I've promised to divulge to Ainsley later today. I replied to Drew's texts from this morning, but we made a pact to keep our distance at school so as not to arouse suspicion. But I'm only one and a half periods away from confession time, and I would love his comfort.

M. Alexandre's voice floats in and out. He's going on about Marguerite Duras and her weird book about this girl who has an affair with this older Asian guy in Vietnam.

"It's the authenticity of the voice, the purity and innocence of the speaker that makes this so memorable a work," M. Alexandre is saying in French. "Not to mention the lush imagery depicting the exotic lands and their mysterious people . . ."

I furrow my brow just for a second, wondering if people are allowed to say *oriental* in French. If there are different rules for different languages. Like, is oriental*e* different from oriental?

M. Alexandre, noticing my barely perceptible flinch, stops mid-sentence. "The person I'm most interested in hearing from," he says, breaking into English, after a beat, "is Hannah."

My eyes dart to his face in alarm. His eyes are sparkling and encouraging, like they always are. But I'm stunned into silence.

"What do you think about this taboo relationship? Young and old . . . crossing ethnicities, generations, class? Most important . . . is the depiction of the Orient authentic? Does it ring true?"

"Ah yes . . . Hannah-san . . . does it ling tuh-lue?" I recognize MacKenzie's nasty voice without having to turn to see who is speaking. I recognize it even through the nasal racist accent she's putting on. I also hear Sarah, MacKenzie's sidekick in shittiness, egging her on, tauntingly repeating "Hannah-san" in an equally offensive fake accent. They're encouraged by this rare chance to speak in English without penalty.

"I'm . . . I don't . . ." Everyone is looking at me as I stammer and stutter and blush fluorescent pink. "I'm not from Vietnam!" is all I can manage in the end. I want to disappear. I don't know what to do or say. I especially hate the way Drew and the other kids are watching. Drew looks both worried and curious about what I'm going to do. If I'm cool enough to brush it off. I can feel it. I don't even need to look up to know his expression.

"Well, Léo is actually Chinese . . ." M. Alexandre corrects, his smile an attempt to be encouraging. To draw some pearl of wisdom from my empty head.

"I'm not Chinese, either."

With that, he lets it go, and I slouch deep into my sweater, trying not to cry. When the bell rings, I can't get out of there fast enough. I hear Drew calling after me as I rush past him and out the door.

My last period is free, thank the Lord. While I wait for Ainsley's science class to end, I take up an entire table in the library and spread my stuff out, to be uninviting. The day's been an emotional roller coaster, and I feel like I filled up on funnel cakes and corn dogs before going on back-to-back rides.

I shake my head, as though maybe those bad thoughts can be erased. Like my brain's a giant Etch A Sketch. When I stop, I notice that Drew has attached a purple Post-it note tucked into my French book, like a bookmark. He must have snuck it in when I was staring out the window during class. There's a doodle of a pineapple (his nickname for me) and about fifty little hearts and a thing that I guess is supposed to be the Eiffel Tower. I can't stop the corners of my lips from curling into a smile, and I try to forget my humiliation from French class.

I remember the first time he called me H-*ananas*—a play on my actual name and the French word for pineapple. It's all because of our first "date"—if you can even call it that. Back in October, I told my moms I was going to study at Ainsley's, but really, I took the metro to the Bloor and Bay station and then sat at a corner table in the brightly lit and newly opened Paris Baguette. The workers eyed me suspiciously because I hadn't yet ordered a pastry, just sat nursing a small hot chocolate for over an hour. It's like I was frozen in place, unsure of how to choose from what seemed to be hundreds of foreign-looking treats—and of how to eat it.

"Try this, if you can't decide."

He appeared and slid a tray in front of me. On it was a plated puffball pastry dusted with sugar. There were other little plates too, but it was obvious which dish was meant for me.

"It's pineapple," he said, never hesitating. He sat in the empty chair opposite me without asking. Without breaking eye contact, he smiled the most dazzling smile, winked one shockingly blue-gray eye, and picked up something made of dough twisted around pieces of cut-up hot dogs. I felt flush all over, which is the same feeling I got when I'd see him at school, but at the café it was like times a million. Nervous and excited, at once.

We sat together for hours. Talking about serious as well as unserious things. "I spent a term in Korea," he said. "Beautiful culture." He tried to teach me the Korean alphabet, but I got frustrated. "It's really easy," he said, trying to assure me. "You'll pick it up one day."

When I passed him my phone so he could add his number ("Let's do this again sometime. I'll shoot you a text"), his eyes twinkled. "And none of this Mr. so-and-so formality, by the way. Just call me Drew. I only let the prettiest girls and my granny do it. Only you don't have to roll your *r*'s like she does when she says it," he said with a small laugh. "Though from what I've seen in French, you're up for the challenge."

I basically died on the spot.

I'm brought back to the library when I get a text from him.

> Hope you're okay, doll. 🖤 🍍 🧑🏻 French class was rough today. I'm sorry.

I'm glad to hear from him but annoyed to be reliving more emotional turmoil. I'm fine, I reply, adding, You could have had my back more in French, you know. Then, You know damn straight why I don't know anything about *the Orient*.

The flashing dots tell me that Drew's writing something long. But after a few minutes, when the message eventually comes through, it just says, You're right. I'm sorry. Can I make it up to you? Pineapple bun at our usual place? 🥺 Please?

I wish I was more torn than I actually am. Since my moms are going to be out until at least nine, maybe Drew and I can go out for dinner together. And even though I'm awkward over how alone I felt and how obnoxious it was for him to not only watch me get roasted in French class, but to abandon me and practically send a formal invitation to those monsters to tear me apart, I can't help but remember how the last time we went out for dinner, Drew was so charming with the waitstaff they didn't card me or bat an eye when he ordered a bottle of what I guess was fancy red wine. I really want him to like me. I want anyone to like me. So against any sense of self-respect, I sort of accept his half-assed apology.

My mind flashes back to Ainsley's anger and sad vulnerability earlier this morning, and I hesitate. But then, just as I'm about to text back, suggesting we meet another day, I see her walk past the library entrance with MacKenzie and her lapdog, Sarah, in tow. They're laughing loudly, and Ainsley is laughing too, and I swear I hear MacKenzie say my name and Sarah doing that racist dubbed "Kung Fu" movie accent. MacKenzie loops her arm through Ainsley's, and I'm gobsmacked to see Ainsley let her. She knows how much those girls have tormented me for years.

Fuck it. She's just made my decision a whole lot easier. I purse my lips so firmly they hurt when I type I'll meet you there 🖤 🖤 🖤 🖤 🖤, knowing Drew is cautious about us being seen leaving school together. I hit send so hard it's like I'm launching a nuclear missile. I'll send Ainsley a rain check text later.

The cashier at Paris Baguette recognizes me now and doesn't pester me to buy something or get out. She knows I'm waiting. I don't know why, but I keep my jacket on.

Under the table, I cross and uncross my legs a thousand times.

"Babe. Sorry. I had to wait for three overcrowded trains to pass before I could squeeze into one at last."

Drew drops a Marc Jacobs messenger bag onto the chair across from me and shakes some snowflakes off his scarf. He winks one of his slate-blue eyes at me. I start to release some of my stress under his gaze, now that we're away from everyone else's nosy and judgmental ones. But I'm still kind of pissed that he stood by watching me get eaten alive by those pit bulls at school. And something else. There's something else that I can't fully put my finger on, and strangely, I wish Ainsley was here. It's like, sometimes things happen and I don't know how to handle them in the moment. I'm confused, and my head is spinning because I recognize something bad is going on, but I can't name it. *It's racist*, Ainsley would state matter-of-factly in a way I can't seem to say.

Oh fuck . . . Ainsley . . . I was supposed to text her.

I'm frantically trying to send an apology to her by the time Drew pays for the food and drinks and rejoins me. He still doesn't register my worry or anger. I look up. He has icing sugar on his lips. They curl into a familiar smile, and I try to relax. Try to forgive him. Everything is normal, I tell myself, not sure I truly believe it. Everything is the same as it was before my meltdown in French class. Everyone makes mistakes. But not everyone has a boyfriend who actually makes her feel sexy. But does he? I immediately vanquish the question from my mind.

He nudges the pineapple custard bun toward me. I pick at the flaky crust on top and resign myself to pushing past my feelings of awkwardness.

"You look so sexy today in your little skirt and leggings," he says. "You're the prettiest girl in school."

I'm blushing. I lean forward so my hair is covering my face. In the past, I would have beamed at his compliments. Felt them like sunshine on my face. Now, because of what happened in class, I'm unsettled. Like my muscles are detaching from my skeleton. Still, I let him inch closer, intertwine his fingers with mine.

Drew is in the middle of brushing my hair back, tucking it behind my ear when we hear it. A trio of screams followed by "OH MY GOD!"

We snap to attention and see Ainsley, MacKenzie, and Sarah standing in the doorway of Paris Baguette. It's like someone's poured ice water all over me. How did they find us here? Did they follow me? It's at least a half-hour train ride from North York! The three of them, like those horrible witches in Macbeth, peer around at the pastries, the workers, and the other people at the café like they've landed on an alien planet. MacKenzie's nose is crinkled up like she's looking for something to find disgusting.

I stand up abruptly, knocking into the table and spilling Drew's chai latte. He's already backing away mechanically, with swift and robotic movements, reaching for his jacket that he tossed over the back of his chair. His palms are up, facing away from him, in the universal sign of innocence.

The hyenas are already howling, shrieking, and snarling. Ainsley is with them, but I can't face her. I don't know what she's thinking. But from what I witnessed from the school library earlier today, that backstabber is probably enjoying it.

"You fucking slut! A teacher? You're banging a teacher?" *"Voulez-vous coucher avec moi?"* and "What a whore. She probably was like 'Me so horny'!"

The insults blur together, making their speaker indecipherable, except for the last thing, which is clearly MacKenzie making a grotesque accent as she squints her eyes and juts her overbite out into fake buck teeth. I turn to Ainsley, who just looks shocked. Shocked and worried.

Drew has his coat on. His wolf's eyes are wild with fear. He doesn't look back at me as he flees the café. "Where are you going, Monsieur A?" Sarah calls after him, screaming with joy at our terror.

MacKenzie joins in, exaggeratedly rolling her *r*'s in a mock French accent. "Yeah, why are you taking off, M. Alexandrrrre? We all want extra crrrredeet in Frrrrench!"

I hear Ainsley say to them, quietly at first, "Calm down." Then she repeats herself more loudly.

"Oh, fuck you, Ainsley, you little traitor. This was your idea to follow her in the first place!" Sarah says.

Ainsley opens her mouth, but nothing comes out. My eyes narrow in her direction, but I still can't really see her. I start to hyperventilate and hiccup at once. This makes MacKenzie and Sarah laugh even harder. Desperate, I turn away from them to face my friend. Somehow it's easier to take my anger out on her, though in reality I am angrier at myself. And Drew. I'm still furious at Drew for his shitty behavior in class, his BS apology, and now, his ridiculous face, frozen, his mouth agape like a cartoon character.

"I only followed you because you stood me up. I thought maybe you were in trouble or mad or . . ." Ainsley is stammering out lies, because if she really cared, she wouldn't have brought Sarah and MacKenzie along.

"You know what? Fuck you," I say. "I'm glad to see the person you really are. And the kind of people you're friends with." I jut my chin in the direction of the others, who mock indignation.

"OooOOOoooo . . ." they taunt. And, "Look out, she probably knows karate!"

"Shut up, Sarah!" Ainsley hisses.

"No," I say. "Listen to your new friends, Ainsley. You're just like them. You've been one of them this whole time. You just used me to make yourself seem more interesting. More woke. Less boring!"

I know I'm being hurtful. And I don't really believe the things I'm saying. Or at least I didn't until Ainsley looked at me, her eyes red and full of tears. It's like she's debating

257

between running to hug me or to slap me. But then Mac-Kenzie quietly says, "What an ungrateful bitch. Some friend. How long has this even been going on?" And then Ainsley, briefly turning to look at MacKenzie and Sarah and then back to me, says something so mean, so out of character, that I feel like I've been hit by a sledgehammer.

Ainsley also looks shocked. Like she didn't know she had it in her. Even MacKenzie and Sarah go silent.

Before I know it, I feel the cold air of the street on my face. And I'm running. I'm alone and running.

Three Weeks Later

Everything looks the same in Ainsley's room. The pile of *Game of Thrones* paperbacks lined up on the windowsill. The IKEA desk and matching chair that wobbles if anyone sits on it. Even the string of Edison lightbulbs with tiny clothespins interspersed, attaching mini Polaroid pictures of Ainsley and me through the years.

Everything looks the same, but the energy of the space is a 100 percent different. I'm awkward and sheepish, and Ainsley is cold and uncomfortable. We've been working on our report on Parliament for nearly an hour and a half in practically dead silence.

"So the upper chamber is appointed, the lower chamber elected?" Ainsley tries to break the ice with something we both know.

I ignore her. She keeps typing on her laptop, but her fingers slow to a stop.

"Listen," she says, her voice low and thick, like she's about to cry. "I'm sorry about what happened. You know. At the Korean bakery, with you and M. Alexandre."

I look up from my spiral notebook, where I've been drawing stars in the margins. My bottom lip starts to quiver, even though I try to stop it. I am still so upset and feel betrayed by Ainsley, but I've spoken to no one about it since it happened. I left Drew and his eighty-nine text messages on read. And with MacKenzie and Sarah telling everyone at school and then the fallout, with Drew being put on leave while the investigation goes on, life has been a living hell. I had to talk to the guidance counselor, some police detectives, child protective services. There was a subreddit about me.

The worst was how disappointed my moms were. "We didn't raise you like that!" my one mom said. "Why do you always feel the need to be different?" My other mom just cried and went on stress leave from her job.

Most of my teachers have been nice and are letting me do remote learning as long as I email all my assignments by their due dates. My moms immediately enrolled me in therapy when it became clear that talking to them was not going to go anywhere. I was just too ashamed sitting through their lectures about how concerned they are about the choices I'm making, inquiring if Drew gave me drugs, and asking if I need more male role models in my life. It's just too embarrassing to admit that it's something so basic as I felt ugly, and this older guy, this teacher everyone had a crush on, told me I was pretty.

I miss Ainsley, even though I don't trust her anymore. I miss her, but I'm sad because I don't see a way forward with our friendship.

Ainsley goes on: "I didn't mean for things to get so out of hand. And for the record, I didn't ask MacKenzie and Sarah to come with me. They just got so into the drama of me following you after we saw you taking off after school when we had plans." She's picking at her nail polish, and I can't see her eyes, so I can't tell if she's telling the truth. "I still don't understand why you kept all that from me. I wouldn't have judged you."

It's nice to talk to someone. Not to be completely isolated. I can't forgive her for what she did. She proved I couldn't trust her. She turned on me because she was insecure and couldn't stand the thought that she didn't belong. It's ironic that she couldn't register that I am the one who never could, never would belong, and what that turned me into. How it made me vulnerable.

We work in silence for a while.

"Were you embarrassed?" she asks.

I know Ainsley's not being judgmental. Not right now, at least. She's genuinely curious. I decide to let her in a little bit, not to alleviate her guilt, but because I want to have a witness to what I was actually thinking.

"It wasn't embarrassment, not like you think, at least. It was more like shame. Or confusion," I say. "No one has ever treated me like someone special. Like something valuable . . ."

"Your moms tell you every day how you're their most prized treasure."

"A prize, a treasure . . . something to be looked at through a museum glass case. Drew, he made me feel like a human who was attractive and interesting on my own." I feel my face reddening at how ridiculous I sound. "Now, since the blowup, I can see just how shitty the whole thing is. How he was using me to feel special, maybe to feel powerful."

I can't tell if Ainsley gets it. She's nodding, but there's something about her expression that makes me doubt her. Makes me know that in a few months I'll leave her, and my schoolmates, and this entire experience behind. At least I hope I can. I hope my moms are right when they promise that will happen.

For now, I'm done talking about it. I pick up the notebook again. Maybe this is something only I can understand.

DEADWOOD

BY KELLEY BAKER

Allison stood near the curb outside the arrivals terminal of the Tucson airport, holding her forest-green backpack as sweat beaded under her nose in the sizzling heat. She leaned onto the handle of her wheeled suitcase, standing on the tips of her toes as she craned her head to see over the roofs of the oncoming cars shuffling through the terminal. She'd considered walking back into the airport to avoid the heat while she waited, but she worried that she would miss Grandma's car coming to pick her up.

Her mom was forcing her to visit her grandmother alone over Memorial Day weekend while she and her new boyfriend, Martin, went to Las Vegas. Mom kept referring to the trip to Vegas as a "romantic getaway," which repulsed Allison and her sister, Beverly, who would be performing in a marching band competition in Florida that weekend.

Beverly was only eleven months younger than Allison—their parents had been astonished to discover that they were expecting another baby just weeks after their long and arduous journey to become parents ended in Allison's adoption. Although their family called Allison and Beverly "the twins" because of their closeness in age, they looked nothing alike.

Allison would often stare at Beverly with an inexhaustible curiosity, analyzing Beverly's resemblance to their parents, from the stringy strawberry blond hair and cloudy blue eyes that matched their mom's in old photos, to the bony, angular nose she shared with their dad. She didn't envy her sister's looks, exactly, so much as the fact that she looked like their parents' daughter.

Allison's brown eyes strained against the brilliance of the blue sky as she scanned for Grandma's car. She was beginning to sweat through her loose black T-shirt and was tempted, briefly, to pull her straight brown hair up into a ponytail to cool off. She preferred to wear her hair down, tucking the left side behind her ear while leaving the right side hanging over her face—an attempt to conceal a quarter-size birthmark near her jawline. She could remember children in kindergarten pointing at her and asking questions about what happened to cause it. Every time she complained about it, her family insisted the birthmark was "hardly noticeable" and "nothing to worry about." Now fifteen years old, Allison had long since learned to internalize her fixation on how unsightly it made her feel.

She opened her backpack to retrieve a pair of sunglasses and checked her phone to see if Grandma had tried to reach her. Her phone's home screen showed an old photo of her family at the water park. Although Allison felt she belonged in her family, she was often reminded that she didn't. Photographs like this one, taken during the summer when the sun had browned her skin to a toasty bronze, highlighted the contrast between her and her white family.

She typed out a text message to let her mom know she had landed in Tucson safely, but her thumb hesitated over the send button. Allison resented her for prioritizing the trip to Las Vegas with Martin, which left Allison in need of adult supervision for the long weekend. She had begged Mom to let her stay home alone instead of traveling to Grandma's.

"Over my dead body," Mom yelled. "You can't stay home alone, Allison!"

"Mom, I'm *fine!*" Allison insisted, despite being perfectly aware that she was not.

Two months earlier, she'd blinked her eyes open to discover that she was lying in a hospital bed, wearing a blue hospital gown and loose, scratchy anti-slip socks, fluorescent lights blaring overhead. She'd immediately recalled the reason she was there, and that when she fell asleep earlier that evening, she hadn't intended to wake up at all.

"Allison, we are not going to pretend everything is 'fine.'" Mom's use of air quotes was a recent tendency she'd acquired when she started dating Martin. It made Allison and Beverly cringe. "You're going to Tucson. End of discussion."

"But Mom," Allison whined. "I'll have so much homework." She could think of several excuses to try to justify why she could stay home alone all weekend, but the simple truth was that she wished her mom would cancel the trip with Martin to stay with her.

"You'll have plenty of time to do homework during Grandma's *Matlock* marathons," Mom said, looking at Allison as she perched her glasses on top of her head. "You know why we need someone to keep an eye on you while we're gone." Mom's other new habit was using *we* to refer to her and Martin, which gave Allison a grave sense that Martin was part of a separate family entity with Mom that apparently didn't include her.

Allison's incident had occurred when Mom and Martin were first seeing each other, a few months after her parents divorced and Dad moved abroad for work. Beverly was staying overnight at a friend's house, and Mom was getting ready to go out with Martin, leaving Allison alone for the evening. She was sitting on her bed reading when Mom rapped gently on her open door.

"Knock-knock," Mom said as she entered. "Could you help me with this clasp?" She held up a bracelet with an

Eiffel Tower charm. "Martin is taking me to a French restaurant this evening."

Allison fastened the bracelet for her mother. The doorbell rang, and Mom leapt up and checked her hair in the mirror. "C'est magnifique," she said to herself before kissing Allison goodbye. "Pizza is in the freezer when you're ready to eat. Please don't forget to remove the cardboard before you put it in the oven."

"I got it, Mom," Allison said with an assuring thumbs-up. "Have fun."

"Au revoir!" Mom said as she made her way downstairs to greet Martin.

Allison watched from her bedroom window, wincing as Martin draped his arm around Mom's shoulder as they walked down the driveway. Seeing her mom walking away with a man she had never met, she felt an unexpected, primal, desperate need for her to return. Her blood rushed suddenly to her head in a hot, fuzzy panic, and she realized she was crying.

The quiet stillness in the house began to turn sinister and overwhelming. She could feel her pulse throbbing behind her eye sockets. Despite what she knew intellectually—that Mom and Beverly would be back, that she wasn't really alone—Allison couldn't help but feel completely abandoned.

She wailed into her pillow, her body shaking as long spasms of anguish erupted from deep in her chest.

Ashamed of how childish it felt to admit it, she wanted her mom, and she sensed a familiar, visceral conviction that she was never coming back.

When Allison came to in the hospital later that night, her first words were "I'm sorry," though she didn't feel apologetic so much as an aching loneliness, even with her mother holding her hand, the Eiffel Tower bracelet still affixed to her wrist.

"I didn't even know you were depressed," Beverly said to her later. "How could you not tell me?" There was a sorrow in her voice that Allison had never heard before.

Allison looked at her sister blankly. "I guess I didn't know either."

"How could you not know?" Beverly asked mournfully. Allison didn't have an answer.

The scorching heat was becoming unbearable when Allison finally spotted Grandma's tan Buick nudging its way through the sunny terminal. When Grandma parked at the curb, she popped the trunk open and Allison swung her suitcase inside. Through the purple-tinted glass of the rear window, she could see Grandma's perfect sphere of wispy white hair as she extinguished a cigarette in the center console. She was wearing an ivory crewneck sweatshirt that nearly matched the sun-bleached beige of the car's interior. Allison closed the trunk as noiselessly as she could and opened the passenger door.

"My little tulip!" Grandma said as she hugged Allison, squeezing her tightly with one arm. "I am so happy to see you!"

"Thank you for picking me up. How are you?" Allison asked as she soaked in the cool air from the air-conditioning.

"I'm marvelous, now that you're here. You seem taller," Grandma said, studying Allison carefully through her enormous horn-rimmed sunglasses. Allison wondered how anyone could accurately assess her height while she was sitting down, but she didn't object. In fact, she had not grown at all since she last saw her grandmother a year ago.

Grandma looked much the same as always: a tall woman, somewhat gaunt, with cheeks that drooped limply and her signature feathery white hair that seemed to stand straight off her scalp. *Antigravity hair*, as Beverly called it. She wore gold and silver rings on every finger. When they were younger, Allison and Beverly had loved it when Grandma would take one off so they could try it on, gawking at how massive the ring was compared with their tiny hands. Now Grandma leaned into the steering wheel as she drove, and her head seemed to sink into her shoulders, making her appear shorter than she was. She fiddled with the audio buttons on the dashboard. "Do you like Buck Owens?" she asked.

"I don't know who that is."

"Well, prepare to be delighted. He was your grandpa's favorite," she said. The opening bars of a twangy, upbeat country song rang out of the Buick's speakers. "We're going to have ourselves some fun this weekend."

Allison exhaled slowly. She felt like she had been holding her breath since Mom dropped her off at the airport earlier that day.

"Do you mind if we make a quick stop on the way home, sweet pea?" Grandma asked, patting Allison's knee lightly. "Grandma has to run an errand for work."

Allison shook her head. She hadn't realized that Grandma had a job.

They passed rust-colored gravel landscaping and scattered cacti for miles, the Santa Catalina Mountains sprawling in the distance. Grandma turned into a strip mall and swerved into a parking space in front of a massive storefront called Rugs Plus. "I'll be right back. Are you okay here for a few minutes by yourself?" She left the engine running as she got out of the car.

"I'm not alone, Grandma, I'm with Buck Owens," Allison said, tapping the CD player on the dashboard and smiling sarcastically.

Grandma let out a laugh. "You kids behave yourselves," she said before shutting the door.

In the car, Allison unzipped her backpack and rummaged for her anatomy and physiology textbook. She had just put a new yellow stretchy fabric book cover on it, but she could still smell formaldehyde emanating from its pages and wondered if the scent would ever work its way out of her memory. When she enrolled in the class, she had imagined that dissecting a cat would be interesting, possibly even fun, but she had been dismayed at the sordid reality of the project. The tangy pickle scent that lingered relentlessly. The way the cat's teeth looked creepy and menacing set in the skull. Last week, she had been unexpectedly upset when her classmate realized his cat was pregnant. Their teacher, Mr. Reynolds, was utterly enraptured by this discovery, ogling the baby kittens as they were extracted one by one.

"This one's enormous!" wailed Mr. Reynolds, holding up a tiny kitten in the palm of his hand. It made Allison wonder where these dead cats had come from in the first place. What was their journey between becoming pregnant with kittens and ending up pickled in a thick vacuum-sealed plastic bag?

As class was about to end, Allison got up from her stool to wash her hands in the sink at the back of the classroom. She stared at her shoes as she walked past Madeline, who was sitting tall and upright on her stool with her legs akimbo, her sneakers hitched around the footrest. Although Madeline seemed to enjoy ridiculing pretty much anyone for any reason, she had a special ability to make Allison feel like an outsider. It was incredible to think that they'd been friends in elementary school: their friendship had ended in the fourth grade when Madeline accused Allison of failing to demonstrate adequate sympathy when her pet gerbil died.

She knew how self-conscious Allison was about her birthmark, and she exploited that vulnerability every chance she got.

At first, Allison had complained to her mom, thinking she'd be able to ask the school for help, but she quickly learned it only made things worse. This made her a snitch on top of everything else Madeline hated about her.

When Allison returned to her workbench that day, she'd seen the scrawling black permanent marker on the cover of her textbook right away. PIZZAFACE. She'd hastily stuffed her textbook into her backpack and tried to look composed, but she could feel heat rising to the surface of her skin, burning around her eyes. The bell rang, and she ran for the door, chancing a micro-glance in Madeline's direction. As she had predicted, Madeline was staring directly at her under a curtain of black hair parted down the middle; she was holding a retractable permanent marker that she clicked in and out so rhythmically that Allison could feel it rather than hear it.

She tried to erase Madeline from her mind now as she saw her grandmother walking back to the car holding an envelope stuffed with cash. "Wow, is that for me?" Allison asked, trying to joke.

"Fat chance," Grandma said, raising her eyebrows conspiratorially as she stashed the money in her bra and backed the car out of the parking space. "We're taking this straight to the bank."

The next day, Allison woke up late. The suitcase she hadn't bothered to unpack was splayed open on the floor beside a wicker armoire. To the right of the window was a framed poster of the Serenity Prayer, written in Papyrus font, a sandy beach trail overlooking the ocean in the background.

Allison wandered into the living room in her pajamas, treading barefoot over the light maroon carpet. Grandma's threadbare brown velour recliner with enormous armrests was sitting empty in front of the TV, which was tuned to the local news.

She found Grandma on the patio, sitting in a camping chair smoking a cigarette and drinking through a straw from a can of iced tea. She wore a white visor and another crewneck sweatshirt, this one with a purple mountain landscape graphic. Allison tried to shove the sliding-glass door open, needing all her weight to heave the door to the side.

"Good morning, Grandma," Allison greeted as she poked her head out the door. It was already blazing hot outside.

"Good morning, petunia. Do you want some iced tea? I have Pop-Tarts for breakfast if you're hungry."

Although Allison hated iced tea, Pop-Tarts were one of her favorites. Grandma dragged herself out of the camping chair to follow Allison back into the house. Allison's heart sank as Grandma retrieved a carton of generic toaster pastries from the cabinet—she considered generic Pop-Tarts so inferior to the original that they were practically inedible. Not wanting to seem ungrateful, she broke her breakfast into small pieces and chewed them very slowly one by one.

"What are we doing today?" Allison asked as she swallowed a dry, miserable bite of food.

"Well, we could visit the shoe store," Grandma suggested. Allison perked up—she loved to shop, and perhaps Grandma would treat her to some stylish souvenir. "I need new orthotics, my plantar fasciitis is killing me. Or there's a *Matlock* marathon this afternoon. We could make popcorn." Allison tried to conceal her disappointment. "Or . . . we could play a game."

Allison noticed that Grandma wore the same conspiratorial expression she had when she returned to the car yesterday in the Rugs Plus parking lot. "Do you know gin rummy?" she asked.

"No, but I'm happy to learn," Allison said, trying to appear confident—or at least accommodating.

"There's a deck of cards in the drawer." Grandma pointed at her kitchen junk drawer. As Allison rummaged through the clutter, she found a trove of nubby golf pencils, chip bag clips, assorted condiment packets, and an ancient silver plastic membership card for the Desert Diamond Casino. She located a box of cards featuring a photo of a red steam train, the words *Silver Dollar City* written in a yellow Western font.

Grandma shuffled the deck and dealt them each eleven

cards, placing the remaining cards facedown in a neat pile in the center of the table. She turned the top card of the deck over and explained that the goal was to create melds of sets or runs. She showed Allison how to match combinations of cards while discarding "deadwood," which were cards that didn't belong with any of the sets or runs you were collecting. The hand ended when a player "knocked" or "went gin," and the first player to reach one hundred points won the game. Allison was surprised at how intrigued she was—she felt alert and engaged for the first time in weeks.

Grandma's column on the sheet of scrap paper they were using to keep score quickly filled up and totaled 121. She continued to dominate the next several games as the rules she had explained slowly became more concrete in Allison's mind. But even when Allison thought she had an intellectual grasp on the mechanics of the game, she felt embarrassed when some turns took her several minutes to deliberate. Eventually, she'd hear Grandma's rings tapping on the table restlessly and she would discard a random card to select a new one from the deck.

By the middle of the seventh game, the thrill Allison had experienced when they first began playing was wearing off. Despite feeling like an abject loser, she was determined to keep playing, hoping to win at least one hand. The tarnished cover of her anatomy textbook flashed in her mind, and the *click-click-click* of Madeline's permanent marker pulsed in her ears.

"I can't get the hang of this. None of my cards belong together," Allison said, finally exasperated.

"Allison, you just learned this game. Take your time, don't rush, and try to look at things carefully. If you want my advice, don't reject the cards in your hand until you've really given yourself time to consider how each one might fit with the others."

Allison studied her cards and organized them by suit, scanning for combinations.

"While we're on the subject," Grandma said, "don't be so quick to reject yourself, either. You are so bright and beautiful, even if you can't see it right now. You just have to keep playing one hand at a time."

Allison kept staring at her cards. She worried that if she looked up and met Grandma's eyes, she'd start crying and never stop. The loss and rejection she had experienced felt like a second skin, part of her identity. Mom. Martin. Madeline—they all felt so close, like they were living inside her head even though they were hundreds of miles away.

Allison rearranged her cards into numerical order and was shocked to see two runs and a set of three of a kind. She didn't know how she hadn't seen them before.

"You want to keep playing?" Grandma asked.

Allison nodded firmly as she laid a card facedown. Knock. When they totaled up the score, Allison had won the hand by three points.

"Is it my turn to deal?" she asked, snatching up the deck

to shuffle the cards. "Eleven cards, right?"

Grandma leaned over to pinch Allison's cheek lightly as she stood. She pulled another carton of generic Pop-Tarts from the cupboard and found a new sheet of scrap paper to keep score. "I think it's snack time," she said.

The following day, Grandma drove Allison to the grocery store to pick up more Pop-Tarts. They passed thorny saguaros and smooth, grassy golf courses as Allison wondered how anything survived in this heat.

"Your mom and I used to play gin rummy," Grandma said. "She really had a knack for it, even as a little girl. I just had to help her with the math."

"Did she ever win?" Allison asked.

Grandma scrunched her eyebrows as her lips tensed. "Once in a while," she said after a pause. "I got a whole lot of practice back in those days. Too much practice . . ."

Allison could see Grandma's bejeweled knuckles turn white as they tightened around the steering wheel. "Your mom forbade me from smoking around you, but I'm dying. Would you mind if I have a quick cigarette?" she asked as she rolled down the front windows of the Buick. Allison squirmed as the stifling heat permeated the car.

"No," Allison said. She genuinely didn't mind, and she could sense that Grandma was getting a little distressed.

"I did the best I could for your mom," Grandma said as she blew smoke out the window. "And I know your mom is doing her best for you. But you really scared her, Allison."

She nodded quietly, looking out the window. "I know, Grandma."

Grandma parked outside the grocery store and handed Allison a twenty-dollar bill from inside her shirt.

"Why don't you go on ahead? I'm just going to finish this smoke." Allison was delighted to have an opportunity to buy brand-name Pop-Tarts before Grandma could suggest generic ones.

Allison scampered into the supermarket and quickly filled her basket with as many Pop-Tarts as she could afford for twenty dollars. She chose an empty checkout line and waited for a gaunt bald man with liver spots covering the backs of his hands to motion for her to approach.

"Would you like a bag, young lady?" he asked.

"Yes, please," she answered as she handed him the cash.

"You live around here?" he pried. He gave Allison the creeps, and she could feel his eyes fixating on her, scrutinizing her appearance.

"No. I'm visiting from Oregon," she said.

"Oregon, eh? You look pretty exotic to me. Where are you really from?" he asked in a suspicious tone.

Allison suddenly felt light-headed, and her eyes narrowed with indignation. She had gotten this question from strangers periodically throughout her life, and it always rattled her. She did not have much information about her birth parents, or their ancestry, and as offensive as she knew this question was, she longed to know the answer.

"Um, Oregon," she said in a monotone voice as she stared down at her sneakers.

That instant, Grandma appeared behind Allison and gripped her shoulder protectively. Her heavy rings almost felt like armor. The man's eyes widened in shock.

"Good grief, she just told you that," Grandma said impatiently as she held out her hand for the receipt.

"I was just being friendly," he said defensively.

"Don't worry about him, Allison. He's clueless," Grandma said, fishing for her keys in her handbag as they walked back to the car.

"It's no big deal, Grandma. It happens."

Grandma stopped to look at Allison appraisingly, as though she could ascertain just how "big of a deal" it was based on her countenance. After a few moments, she asked Allison if she had her driver's license.

"No. Just my learner's permit. I can't take the driver's test until I'm sixteen."

Grandma threw her the keys to the Buick. "You'll take us home."

"I think that's illegal," Allison protested weakly after she caught the keys with both hands. "I'm not allowed to drive out of state."

"ILL-EAGLE?" Grandma shrieked dismissively, spitting on the hot asphalt. "No, we won't be deterred by a sick bird."

Allison looked at her incredulously. "What if I get pulled

over?" she said, feeling as enticed by the prospect of driving Grandma's car as she was anxious about getting caught driving out of state.

"I'm sure you're a better driver than most of the folks on the road here."

Allison pulled her lips to one side, still unsure.

"Let's boogie," Grandma said as she opened the passenger door.

After buckling her seat belt, Allison adjusted the driver's seat and the mirrors, like her mom had shown her. She was about to turn the key in the ignition when Grandma stopped her.

"I think we need to get your hair out of your eyes," Grandma said as she tucked Allison's hair behind her right ear, revealing her rose-colored birthmark.

"There's Grandma's little strawberry," she said, giving Allison's cheek a slight pinch between her fingers.

"Ew, Grandma! It's disgusting," Allison said, swatting Grandma's hand away.

"How dare you! It's adorable," Grandma retorted as Allison turned on the engine. "I think it looks very distinguished."

As Allison pulled out of the parking lot, Grandma turned the stereo off. "Sorry, Buck," she said. "It'll help you see better."

Allison had to sit as tall as she could to see over the long beige hood. The purple tint on the back window distorted the clear, sunny sky in the rearview mirror.

Grandma gave directions on the drive back home, sometimes delivering her prompts too late for Allison to make the turns comfortably. The route was consequently circuitous and took much longer than it should have, but when Allison finally pulled into the garage, she felt the same sense of accomplishment she had after she won her first hand of gin rummy. This boost of confidence thrilled her, and she dreamed of the independence she'd enjoy when she finally got her driver's license.

Her phone rang a few minutes after they arrived back at Grandma's house. It was Beverly calling to let her know her marching band had failed to place in the competition. They were about to leave for a medieval-themed dinner theater.

"I'm so sorry," Allison said consolingly.

"About not placing? Or about the ridiculous dinner theater?" Beverly asked.

"Both," Allison said as they laughed.

"Also, Madeline's cousin Terry plays trombone in the band, and he says that Madeline got suspended next week. Something about defacing school property. Anyway, how are you doing?" Beverly asked.

"Not as bored as I thought I'd be," Allison admitted. "Grandma taught me this card game she used to play with Mom."

"That's cool. But how are you *really* feeling?" Beverly pressed.

Allison hesitated, trying to honestly assess her emotions. Somewhere between her distress about Mom and Martin, her shame about her birthmark, and her anxiety about Madeline, she could sense a small but sturdy bit of space opening up for herself. She recalled the pride she felt when she won her first hand of gin rummy after so many losses.

"I'm feeling hopeful, I guess," she finally said. She started to tell Beverly about getting to drive Grandma's car, when her sister interrupted her.

"I'm sorry! I have to go, we're leaving for dinner," Beverly said. "Give Grandma a hug for me."

Allison entered the kitchen, where Grandma had set up another game of gin rummy.

She walked to Grandma's seat at the kitchen table and put her arms around her shoulders. "This is from Beverly," she said. "Her band lost the competition."

"Can't win them all," Grandma said with a shrug as she sorted the cards in her hand.

"I suppose not," Allison said as she picked up her hand and examined the cards with an unfamiliar ease.

On her last day in Tucson, Allison was scheduled to fly home at noon. As she was packing, Grandma came into her room and threw the deck of cards into her suitcase.

"Something to remember me by," she said as she sat on the bed. "You should play with your mother—maybe she will remember this deck of cards. We bought it as a souvenir from our family reunion in Branson when she was about your age."

Allison turned the box of cards over in her hands, staring at the photo of the red steam train.

Grandma was quiet for a few seconds, her eyes fixed on the framed poster of the Serenity Prayer, seemingly lost in thought. "Well, are you nearly finished packing? We should get you to the airport soon," she said.

At the airport, Grandma got out of the car in front of the departures terminal and gave Allison a long, tight hug.

"Before you go, one more thing." Her hand dove into the collar of her shirt, and she seemed to be fishing something out of her sweatshirt. She handed Allison a hundred-dollar bill. "This is for you. Don't tell your mother or Beverly."

"Wow," Allison said, stunned, as she stared at the crispy green bill in her hand. "I don't deserve this."

"Consider it your prize money for beating me at gin rummy."

"Beat you?" Allison argued. "I could hardly keep up with you."

"Just take it, Allison. You don't have to earn every nice thing someone does for you."

Allison folded the bill gently and tucked it into her front pocket. "Thank you, Grandma," she acquiesced.

"I love you so much, daffodil," Grandma said. "Please look after yourself."

"I will," Allison said, again afraid that she would burst into tears.

She made her way to the terminal door, toting her suitcase behind her, and turned to wave at Grandma as she drove away.

As she waited at the gate for her flight, she looked up the rules for gin rummy on her phone and realized that Grandma's rules were not correct. She should have dealt ten cards, not eleven, but Allison knew that she would continue to play Grandma's way for the rest of her life, dealing one extra card to meld or discard.

GLIDE

BY LISA NOPACHAI

It's a weird feeling: one that doesn't happen a lot, but is hard to describe when it does. It happened again during an after-school yearbook meeting with my best friends, Emily and Gwen. We were supposed to be doing photo layouts for the senior class, but instead, we were trying to find a date to throw a surprise birthday party for our friend Michaela. We'd all known each other since preschool.

"That weekend isn't going to work for me," I said when Gwen mentioned a date a couple of weeks out.

Emily turned to me. "Isn't that your *colored people's* weekend *thing*?" she asked, in a tone that was . . . condescending? Annoyed? I couldn't put my finger on it. But does anyone even say "colored people" anymore? Ugh. I tried to hide my eye roll.

"Yes," I said. "The diversity open house at a college I'm looking at." I had mentioned to her last week that the school invited students of color.

"Right," she said, and the conversation moved on.

But I couldn't shake that feeling so quickly. That weird, uncomfortable feeling. I guess it's the sense of being so close to someone, yet realizing that our experiences are so far apart.

I also couldn't stop thinking about the upcoming open house.

A letter had arrived in my mailbox a couple of months earlier, inviting me to attend Ausueden College's Diversity Open House weekend for prospective students. I was one of three brown girls in the sea of white that made up Dalewood High School's senior class of 145 kids. Our small New Jersey town was 96 percent white, something I usually tried to ignore.

Looking at this invitation, I was intrigued. Ausueden College was a good school, and the open house was free, so I signed up.

I wasn't even sure how the school got my info. Maybe through standardized testing? The few times I had to fill out a "race/ethnicity" section on something, I never felt sure of what to put.

Ever since I was little, my parents were super open about the fact that my younger sister and I were both adopted at birth and that we were Mexican American. People always said we looked alike, with our tan skin; thick, wavy black hair; and big brown eyes. I thought it was kind of funny, since we weren't actually blood-related, but I guess, as some of the only kids in town who looked like that, we stood out.

Like I said, I tried to ignore it. I tried to brush off kids touching or sticking objects in my hair because it wasn't smooth and straight like theirs. It was hard to ignore when I went to the mall and got followed around by the sales people. It definitely happened to me more than to my friends, who didn't look like me. I'm not sure it ever happened to them at all.

During the standardized tests we had to take in school, I would move my cursor across the screen and, slowly, with uncertainty, click on the "Hispanic/Latino" box. I would still feel somewhat fraudulent as I scrolled down to the next question.

So I guess that's how Ausueden College got my info.

The rest is history. I went to the weekend. I danced my heart out at a party on Saturday night, where the walls of the dorm were literally dripping with sweat from everyone's dancing. I had great conversations with the other high school kids and the college girls—"hosts"—who let me crash in their dorm room. I went to a class (History 338: The Age of Jim Crow) and enjoyed the pasta and salad bars at the dining hall.

I walked around with awe and freedom, soaking in the fact that for once, I didn't stand out. My hair, my skin, my body . . . could finally blend into a sea of bodies that all looked so different and beautiful—from every background, from all over the country and the world.

I could picture myself there.

I applied, got in, and that's how I ended up as a student at one of the most diverse liberal arts colleges in the country.

My roommate's name was Anna. She was five feet one and small-framed, with a short bob haircut. She was Korean American, from Queens, New York, and she loved playing Ultimate Frisbee. She drank more cups of coffee each day than I could count. And she was a painter. When I walked into our dorm room on the first day and saw her artwork, I was stunned. The first one I saw was a painting she'd done of a teddy bear . . . a childhood toy, maybe? It was so realistic that I felt like it was a photograph.

We'd gotten along well, which was great, especially since neither of us had known anyone else in the freshman class as we'd entered college.

"Hey, Emma!" Anna burst into our dorm room breathlessly, sweat dripping down her face after jogging up four flights of stairs to our hall. She preferred the stairs over elevators because she never wanted to waste an opportunity to exercise. It was a Saturday morning. I was in the middle of typing up a paper on Piaget for Psychology 101.

"Do you wanna go to New York?" she asked, collapsing

on her bed. I looked up at her.

"TODAY?!" she added, sitting up with enthusiasm.

"Um. What??" I stared at her, slightly annoyed that I lost track of the sentence I was in the middle of writing, but also curious.

New York City was nearly four hours away from Ausueden by car.

"My mom has been trying to get tickets to *KPOP*, the musical, *forever*, and she finally got some for me and her to go tonight. I don't have an extra ticket for you, but you said you have a friend from high school who's in Manhattan. You wanna go with me, and I could drop you off by her?"

Hmm. I forgot about Piaget and started imagining New York City.

"Sorry for the short notice, but . . . think about it!" she said enthusiastically, hopping off the bed and grabbing an overnight bag from her closet. "I'm going to leave sometime in the next couple hours, so just let me know, okay?"

Oh, man. How was I supposed to write this paper? I tried to get back to it, but my mind kept wandering to skyscrapers. Walking down Fifth Avenue. Seeing Gwen, who went to school at NYU.

Who was I kidding? I was in.

In New York City, I got out of Anna's car with my peacock-blue backpack and stepped onto the sidewalk in front of

288

Gwen's building, a few blocks north of Manhattan's famous Washington Square Park.

Dalewood, where I grew up, was only about thirty miles away from there, but my parents had never been really big on letting me go into the city. They got nervous about safety.

I waved goodbye to Anna, turned around, and watched as Gwen burst out of the building. She ran up, threw her arms around me, and practically lifted me off the ground. "I've missed you, girl!"

"Ah! I've missed you, too!"

She barely took a breath when she talked. "Welcome to NYC! You're really here! So, I'm interning as a DJ at the college radio station and don't get off till late, but we can meet up later and go OUT, girl!" She added, "I tried to change my shift, but no one else could take it on such short notice. I wish I could hang out now, but feel free to explore the city! Let's meet up back here at eleven fifteen and we'll go to a couple of parties I heard about. Sound good?"

"Yes! I can't believe I'm here either."

"And I don't wanna forget to give you this." She slipped a card into my hand. "You need this to get anywhere around here."

She gave me a few tips for riding the subway from her stop, recommended riding up to Times Square and walking back down to NYU for some good exploring, said she needed to get going, and told me to have fun until we met up. And then she was gone.

Wait. What?

Am I actually in New York City? By myself, with hours to explore?

I looked all around me, taking it in. I looked up, feeling tiny in the shadow of skyscrapers.

Emma, don't look up. It makes you look like a tourist, which makes you a target. Come on, be safe. My parents' voices in my head.

Instead, I looked around at eye level. Again, taking it all in.

New York City seemed to me to be a sea of bodies and cars and buildings and concrete and pavement. A whirlwind of exhaust fumes and blaring car horns paired with road rage. It was snippets of conversations in dozens of different languages.

A man yelling into his cell phone over here. A bodega owner sweeping out front over there as a jogger passed by. Ceramic cups and plates clinking against each other, tossed into a brown plastic bin by a busboy at a sidewalk café with a vine-covered trellis. Bodies trying to maintain some personal space, but inevitably brushing up against each other, because that's just what 8.8 million people do.

I breathed out, not even realizing I'd been holding my breath.

Joy. To me, it all just looked and sounded like joy.

On Forty-First Street, I ate the best slice of pizza of my life.

I sat on a stool at the three-seater Formica counter overlooking the sidewalk on the other side of the glass. Every kind of person walked by. Young, old, from every ethnic background. Some dressed trendy, looking like they walked off a magazine shoot. Some wearing probably the only shirt they owned.

I couldn't get enough of people watching. If each person's life was a book, I would have an incredible, endless library before my very eyes. What were their lives like? Where did they come from? What did they love? What were their deepest—maybe even secret—dreams and hopes?

I threw away my greasy paper plate and napkin and wandered toward Bryant Park, gaping at Fashion Week banners and tents and feeling the infectious energy as I got closer. I watched rich people dine luxuriously on the open-air patio at the fancy restaurant on the green, imagining what it must be like to see the world through their eyes. I was having a hard time imagining it. My family never ate at places like that.

I continued on, walking past store after store containing endless rolls of fabrics in every color and pattern and intricacy imaginable. I didn't even know places like this existed.

I entered the cavernous halls of Grand Central Station and enjoyed the echoes that filled its cool marble floors and walls.

As the sun began to set behind the buildings, I could picture myself living and working in this city one day.

It was the music that drew me in.

I heard the bass pulsing in the distance, which was nothing new for a city that never sleeps.

But it was the trumpet crescendos, the shakers and the overlapping percussion beats. The complexity of chords, or at least chord changes I wasn't used to in the Top 40 pop or hip-hop I listened to.

The strings in the background. The fun staccato piano riffs. The Spanish that I didn't understand much of, sounding beautiful.

The feeling that this music ran in my blood.

I didn't know my own blood very well, not nearly as well as most other people knew their roots, probably. But I knew how to explore. That's what I'd been doing all day.

The salsa music drew me in.

I walked down a long hallway that connected the city street to the inside of what looked like a restaurant-nightclub combo. It felt like I was being transported into an entirely new world.

The hallway opened into a narrow ballroom with a tall ceiling and a stage. There were empty tables and booths, where it looked like people might eat and drink later. The night was still young, though, and the room was brightly lit.

"Are you here for the salsa lesson?" a young woman at the entrance said to me. Her long black hair flowed down her back, and she was wearing a white-beaded crop top, jeans, and heels. "They just got started," she said.

"Um. Sure!" I had enough cash on me to cover the cost of the lesson.

I knew that Gwen and I would be going out to a party or something fun later on, so I had stashed some cute golden heels in my bag. After sitting at one of the empty booths to change into the shoes, I stuck my things under a dark-looking table, where I could keep an eye on them from the dance floor. I joined the group. Everyone lined up facing the teacher, to warm up by following some simple moves.

I had never danced salsa, but it seemed like a fun Latin style. Much more fun than, say, tango. During college orientation week I'd attended a free tango workshop at one of the Campus Center events. We were partnered with some experienced students from the Ausueden Tango Club, which was made up of a few kids who had studied abroad in Buenos Aires, Argentina, and fallen in love with the sultry and serious dance style. Dancing during that workshop with people I had just met was just . . . low-key embarrassing. We kept rotating partners, and I kept stepping on toes, resisting getting too close, and just not getting it. I'd been paired up with one especially serious guy, and I couldn't help it; I burst out laughing in his face, completely unable to embody the lustful nature the dance called for. Or, maybe, unwilling.

"You haven't done this before, have you?" he'd said dryly. So awkward!

But it seemed like salsa was different. Salsa even *sounded* more fun. And from what I had seen walking in and watching the teachers dance together before class, salsa was twirls and hip-shaking and flair. Positive energy. I could do that. That was much more . . . *me*.

The teacher had us do some basic steps side to side and front to back. *Okay, I can do this!*

One-two-three . . . five-six-seven . . .

Over and over, we counted . . .

Soon the teachers brought us into two circles of people facing each other. We each paired up with a partner from the opposite circle. In salsa, it turns out, there are leaders and followers. The leader guides the follower and is in charge of deciding what moves they're going to do together. The teachers said that the followers' job is to "listen" to the body movements of the leader and to respond with our own bodies.

I saw some women in the leaders' circle, which was mostly made up of men, and one guy in the followers' circle, which was mainly ladies. *Cool, cool*, I thought. *Maybe I should join the leaders*. I was used to leading things. In high school, it seemed like I was always taking on some student leadership role or organizing events. Or party planning with and for friends. I loved that kind of thing. If I was honest with myself, I liked being in control of what was going on and when. It gave me a kind of peace.

Maybe that's why a little voice—my heart? . . . my conscience? . . . God?—told me that I needed to stay put. Maybe it was my turn to learn how to follow. I guess I always thought that following meant I was just being passive, or even irresponsible. *Don't be a follower,* my parents always said. I never thought of following as something that could be learned, or that there might be something good about it.

I stayed where I was. The teachers encouraged us to introduce ourselves to the person from the opposite circle who was standing in front of us.

"Soy Alejandro," my first partner said. He was probably a little older than me, a tall guy with kind eyes and a form-fitting collared shirt. "¿Vienes aquí a menudo?" he asked.

Oh. Um. I guess I look like I speak Spanish. I've gotten this before. And I've *always* frozen. Because despite trying to learn some of the language in school, I've been terrible at actually using it in real life. To me, it's always been a classroom thing, like biology or algebra. If you put me behind a desk with a test on what he just said, I'd be good. I would've prepared and studied. I probably would've gotten an A or B-plus, for sure.

But I had no idea what he just said to me, and now I felt super awkward because I'd been staring at him for a few seconds with, I'm sure, a strange and panicked look on my face.

"No . . . um . . . hablo mucho español," I said awkwardly, with none of the inflection of a native speaker, because, well, I wasn't a native speaker. Trying to add that felt strange to me, even though this language was probably somewhere in my blood. A language I had learned as the only Latina—besides the teacher—in classrooms filled with white, non-Latino students. In seventh grade, my teacher had even been a non-Latina white woman who was learning the language herself.

So. This was an uncomfortable moment.

"Got it," Alejandro said, smiling and switching effortlessly to English. His warm smile and his English made me feel relieved. We talked a little bit before trying out the dance moves we were supposed to practice together.

"Switch!" one of the teachers called out, letting us know it was time for the circle of followers to move to the right, to the next partner.

Round and round we went with different partners, learning footwork and spins. "Make your arm into an *L* shape when he holds your hand to spin you," the teacher said, "and you'll be able to turn in a more stable way." When I tried it, it made a huge difference in how fast I could go. It was fun to see results.

The lesson flew by, and soon enough, as we were practicing the final short routine in pairs, the lights started to dim and more people started trickling into the ballroom.

Serious dancers started coming out on the dance floor as we newbies drifted to the edges with *one-two-three . . . five-six-seven* ringing in our ears.

A thirtysomething Latina woman—wavy hair, bright red lipstick, and a vibrant, flowing emerald-colored dress—was asked to dance. Her partner took her by the hand and led her out to the floor, where it seemed like they had some beautiful secret between them, expressed through their bodies. They were in perfect sync with each other and the music. She laughed when he did certain moves, and he spun her around and around. Was that four times in a row? How did she not fall on her face?

Her arms flowed through the air with ease and grace and beauty as her hips swayed and her feet went exactly where his body guided her. There were times when each of them danced on their own, across from each other, playing off of each other's moves.

It was her laughter and the glint in her eyes that stood out to me the most. It all seemed so easy. And so fun.

Very different from my own *one-two-three . . . five-six-seven* and stepping on toes. Seeing this couple's ease, along with others now out there on the dance floor, made me want to learn so badly.

I caught Alejandro's eye. He came over with his hand out, inviting me to dance. We stiffly practiced our beginner's routine from class, trying hard not to bump into anyone else. The dance floor had filled up fast.

The night went on, and slowly others from the class trickled out of the ballroom. Two of the more experienced dancers asked me to dance, but I could tell that they were kind of disappointed when I kept missing their cues. One was really nice and helped me learn a few things. The other guy was either super bored or annoyed, or both. I couldn't tell.

Sweaty, thirsty, and with tired feet, I grabbed the water bottle from my backpack under the table and plopped down. Wow, I was exhausted.

I looked at my watch. It was almost time to meet Gwen downtown. I drank in my final gazes at the flowing dresses, the bodies moving seamlessly together.

The subway ride downtown gave my aching feet a chance to rest before meeting up with Gwen and her friends at a party near their place.

A bearded man, probably in his forties, entered the subway car. He had a suit and a hat made entirely out of aluminum foil. Entirely. A wire hanger stuck out of the top of the hat. The antenna, I was guessing. This was just another evening in New York City.

What stood out to me more than the man's outfit was how nobody around me looked at him twice. I was surprised when a warm feeling washed over me. I didn't know where it came from, but I savored it.

And then it hit me. Here I was, in another place where I didn't stand out. I had never in my life been in so many spaces where my hair, my skin, and my body could blend into a sea of bodies that all looked so different. And no one looked twice.

The next morning, Anna pulled up to the curb in front of Gwen's building.

"Hey, Emma! How was your night in New York?" she asked as I settled into the seat of her SUV and put my backpack on the floor between my feet.

Liberating. Illuminating. New. Exciting. Revealing. Confusing. Fun. Scary. Interesting. Awkward. Maybe . . . life-changing?

"It was good," I said. "Really good."

I looked out the window at the bodegas and buildings and people as we drove down Fifth Avenue, starting the four-hour trek back to Ausueden. The beat of the salsa music from last night was still ringing in my head: *One-two-three, five-six-seven. One-two-three, five-six-seven.* I thought of the women who twirled and glided through the air. They had long ago stopped counting every beat.

Maybe that's what growing up was kind of like. Moving from the awkwardness of counting each and every step to dancing through it with flow, confidence, grace. Joy. Effortless, in large part due to the work and effort put in over years.

I hope I get there one day. I want to be one of those gliding, twirling, laughing women.

Not just with salsa dancing, but with everything. With being in new places. With friends. With romance. Maybe even with speaking Spanish. Getting to know who I am as a person, with so many parts of myself and my story, with so many of those pieces hidden from even my own view.

One day, I will glide.

THE DREAM DEALER'S AUDITION

BY SUN YUNG SHIN

It was hard for most people to believe that there was a time when nearly everyone dreamed, every night, sometimes multiple times a night.

Eleanor had been born into this new dreamless world, but she was different.

Twelve years ago, one morning when she was five years old, she woke up in her toddler bed with the owl print, picked up her blankie, walked down the hallway to her parents' bedroom, and started telling them everything she remembered about her dream. She was in the ocean, floating gently on her back, just like at swimming lessons, and she was looking up at the big blue sky, except instead of clouds, there appeared to be islands hovering far above, peacefully and slowly cruising overhead, their green trees and violet mountains visible at an angle. Her parents looked at each other in wonder and began to weep gently, as neither of them had ever had a dream in their lives without the help of a "dream dealer."

"Why are you crying?" asked Eleanor, rubbing her eyes.

"We're just happy," said her father, his eyes bright.

"Our daughter is a dreamer," her mother said, half to herself. No one in their families had been a dreamer. They knew when they adopted Eleanor that she might be a dreamer, but it was a very remote possibility, and they didn't dare to hope. Being good parents, they also didn't want to put unrealistic expectations on their child, who had already been through the ordeal of losing her mother, and everything that went with that loss, and had been relocated halfway around the globe to be raised by a pair of strangers.

"She can become a dream dealer when she gets older," Eleanor's father whispered. "She can help people."

"I don't want to be a dream dealer, I want to be a raccoon," said Eleanor.

"Oh really, what's so fun about being a raccoon?" said her father, reaching over to tousle her dark hair, mussed from sleep.

"They have *snack journals*," Eleanor said proudly, gesturing boldly with her old blankie like a miniature conductor leading an orchestra with a floppy, faded blue flannel rectangle that had frayed edges.

"Um. Do you mean they're *nocturnal*?" asked her mother with an inquisitive look.

"That's what I said, silly," replied Eleanor, who then yawned, flopped down at the foot of her parents' bed, and promptly fell asleep. Her parents gazed her at for moment as if seeing her for the first time. Then her father picked her up and tucked her back into her own bed, and then they both went to their laptops and began frantically research-ing everything they could about the best ways to raise a dreaming child.

Dreamify was the name of the massive global corpora-tion that had purchased and then further developed the most successful dream-dealing methods and technologies, and Eleanor's parents had worked there during their entire careers. Her father, James, was a sound engineer, and her mother, Anne, was a biochemist. They knew all about the science of what was called "dream dealing," but hadn't, until now, needed to know anything about raising some-one who practiced it.

As the years went on, it became clear that Eleanor was becoming a powerful dreamer—a lucid dreamer, which was even rarer among the tiny population of dreamers—and had a possibly unlimited future as a dream dealer, should she choose it. And Eleanor downplayed the ability, didn't talk about it, and tried to be a kid just like everyone else.

Not every dreaming person wanted to be a dream dealer, even though there was fame and fortune to be had. A dreamer might have another talent, such as music, or math, and want to pursue those. A dreamer might not want that kind of contact with other people, which could feel too intimate. A dreamer might not want the responsibility for so many other people's well-being. And there were some risks to the psyche of the dreamer. As with any gift, one had to take care not to burn too bright or burn out like a supernova, not to disappear into the dreamworld or succumb to the magic of that sometimes intoxicating and slippery realm.

The ability to dream seemed to be genetically inherited, but Eleanor had been adopted from Korea, and the Korean agency said she was abandoned and found at a police station with no name or identifying information. Thus her adoptive parents, Anne and James, could not tell her how exactly she had inherited the means to spend some of her sleeping hours not in blank nothingness, but in dreams.

A dream dealer could transfer their dreams to another person, or could create a new dream for them or recombine pieces of their or other people's dreams, depending on the "bets" the person had made and whether they had won or lost. A losing bet didn't mean a nightmare, it just might mean a less intense dream, or a less personal dream, but that wasn't a bad thing. The combination of free will, choice, randomness, memory, imagination, the subconscious, and collective imagery was what was nourishing to the human mind, the body, at sleep.

Eleanor's desire to audition had taken her by surprise, but she had to admit that something had shifted inside her recently.

When she saw the notice on the board at her high school, it had been a day like any other, but she had had intense dreams the night before, which she didn't remember, but she had woken up crying, her pillow wet with tears, which was unusual. She wasn't a particularly sad or even passionate person—she tended to be a bit on the aloof side, self-contained, an observer—but something was happening in her dreams. As Anne's belly grew bigger over the months and the baby inside was becoming more and more of a person, kicking and stretching, Eleanor's dreams were getting more emotional.

Eleanor often dreamed about her family. Her mom, dad, and now her sister. Except, in her dreams, they were faceless, more iconic than real people. Her dreaming mind identified them as *Mother. Father. Sister.* But in her dreams, something like parentheses, or the feeling of parentheses, had begun appearing. And then, against her will, they leaked into her waking day. She found herself using silent parentheses in casual, functional, unremarkable conversation with others, as in, *Hey, Luke, thanks for the offer, but my (adoptive) mom is picking me up from school.* Or *Sarai, do you want to come over? My (adoptive) dad is making dinner tonight.* Or *Sorry, Mx. H, I can't babysit for you Saturday night, I have to watch my (adoptive) baby sister at home.*

One thing that correlated with the gift of dealing dreams was a facility with gambling—the complex set of skills and temperament that successful professional gamblers possessed. This didn't mean that everyone who dreamed enjoyed gambling, or even enjoyed dreaming, but a significant portion of the population had to either gamble for dreams or buy them outright from professional dreamers. Buying them didn't offer the same sense of excitement, surprise, and mystery, but the super wealthy generally preferred it because the dreams were pre-sanitized, and nightmares could be and were filtered out.

After various types of systems—including a brief prohibition on any exchange of dreams, which failed utterly—the governments eventually encouraged and underwrote the institutionalization and regulation of the gambling of dreams, because they eventually found, and accepted, that the more dreams were in circulation, the calmer, happier, and even healthier people were.

Nobody quite knew why the gambling, as opposed to simply purchasing, worked better than most other arrangements, but of course there were many theories and conjectures. The most logical was that gambling most closely matched what used to be the natural pattern of dreaming, as no one had ever understood why we dream in exactly the manner we do. Broadly, perhaps, it had been concluded over the millennia of human experience: You will dream about that which is preoccupying you during the day, that which you have suppressed, that which you have unresolved. You will dream about past lives, about collective ancestral pasts. You will dream about the future. Or futures.

Nevertheless, it could not be predicted exactly what any person would dream about each night and in what order, and how they would feel about it all when they woke up. Dream dictionaries, game theory, swarm theory, string theory—none of it was complex enough. There was something deeply wild about dreams that made their own cosmos each night and unmade it by the morning, leaving only traces of light, glimpses of understanding.

Eleanor had never been to an audition—which meant going in a "dream pod" for the test procedure to become a "dream intern" on the path to potentially becoming a full-time dream dealer, a lucrative job with high job satisfaction, according to research sponsored by life insurance companies and analyzed by their actuaries. Dream casinos accepted interns as young as ten years old. Her parents, believing in career autonomy for young people, hadn't pressured her. They in fact had been surprised when she announced that she wanted to apply for the internship at their local dream casino, which jutted boldly between the farthest point on the beach and the new concrete foundation, meeting the edge of the soft yellowish sand beach and the craggy black rocks and the crashing white waves of the dark blue sea.

Eleanor walked around the bright white building toward the back entrance at exactly five minutes before noon, five minutes before her interview. With the sun high in the sky, she barely made a shadow, which she always found a little unsettling.

Whenever the sun was low in the sky and her figure made a long, dark echo, Eleanor felt solid, like she knew she was *there*, in this world, in this moment, blocking the light that would otherwise go everywhere and through anything that had transparency, cracks, or gaping holes. On a bright day, when shadows were particularly dark, she had the sense of being accompanied, perhaps the way some sets of twins seem to. She knew there was nothing mystical about shadows, that they were just about light and its absence, but she still found them comforting.

As she walked toward the arched entrance and the double doors, she couldn't help but notice that the sand on the nearby beach was the exact color of her mother's hair, and would be the color of her baby sister's hair when she was older. Everyone remarked at how *wow, so blond* her little sister was, admiringly, as if it were an achievement, and although her parents tried not to encourage praise of that nature, Eleanor could tell by their faces that they were pleased. How could they not be? Anne and James had produced a child that other people found beautiful, valuable, literally remarkable.

Eleanor's hair, on the other hand, was the exact same pure black as it was when she arrived, which she didn't mind, although no one except hairstylists ever commented on it—*wow it's so coarse*, or, *it's so black it's almost blue*, or, *it's so stick straight*—but these weren't compliments. Neither were they really insults, but more like when people commented on exotic animals at the zoo. *Hey, look at that one, it can regrow its tail if it gets bitten off!* or, *Amazing, this fish can live on the land for up to eight hours before it needs to go back in the water!*

A young man, slight build, with tortoiseshell glasses, answered the door and looked at her with an air of expectation and polite curiousness.

"Can I help you?" he said.

"I'm Eleanor O'Connor. I'm here for the internship interview."

"Of course! Yes, they're expecting you. Come in, I'll take you to the room," he said, gesturing for her to follow him down the hall.

The young man, who had during the short walk introduced himself as Thomas, delivered her to the promised room and said with a sincere smile, "Good luck."

Eleanor walked into the small, windowless room, which had white walls like the rest of the building, a small table with a raised, tilted screen interface, a white plastic chair, and a seven-foot white metal pod, a new DreamPod3000 with a clear plexiglass shield, lying lengthwise in the middle of the room. It emitted a faint but audible, not unpleasant hum. The shield was up and open.

She sat in the chair and touched the screen. An electronic form appeared, and she began typing in the boxes with the requested information: ELEANOR MIN-YOUNG O'CONNOR, birthdate, address.

Typing her birthdate made her feel strange. Like the feeling she had with her shadow, she couldn't quite put her finger on it. It had never been a secret that this was not her real birthday, that her birthdate had been made up and given to her by social services in Korea, but she had never given it much thought until lately, since her little sister arrived. She was there when tiny Maeve was born; she saw her wet and wrinkled and blind like the motherless kittens she and her friend Luke found in his backyard last summer; she saw her take her first breath; she saw her weighed and measured and given an Apgar score, and saw her swaddled and then returned to the arms of her mother, to reunite with the warm body she had just emerged from.

Although Eleanor could now say, if she wanted to, *This is my little sister, Maeve. We are with our mother,* and it was *legally* true, it felt like a fiction. They weren't the same kind of daughter. Compared with the indivisibility of her mother and Maeve, Eleanor felt a bit like a faraway planet in orbit, visible but not touchable, not connected, not of the same material, not the same color or temperature, locked in a certain fixed distance. Light-years away.

In fact, the first time she held tiny Maeve in her arms, Eleanor felt a strange sensation, as if she were being lifted away, and then all of a sudden she was outside her own body, floating near the ceiling, and looking down on herself, a darker person, a black-haired person, a person who was not related to anyone in the room. In that moment she realized that this baby she was holding—this person, this human—was not going to be separated, processed, renamed, and sent to a different country to listen to a different language, to try to understand what had happened to her, without her consent.

Throughout the whole nine months of her mother's pregnancy, Eleanor had been amazed at the process of forming a new life, how it progressed on its own without much help, how her mother's body changed to accommodate this growing but still tiny person. When the baby began kicking and pushing outward against her mother's belly, Eleanor would put her hand there and marvel. There, inside Anne, was a room in which another human being was growing, safe and protected.

Eleanor's father, James, was a good dad—a laid-back "modern cool dad," caring and attentive—but ultimately, she realized, he was a bit like her, on the outside of the *mother-child*, as Eleanor had started to think of her mom and her sister, even though he had been an essential part of the equation.

After Eleanor typed in her birthdate, the numbers blurred and swam a bit before her eyes, losing meaning, like when you say a common word over and over again. *Umbrella. Umbrella. Umbrella. Umbrella.*

She reached the last section of the intake form.

Do any of your genetic relatives have dream-dealing abilities? Please select all that apply:

- Mother
- Father
- One sibling
- More than one sibling
- More than two siblings
- More than three siblings
- Mother's full sibling
  - How many _____
- Mother's half sibling
  - How many _____
- Father's full sibling
  - How many _____
- Father's half sibling
  - How many
- Maternal grandmother
- Maternal grandfather
- Paternal grandmother
- Paternal grandfather
- First cousins on mother's side

- How many _____
- First cousins on father's side
- How many _____
- Second cousins on mother's side
- How many _____
- Second cousins on mother's side
- How many _____

SUBMIT

She left them all blank. There was no option, no text box for "I do not know any of my genetic relatives."

She clicked the submit button.

Thank you for filling out this application. Your responses have been recorded. Please remove your shoes and then carefully enter the pod to complete this process. The pod session will last 60 minutes, after which time you may leave the building. You will be contacted within 24–48 hours.

Eleanor took off her Vans and left them under the small table. Stepping into the white pod as if it were a bathtub, one foot and then the other, putting her hands on the rim of the pod for balance, she eased herself in and sat down. Once she was inside and sitting up in the reasonably comfortable but narrow encasement, no space wasted, it reminded her of a year and a half earlier, when her dad took her sea kayaking for the first time, for a "fun dad-daughter trip." The plastic kayak didn't look like it would be comfortable, but it was. That was also when he told her that she was going to have a sibling—not because they were adopting, again, but because Anne was pregnant. New drugs had been developed, and one that Anne was taking had worked; suddenly they were no longer dealing with infertility.

"It's a miracle," James had said, smiling, squeezing Eleanor's shoulder reassuringly. Eleanor looked surprised at this use of a religious term. James took the expression on her face as one of concern.

"Don't worry, you'll always be our number one kid."

"I'm not worried, Dad," Eleanor said.

When the baby was born, Eleanor had been there and had watched in amazement as Maeve opened her eyes and stared into Anne's face as if this were the thing she wanted to see most in the world, and vice versa. Later, in the hospital room bathroom, Eleanor looked in the mirror and wondered if her eyes looked the same as they did when she was born. She looked into her own eyes and wondered if they retained the images of the first things she ever saw. She wondered if those images would arrive one day, like long-delayed mail, in her dreams.

The pod began a soft but insistent beeping, and the clear lid began slowly lowering. Eleanor leaned back and lay down inside. The surface running the length of the pod was padded and comfortable, with an attached pillow that cradled her head. The lid shut with a soft click, and the recessed ceiling lights in the room dimmed and then winked out completely, leaving the room in soft darkness, a sliver of light entering from underneath the closed door to the hallway.

Eleanor was comfortable, her breathing deep and even. She'd never had a problem with small spaces. Her parents had told her the story many times of how, after she arrived in their country, their home, she would climb out of her crib in her new bedroom, fall with a thump onto the soft rug, crawl under the crib, and fall asleep there until morning. How at daycare she would hide in the closet before naptime, only to be found by the caregiver every time and placed on her assigned mat, when she lay on her back and looked at the ceiling until it was time to play again. And how even now, as a teenager, she had moved her mattress into her sizable closet and slept there, which her parents allowed with a bemused shrug. She liked small spaces, being able to touch each wall, having her back to the corner. In restaurants and public places, too, if she had a choice, she sought out the most secure location, away from windows, never with her back to the door.

Inside the cool, comfortable DreamPod3000 it was surprisingly pleasant, even though it was made of metal and plexiglass. Its gently curved lines and soft interior made it soothing, as homey and relaxing as if it had been made for her—and she began to dream. The machine began to record not the dream itself, not the images, sounds, places, actions, but the intensity of the feelings, the emotional architecture. This is what people needed, what they needed to borrow from the dreamer.

Sixty minutes was passing inside the pod according to the laws of physics, but in dreamtime, it could feel like days, even though REM sleep sometimes lasted only a handful of minutes. Dreaming was like that, bending time, expanding and contracting space, folding the universe inside the mind. Castles in the inner skies of the body. Museums built then brushed away like dust. Memory palaces, rooms after rooms to enter, then exit.

Eleanor dreamed of her sister Maeve's birth, of her father holding her mother's hands, of herself, Eleanor, holding a baby, having an out-of-body experience. As she relived that memory in her dream, she wasn't afraid. She knew she would come back to her body, as she did in her waking life, after a few minutes.

In her dreams, her shadow was always with her, solid, reliable. She was never truly alone. Even in what others would call nightmares, she wasn't afraid. One of the worst things had already happened to her. She had been abandoned, given away to strangers, as in a lottery. She was a prize, a random one, and that was a lot of pressure to put on someone. In her dreams, her shadow never left her, regardless of the amount of sunlight or the direction she was walking.

Time was up. The pod opened as gently and quietly as it had closed. The lights came back on and the room was once again brightly but comfortably lit from above. Unlike a baby bird, Eleanor didn't have to fight beak and claw to emerge from the egg, she just sat up and stood in the pod, then climbed out, one leg at a time. She felt some affection for the pod that had cradled her, kept her safe for the hour, listening to her, transmitting information, but not invasively. She gave it an affectionate pat, as if it were a nice dog she had just met. "Thanks," she whispered.

She envied the pod its simplicity, its focus of purpose. Built for one thing. It was a dream ship that never had to leave Earth; unlike her, it didn't need to change orbit. She had dreamed of her sisterhood, her daughterhood, but there was something on the horizon in her dream that she couldn't make out. It wasn't necessarily her past or memories, and it wasn't necessarily her future. It wasn't about time. She somehow knew it was about her relationship with herself and living with the promise and the mystery of that. Knowing that there would be things about the real world she would probably never know, like her real birthday, her "real" mother and "real" father and their—her—ancestors.

It wasn't that she didn't care, she *did*, and it burned, the not knowing, and the older she got, the more curious she was and the more keenly she felt the losses, which were in fact innumerable, even as she was aware of the goodness and safety of her present life with her adoptive family. She wasn't that naive. She tried not to romanticize the life she would have had.

Yet, regardless of how she thought about it, she *felt* untethered, and she had the sense she might always feel that way, because she always had. But recently, the dreams had told her that her inner life was as important as her outer life, and that despite humanity's ongoing attempt to organize and categorize everything, there was something universally wild within every living thing.

That she was in fact, like all beings, in some sense, unlimited. Not because she was immortal; she wasn't, at least not in this form. But energetically, yes. Dreams had taught her that *everything* was energy, and energy could neither be created nor destroyed, as her physics teacher had taught her—the first law of thermodynamics, or the law of conservation of energy.

But what had intrigued Eleanor in her physics textbook the most was the zeroth law of thermodynamics, which states that if two systems are in thermodynamic equilibrium with a third system, the two original systems are in thermal equilibrium with each other. Heat, sun, light, energy, matter, equilibrium.

Eleanor intuited that her Korean family, her people, her lineage, the bodies from which she had come, and the DNA from which she was made and carried inside her were the first system. That her American family was the second system, and she herself was the third system.

She felt that there was an equilibrium she carried within her, as one person connecting many. She wasn't connected by DNA or blood with her adoptive mother and her adoptive parents' new child, she was the odd one out there, and would always be, but maybe it was something like *okay*. It was what she had, and it was a life, regardless. What choice did she have but to continue to adapt, to continue to seek equilibrium?

Inside the pod, it seemed that her body remembered the time before being born, the time of development, when she was cells dividing, preprogrammed to do exactly what they had evolved to do, without any external force of direction. The direction was inside, already encoded, millions of years of life on Earth. Her time enclosed in the pod, more enclosed than she'd ever been, truly, since her time in the womb, told her that her ability to dream was for *her*. It wasn't something she had to share or turn into a career.

Eleanor knew she would pass the audition and be offered an internship and, if she wanted, a scholarship to college and a job—a good one—for as long as people needed dreams. It wasn't that she didn't want to help them, but when she emerged from that pod, alone, she realized that she needed to help herself first. She didn't know what she was "born to do," and she wanted to find out.

She bent down and picked up her Vans from under the table, slipped her feet into them, opened the door, and walked out into the hallway. The artificial white glow from the wall sconces fell on her, and she glanced down at her shadow. With no escort in sight, Eleanor walked toward the nearest exit, opened the door, and slipped back into the afternoon sunlight.

AFTERWORD

BY DR. JAERAN KIM

I was that young reader, the one who was constantly being told by adults to put my book down and pay attention to whatever else was happening around me. In one of my favorite photographs of me, I am fourteen years old, holding a book in one hand and loading the dishwasher with the other. The friend who took the photo wrote on the back, "This is how I always remember you, with your nose in a book."

As a Korean transnational adoptee growing up in a white family in Minnesota in the 1970s and 1980s, there were few stories providing what the multicultural children's literature scholar Dr. Rudine Sims Bishop calls "mirrors, windows, and sliding glass doors" for a kid like me. Stories featuring orphans and children informally fostered have always been common tropes in children's literature. But neither my small-town library nor school libraries possessed books that had characters who looked like me or shared my experiences; none of the books featured Korean youths as protagonists, nor did I ever read a story about a transracial adoptee. As a teenager, I would lie on my bed writing stories of girls who looked like me, going to summer camp, longing over a crush, or nervously attending their first day of high school. I was writing stories about myself, for myself. I wish I'd had *this* book and these stories.

As Sims Bishop writes, "Literature transforms human experience and reflects it back to us, and in that reflection, we can see our own lives and experiences as part of the larger human experience. Reading, then, becomes a means of self-affirmation." What does it mean for a young person when what we read offers only distorted mirrors? How can reading offer self-affirmation when we do not see our identities and experiences represented as part of the larger human experience? The human development theorist Erik Erikson identified the adolescent years as the time when the process of figuring out one's identity begins in earnest. Most young people begin to wonder "Who am I?" beyond their roles in their families; research has found that when you are an adoptee, this question is even more complicated. When you do not look like your adoptive family, or if you have little or no information about the people who gave birth to you, trying to figure out who you are can be challenging. Many adoptees have only heard stock responses to the question "Why was I adopted?" If your adoption involved crossing geographic, cultural, and/or racial borders, you might wonder what it would have been like growing up in a different state, country, or racial/ethnic heritage. It is also difficult to feel like you have permission to even ask these questions, in case you are seen as being ungrateful or disloyal to your adoptive family.

Though it is true that more stories featuring adoptees have been published in the forty years since I was a teenager, most of those stories are not authored by adoptees—and that matters. These fifteen adoptee authors imbue their protagonists with insider knowledge of the adoptee experience. The stories in this collection speak to modern adoptee experiences even if the stories themselves take place in the past or the future. The themes of not fitting in, being a racial imposter, and feeling conspicuously different from one's family and community are tenderly expressed. Another theme present is that of ambiguous loss, a concept developed by the family scholar Dr. Pauline Boss to describe the disjointedness and unresolved feelings that accompany relationship disruptions. Although adoption is often seen as being about what is gained (parents, a family, a home), it can be forgotten that for an adoption to happen, a family first had to experience a tremendous loss. A child was separated from their first family, and a family was separated from a child.

And that is why the stories included in this volume are so important. For the millions of youths and adults who were adopted, these stories provide a reflection of themselves and a window through which to see others like them. But, as Sims Bishop would remind us, it is not just that adoptees (especially Indigenous and adoptees of color) need to see their identities and experiences reflected in youth literature. The fact is that those from dominant and majority groups need decentering if they are to develop into compassionate, justice-seeking adults. This book is for everyone—those personally connected to adoption and anyone interested in expanding their understanding of adoptees.

ABOUT THE AUTHORS

Kelley Baker is a transracial adoptee born in Colorado and raised in Northern California. She lives in the San Francisco Bay Area. You can find her on Instagram @kelleydbaker.

Nicole Chung is the author of a new memoir, *A Living Remedy*. Her bestselling first book, *All You Can Ever Know*, was a finalist for the National Book Critics Circle Award, a semifinalist for the PEN Open Book Award, and an Indies Choice Honor Book. Both of her books are official Junior Library Guild crossover selections. Chung's writing has appeared in the *New York Times Magazine*, *The Atlantic*, *Time*, *GQ*, *The Guardian*, and *Slate*, among other publications.

MeMe Collier is a creative writing major turned resident physician who dabbles in various other arts as well, from sketching and painting to singing and writing music. She was raised by her incredible adoptive single mother and grandparents, and the passing of her mother after battling a brain tumor for ten years is a major influence on her desire to pursue medicine and the themes of loss and life afterward that she often explores in her writing. She tries to stay active in the adoptee community, having contributed to the ABC *Adoptees Born in China* podcast, research studies on how international adoptees form their identity, and a discussion panel with the 1882 Foundation. She has never been much for social media, but she has attempted to start a creativity-focused Instagram account and would be happy to chat. You can find her online by following word.doc96.

Shannon Gibney is a writer, educator, activist, and the author of *See No Color* and *Dream Country*, young adult novels that won Minnesota Book Awards, as well the picture book *Sam and the Incredible African and American Food Fight*, and the memoir/novel *The Girl I Am, Was, and Never Will Be: A Speculative Memoir of Transracial Adoption*. She coauthored the children's picture book *Where We Come From*. Gibney teaches writing in the English department at Minneapolis College.

Susan Harness, author of *Mixing Cultural Identities Through Transracial Adoption* and award-winning *Bitterroot: A Salish Memoir of Transracial Adoption*, is a member of the Confederated Salish and Kootenai Tribes as well as an American Indian transracial adoptee. She holds MAs in both cultural anthropology and creative nonfiction from Colorado State University.

Meredith Ireland is a transracial adoptee attorney and writer, born in Seoul. She is a Rollins College and University of Miami School of Law alumna. She writes young adult and children's books. Her debut novel, *The Jasmine Project*, was a Junior Library Guild Gold Standard selection, a Best Book of 2021 according to Boston Public Library, and received a starred review from ALA *Booklist*. Her follow-up, *Everyone Hates Kelsie Miller*, also from Simon & Schuster Books for Young Readers, was named a best book of 2022 by both *Forbes* and *Seventeen* magazine. Her short story is featured in *You Are*

Here, a middle grade anthology and the inaugural title of Allida/Clarion. *Emma and the Love Spell,* her debut middle grade fantasy, will be out in winter of 2024 from Bloomsbury Children's Publishing. Meredith resides in New York with her two children and a county fair goldfish that will probably outlive them all.

Mariama J. Lockington is a transracial adoptee, author, and educator. She has been telling stories and making her own books since the second grade, when she wore shortalls and flower leggings every day to school. Mariama's middle grade debut, *For Black Girls Like Me,* earned five starred reviews and was a *Today Show* Best Kids' Book of 2019. Her sophomore middle grade book, *In the Key of Us,* is a Stonewall Honor Award book and was featured in the *New York Times.* Her debut young adult novel, *Forever Is Now* came out in May of 2023. Mariama holds a master's in education from Lesley University and a master's in fine arts in poetry from San Francisco State University. She calls many places home, but currently lives in Kentucky with her wife, her little sausage dog, Henry, and an abundance of plants. You can find her on Twitter @marilock and on Instagram/TikTok @forblackgirlslikeme.

Lisa Nopachai is a Mexican American transracial adoptee, born in Texas and raised in an Italian American family in New Jersey, where she fell in love with homemade ravioli and loud music. With a BA in psychology from Amherst College and an MA in intercultural studies from Fuller Theological Seminary, Lisa has worked in the fields of child advocacy, interdisciplinary research, and healthcare chaplaincy. Lisa is passionate about creating spaces for people to engage their full range of emotions and process experiences of grief, beauty, pain, and joy. Lisa and her husband live in the Los Angeles area with their two lovely, imaginative kids.

Mark Oshiro is the award-winning author of the young adult books *Anger Is a Gift* (2019 Schneider Family Book Award), *Each of Us a Desert*, and *Into the Light* (Tor Teen), as well as their middle grade books *The Insiders* and *You Only Live Once, David Bravo* (HarperCollins). They are also the coauthor (with Rick Riordan) of the #1 *New York Times* Bestselling *The Sun and The Star*, the first stand-alone Percy Jackson book centered on Nico di Angelo and Will Solace. When not writing, they are trying to pet every dog in the world.

PHOTO BY GRACE SALESSES

Matthew Salesses was adopted from Korea when he was two. He has written about adoption, race, and grief for NPR, the *New York Times, The Guardian, VICE*, and other publications. He is the author of seven books of fiction and nonfiction, including the writing guide *Craft in the Real World* and the PEN/Faulkner short-listed novel *Disappear Doppelgänger Disappear.* He lives in New York with his two kids and is an assistant professor of writing at Columbia University.

DAVID BOYER

Sun Yung Shin was adopted from Korea and was raised in the Chicago area. She is an award-winning multi-genre author or editor of nine books for adults and children, including *Outsiders Within: Writing on Transracial Adoption* coedited with Julia Chinyere Oparah and Jane Jeong Trenka. Her latest books are *Where We Come From*, a picture book co-authored with Diane Wilson, Shannon Gibney, and John Coy, and illustrated by Dion MBD; *The Wet Hex* (poems), and the essay anthology *What We Hunger For: Refugee and Immigrant Stories about Food and Family.* She lives in Minneapolis with her family.

Lisa Wool-Rim Sjöblom was born in Busan, South Korea, and adopted to Sweden at age two. She is a comic book artist and illustrator and has published two graphic novels: *Palimpsest* (2016), an autobiographical account of the search for her Korean family, and *The Excavated Earth* (2022), which follows Chilean adoptees who were stolen and sold for adoption to Sweden. She is a vocal adoptee rights activist and a Swedish Korean Adoptees' Network member, fighting for truth and justice for adoptees and first parents. Lisa lives in Aotearoa, New Zealand, with her partner, two children, and a cat. Follow her on Instagram at @chung.woolrim.

Eric Smith is a literary agent and young adult author from Elizabeth, New Jersey. His recent books include *Don't Read the Comments, You Can Go Your Own Way*, and *Jagged Little Pill: The Novel*, written in collaboration with Alanis Morissette, Diablo Cody, and Glenn Ballard. Together with award-winning author Lauren Gibaldi, he's coedited the anthologies *Battle of the Bands* and *First-Year Orientation*. He enjoys pop-punk, video games, and crying over every movie. He lives in Philadelphia with his wife and son.

Stefany Valentine first fell in love with writing when her elementary school teacher gave her an assignment to create a picture book, and she ended up writing a twenty-page manuscript laced with misspelled words. Since then, she's proudly graduated from writing stories about befriending orca whales to tales about the Taiwanese diaspora and existential sci-fi. Her debut novel, *First Love Language*, in which a Taiwanese adoptee reconnects with her heritage by learning Mandarin, will release with Penguin Workshop in 2025. When not reading or writing, she can be found practicing Mandarin, stuffing her face with street tacos, and trying not to kill her plants. Again.

Jenny Heijun Wills is the author of the multi-award-winning memoir *Older Sister. Not Necessarily Related* (Penguin Random House Canada, 2019). She was born in Seoul and raised in a white family and community in Southern Ontario, Canada. She is currently professor of English and Chancellor's Research Chair at the University of Winnipeg. She is the author of the forthcoming collection of personal essays, *Asian Adopted Queer Hungry* (Knopf Canada, 2024) as well as coeditor of two academic books.

FURTHER READING

Additional materials by adoptees with themes of adoption

Books

A Long Way Home, Saroo Brierley (memoir)

Surviving the White Gaze: A Memoir, Rebecca Carroll

Parenting as Adoptees, Adam Chau and Kevin Ost-Vollmers (anthology)

A Living Remedy and *All You Can Ever Know*, Nicole Chung (memoirs)

See No Color and The Girl I Am, Was, and Will Never Be: A Speculative Memoir of Transracial Adoption, Shannon Gibney (young adult novels)

Bitterroot: A Salish Memoir of Transracial Adoption, Susan Devan Harness (memoir)

The Son with Two Moms, Tony Hynes (memoir)

The Jasmine Project and *Everyone Hates Kelsie Miller*, Meredith Ireland (young adult novels)

I Would Meet You Anywhere, Susan Kiyo Ito (memoir)

Ghost of Sangju: A Memoir of Reconciliation, Soojung Jo

The Adoption Papers, Jackie Kay (poetry)

For Black Girls Like Me, Mariama J. Lockington (middle grade novel)

Disrupting Kinship: Transnational Politics of Korean Adoption in the United States, Kimberly McKee (scholarly text)

The Book of Sarahs: A Family in Parts, Catherine McKinley (memoir)

Black Anthology: Adult Adoptees Claim Their Space, Susan Harris O'Connor, Diane René Christian, and Mei-Mei Akwai, eds. (anthology)

Invisible Asians: Korean American Adoptees, Asian American Experiences, and Racial Exceptionalism, Kim Park Nelson (scholarly text)

Into the Light, Mark Oshiro (young adult novel)

Selling Transracial Adoption: Families, Markets, and the Color Line, Elizabeth Raleigh (scholarly text)

In Their Voices: Black Americans on Transracial Adoption, Rhonda M. Roorda (scholarly text)

The Sense of Wonder and *Disappear Doppelgänger Disappear*, Matthew Salesses (novels)

Unbearable Splendor, Sun Yung Shin (poetry/essays)

Palimpsest: Documents from a Korean Adoption, Lisa Wool-Rim Sjöblom (graphic memoir)

Outsiders Within: Writing on Transracial Adoption, Jane Jeong Trenka, Julia Chinyere Oparah, and Sun Yung

Shin, eds (anthology)

The Language of Blood and Fugitive Visions: An Adoptee's Return to Korea, Jane Jeong Trenka (memoirs)

"You Should Be Grateful": Stories of Race, Identity, and Transracial Adoption, Angela Tucker (nonfiction)

Person, Perceived Girl, A. A. Vincent (poetry)

Older Sister. Not Necessarily Related, Jenny Heijun Wills (memoir)

Tree of Strangers, Barbara Sumner

Approved for Adoption (volume 1 and 2), Jung (graphic novel)

Film

A Story of One's Own (2021, documentary)

Approved for Adoption (2012, animated film based on the comic)

Blood Memory (2019, documentary)*

Closure (2013, documentary)

First Person Plural (2000, documentary)

Geographies of Kinship (2019, documentary)

Girl, Adopted (2013, documentary)*

In the Matter of Cha Jung Hee (2010, documentary)

Off and Running (2009, documentary)*

Struggle for Identity (2008, documentary)

*Although these three documentaries are produced by non-adoptees, I am including them here because they center Native and teenage Black female transracial adoptee experiences and voice—something that is all too uncommon.

Podcasts

ABC Adoptees Born in China podcast

Adapted (explores the experiences of Korean adoptees)

Adopted Feels (Australian Korean adoptees discuss anything adoption-related)

Adoptees On (adult adoptees share life stories and what they've learned)

The Janchi Show (by, for, and about Korean adoptees)

Labor of Love: A Podcast for BIPOC Adoptees Navigating Parenthood (adoptee parents share thoughts and insights)

Websites and blogs

Adoption Mosaic: adoptionmosaic.com

The Alliance for the Study of Adoption and Culture: adoptionandculture.org

Harlow's Monkey: harlows-monkey.com

I Am Adoptee (a community around mental health and wellness): iamadoptee.org

Intercountry Adoptee Voices (ICAV): intercountryadopteevoices.com